Judith of Blue Lake Ranch

Jackson Gregory

Contents

JUDITH OF BLUE LAKE RANCH

BY

Jackson Gregory

I
BUD LEE WANTS TO KNOW

Bud Lee, horse foreman of the Blue Lake Ranch, sat upon the gate of the home corral, builded a cigarette with slow brown fingers, and stared across the broken fields of the upper valley to the rosy glow above the pine-timbered ridge where the sun was coming up. His customary gravity was unusually pronounced.

"If a man's got the hunch an egg is bad," he mused, "is that a real good and sufficient reason why he should go poking his finger inside the shell? I want to know!"

Tommy Burkitt, the youngest wage-earner of the outfit and a profound admirer of all that taciturnity, good-humor, and quick capability which went into the make-up of Bud Lee, approached from the ranch-house on the knoll. "Hi, Bud!" he called. "Trevors wants you. On the jump."

Lee watched Tommy coming on with that wide, rocking gait of a man used to much riding and little walking. The deep gravity in the foreman's eyes was touched with a little twinkle by way of greeting.

Burkitt stopped at the gate, looking up at Lee. "On the jump, Trevors said," he repeated.

"The hell he did," said Lee pleasantly. "How old are you this morning, Tommy?"

Burkitt blushed. "Aw, quit it, Bud," he grinned. Involuntarily the boy's big square hand rose to the tender growth upon lip and chin which, like the flush in the eastern sky, was but a vague promise of a greater glory to be.

"A hair for each year," continued the quiet-voiced man. "Ten on one side, nine on the other."

"Ain't you going to do what Trevors says?" demanded Tommy.

For a moment Lee sat still, his cigarette unlighted, his broad black hat far back upon his close-cropped hair, his eyes serenely contemplative upon the pink of the sky above the pines. Then he slipped from his place and, though each single movement gave an impression of great leisureliness, it was but a flash of time until he stood beside Burkitt.

"Stick around a wee bit, laddie," he said gently, a lean brown hand resting lightly on the boy's square shoulder. "A man can't see what is on the cards until they're tipped, but it's always a fair gamble that between dawn and dusk I'll gather up my string of colts and crowd on. If I do, you'll want to come along?"

He smiled at young Burkitt's eagerness and turned away toward the ranch-house and Bayne Trevors, thus putting an early end to an enthusiastic acquiescence. Tommy watched the tall man moving swiftly away through the brightening dawn.

"They ain't no more men ever foaled like him," meditated Tommy, in an approval so profound as to be little less than out-and-out devotion.

And, indeed, one might ride up and down the world for many a day and not find a man who was Bud Lee's superior in "the things that count." As tall as most, with sufficient shoulders, a slender body, narrow-hipped, he carried himself as perhaps his forebears walked in a day when open forests or sheltered caverns housed them, with a lithe gracefulness born of the perfect play of superb physical development. His muscles, even in the slightest movement, flowed liquidly; he had slipped from his place on the corral gate less like a man than like some great, splendid cat. The skin of hands, face, throat, was very dark, whether by inheritance or because of long exposure to sun and wind, it would have been difficult to say. The eyes were dark, very keen, and yet reminiscently grave. From under their black brows they had the habit of appearing to be reluctantly withdrawn from some great distance to come to rest, steady and calm, upon the man with whom he chanced to be speaking. Such are the serene, dispassionate eyes of one who for many months of the year goes companionless, save for what communion he may find in the silent passes of the mountains, in the wide sweep of the meadow-lands or in the soul of his horse.

The gaunt, sure-footed form was lost to Tommy's eyes; Lee had passed beyond the clump of wild lilacs whose glistening, heart-shaped leaves screened the open court about which the ranch-house was built. A strangely elaborate ranch-house, this one, set here so far apart from the world of rich residences. There was a score of rooms in the great, one-story, rambling edifice of rudely squared timbers set in field-stone and cement, rooms now closed and locked; there were flower-gardens still cultivated daily by Jose, the half-breed; a pretty court with a fountain and many roses, out upon which a dozen doorways looked; wide verandas with glimpses beyond of fireplaces and long expanses of polished floor. For, until recently, this had been not only the headquarters of Blue Lake Ranch, but the home as well of the chief of its several owners. Luke Sanford, whose own efforts alone had made him at forty-five a man to be reckoned with, had followed his fancy here extensively and expensively, allowing himself this one luxury of his many lean, hard years. Then, six months ago, just as his ambitions were stepping to fresh heights, just as his hands were filling with newer, greater endeavor, there had come the mishap in the mountains and Sanford's tragic death.

Lee passed silently through the courtyard, by the fountain which in the brightening air was like a chain of silver run through invisible hands, down the veranda bathed in the perfume of full-blown roses, and so came to the door at the far end. The door stood open; within was the office of Bayne Trevors, general manager. Lee entered, his hat still far back upon his head. The sound of his boots upon the bare floor caused Trevors to look up quickly.

"Hello, Lee," he said quietly. "Wait a minute, will you?"

Quite a different type from Lee, Bayne Trevors was heavy and square and hard. His eyes were the glinting gray eyes of a man who is forceful, dynamic; the sort of man who is a better captain than lieutenant, whose hands are strong to grasp life by the throat and demand that she stand and deliver. Only because of his wide and successful experience, of his initiative, of his way of quick, decisive action mated to a marked executive ability, had Luke Sanford chosen Bayne Trevors as his right-hand man in so colossal a venture as the Blue Lake Ranch. Only because of the same pushing, vigorous personality was he this morning general manager, with the unlimited authority of a dictator over a petty principality.

In a moment Trevors lifted his frowning eyes from the table, turning in his chair to confront Lee, who stood lounging in leisurely manner against the doorjamb.

"That young idiot wants money again," he growled, his voice as sharp and quick as his eyes. "As if I didn't have enough to contend with already!"

"Meaning young Hampton, I take it?" said Lee quietly.

Trevors nodded savagely.

"Telegram. Caught it over the line the last thing last night. We'll have to sell some horses this time, Lee."

Lee's eyes narrowed imperceptibly. "I didn't plan to do any selling for six months yet," he said, not in expostulation but merely in explanation. "They're not ready."

"How many three-year-olds have you got in your string in Big Meadow?" asked Trevors crisply.

"Counting those eleven Red Duke colts?"

"Counting everything. How many?"

"Seventy-three."

The general manager's pencil wrote upon the pad in front of him "73," then swiftly multiplied it by 50. Lee saw the result, 3,650 set down with the dollar sign in front of it. He said nothing.

"What would you say to fifty dollars a head for them?" asked Trevors, whirling again in his swivel chair. "Three thousand six fifty for the bunch?"

"I'd say the same," answered Lee deliberately, "that I'd say to a man that offered me two bits for Daylight or Ladybird. I just naturally wouldn't say anything at all."

"Who are Daylight and Ladybird?" demanded Trevors.

"They're two of *my* little horses," said Lee gently, "that no man's got the money to buy."

Trevors smiled cynically. "What are the seventy-three colts worth then?"

"Right now, when I'm just ready to break 'em in," said Bud Lee thoughtfully, "the worst of that string is worth fifty dollars. I'd say twenty of the herd ought to bring fifty dollars a head; twenty more ought to bring sixty; ten are worth seventy-five; ten are worth an even hundred; seven of the Red Duke stock are good for a hundred and a quarter; the other four Red Dukes and the three Robert the Devils are worth a hundred and fifty a head. The whole bunch, an easy fifty-seven hundred little iron men. Which," he continued dryly, "is considerable more than the thirty-six hundred you're talking about. And, give me six months, and I'll boost that fifty-seven hundred. Lord, man, that chestnut out of Black Babe by Hazard, is a real horse! Fifty dollars----"

He stared hard at Trevors a moment. And then, partially voicing the thought with which he had grappled upon the corral gate, he added meditatively: "There's something almighty peculiar about an outfit that will listen to a man offer fifty bucks on a string like that."

His eyes, cool and steady, met Trevors's in a long look which was little short of a challenge.

"Just how far does that go, Lee?" asked the manager curtly.

"As far as you like," replied the horse foreman coolly. "Are you going to sell those three-year-olds for thirty-six hundred?"

"Yes," answered Trevors bluntly, "I am. What are you going to do about it?"

"Ask for my time, I guess," and although his voice was gentle and even pleasant, his eyes were hard. "I'll take my own little string and move on."

"Curse it!" cried Trevors heatedly. "What difference does it make to you? What business is it of yours how I sell? You draw down your monthly pay, don't you? I raised you a notch last month without your asking for it, didn't I?"

"That's so," agreed the foreman equably. "It's a cinch none of the boys have any kick coming at the wages."

For a moment Trevors sat frowning up at Lee's inscrutable face. Then he laughed shortly. "Look here, Bud," he said good-humoredly, an obvious seriousness of purpose under the light tone. "I want to talk with you before you do anything rash. Sit down." But Lee remained standing, merely saying, "Shoot."

"I wonder," explained Trevors, "if the boys understand just the size of the job I've got in my hands? You know that the ranch is a million-dollar outfit; you know that you can ride fifteen miles without getting off the home-range; you know that we are doing a dozen different kinds of farming and stock-raising. But you don't know just how short the money is! There's that young idiot now, Hampton. He holds a third interest and I've got to consider what he says, even if he is a weak-minded, inbred pup that can't do anything but spend an inheritance like the born fool he is. His share is mortgaged; I've tried to pay the mortgage off. I've got to keep the interest up. Interest alone amounts, to three thousand dollars a year. Think of that! Then there's Luke Sanford dead and his one-third interest left to another young fool, a girl!"

Trevors's fist came smashing down upon his table. "A girl!" he repeated savagely. "Worse than young Hampton, by Heaven! Every two weeks she's writing for a report, eternally butting in, making suggestions, hampering me until I'm sick of the job."

"That would be Luke's girl, Judith?"

"Yes. Two of the three owners' kids, writing me at every turn. And the third owner, Timothy Gray, the only sensible one of the lot, has just up and sold out his share, and I suppose I'll be hearing next that some superannuated female in an old lady's home has inherited a fortune and bought him out. Why, do you think I'd hold on to my job here for ten minutes if it wasn't that my reputation is in making a go of the thing? And now you, the best man I've got, throw me down!"

"I don't see," said Lee slowly, after a brief pause, "just what good it does to sell a string of real horses like they were sheep. Half of that herd is real horse-flesh, I tell you."

"Hampton wants money. And besides, a horse is a horse."

"Is it?" A hard smile touched Lee's lips. "That's just where a man makes a mistake. Some horses are cows, some are clean spirit. You can stake your boots on that, Trevors."

"Well," snapped Trevors, "suppose you are right. I've got to raise three thousand dollars in a hurry. Where will I get it?"

"Who is offering fifty dollars a head for those horses?" asked Lee abruptly. "It might be the Big Western Lumber Company?"

"Yes."

"Uh-huh. Well, you can kill the rats in your own barn, Trevors. I'll go look for a job somewhere else."

Bayne Trevors, his lips tightly compressed, his eyes steady, a faint, angry flush in his cheeks, checked what words were flowing to his tongue and looked keenly at his foreman. Lee met his regard with cool unconcern. Then, just as Trevors was about to speak, there came an interruption.

II
JUDITH TAKES A HAND

The quiet of the morning was broken by the quick thud of a horse's shod hoofs on the hard ground of the courtyard. Bud Lee in the doorway turned to see a strange horse drawn up so that upon its four bunched hoofs it slid to a standstill; saw a slender figure, which in the early light he mistook for a boy, slip out of the saddle. And then, suddenly, a girl, the spurs of her little riding-boots making jingling music on the veranda, her riding-quirt swinging from her wrist, had stepped by him and was looking with bright, snapping eyes from him to Trevors.

"I am Judith Sanford," she announced briefly, and there was a note in her young voice which went ringing, bell-like, through the still air. "Is one of you men Bayne Trevors?"

A quick, shadowy smile came and went upon the lips of Bud Lee. It struck him that she might have said in just that way: "I am the Queen of England and I am running my own kingdom!" He looked at her with eyes filled with open interest and curiosity, making swift appraisal of the flush in the sun-browned cheeks, the confusion of dark, curling hair disturbed by her furious riding, the vivid, red-blooded beauty of her. Mouth and eyes and the very carriage of the dark head upon her superb white throat announced boldly and triumphantly that here was no wax-petalled lily of a lady but rather a maid whose blood, like the blood of the father before her, was turbulent and hot and must boil like a wild mountain-stream at opposition. Her eyes, a little darker than Trevors's, were the eyes of fighting stock.

Trevors, irritated already, turned hard eyes up at her from under corrugated brows. He did not move in his chair. Nor did Lee stir except that now he removed his hat.

"I am Trevors," said the general manager curtly. "And, whether you are Judith Sanford or the Queen of Siam, I am busy right now."

"He got the queen idea, too!" was the quick thought back of Bud Lee's fading smile.

"You talk soft with me, Trevors!" cried the girl passionately, "if you want to hold your job five minutes! I'll tolerate none of your high and mighty airs!"

Trevors laughed at her, a sneer in his laugh. "I talk the way I talk," he answered roughly. "If people don't like the sound of it they don't have to listen! Lee, you round up those seventy-three horses and crowd them over the ridge to the lumber-camp. Or, if you want to quit, quit now and I'll send a sane man."

The hot color mounted higher in the girl's face, a new anger leaped up in her eyes.

"Take no orders this morning that I don't give," she said, for a moment turning her eyes upon Lee. And to Trevors: "Busy or not busy, you take time right now to answer my questions. I've got your reports and all they tell me is that you are going in the hole as fast as you can. You are spending thousands of dollars needlessly. What business have you got selling off my young steers at a sacrifice? What in the name of folly did you build those three miles of fence for?"

"Go get those horses, Lee," said Trevors, ignoring her.

Again she spoke to Lee, saying crisply: "What horses is he talking about?"

With his deep gravity at its deepest, Bud Lee answered: "All L-S stock. The eleven Red Duke three-year-olds; the two Robert the Devil colts; Brown Babe's filly, Comet----"

"All mine, every running hoof of 'em," she said, cutting in. "What does Trevors want you to do with them? Give them away for ten dollars a head or cut their throats?"

"Look here--" cried Trevors angrily, on his feet now.

"You shut up!" commanded the girl sharply. "Lee, you answer me."

"He's selling them fifty dollars a head," he said with a secret joy in his heart as he glanced at Trevors's flushed face.

"Fifty dollars!" Judith gasped. "Fifty dollars for a Red Duke colt like Comet!"

She stared at Lee as though she could not believe it. He merely stared back at her, wondering just how much she knew about horse-flesh.

Then, suddenly, she whirled again upon Trevors.

"I came out to see if you were a crook or just a fool," she told him her words like a slap in his face. "No man could be so big a fool as that! You--you crook!"

The muscles under Bayne Trevors's jaws corded. "You've said about enough," he shot back at her. "And even if you do own a third of this outfit, I'll have you understand that I am the manager here and that I do what I like."

From her bosom she snatched a big envelope, tossing it to the table. "Look at that," she ordered him. "You big thief! I've mortgaged my holding for fifty thousand dollars and I've bought in Timothy Gray's share. I swing two votes out of three now, Bayne Trevors. And the first thing I do is run you out, you great big grafting fathead! You *would* chuck Luke Sanford's outfit to the dogs, would you? Get off the ranch. You're fired!"

"You can't do a thing like this!" snapped Trevors, after one swift glance at the papers he had whisked out of their covering.

"I can't, can't I?" she jeered at him. "Don't you fool yourself for one little minute! Pack your little trunk and hammer the trail."

"I'll do nothing of the kind. Why, I don't know even who you are! You say that you are Judith Sanford." He shrugged his massive shoulders. "How do I know what game you are up to? Wayward maidens," and in his rage he sneered at her evilly, "have been known before to lie like other people!"

"You can't bluff me for two seconds, Bayne Trevors," she blazed at him. "You know who I am, all right. Send for Sunny Harper," she ended sharply.

"Discharged three months ago," Trevors told her with a show of teeth.

"Johnny Hodge, then," she commanded. "Or Tod Bruce or Bing Kelley. They all know me."

"Fired long ago, all of them," laughed Trevors, "to make room for competent men."

"To make room for more crooks!" she cried, her own brown hands balled into fists scarcely less hard than Trevors's had been. Then for the third time she turned upon Lee. "You are one of his new thieves, I suppose?"

"Thank you, ma'am," said Bud Lee gravely.

"Well, answer me. Are you?"

"No, ma'am," he told her, with no hint of a twinkle in his calm eyes. "Leastwise, not his exactly. You see, I do all my killing and highway robbing on my own hook. It's just a way I have."

"Well," Judith sniffed, "I don't know. It will be a jolt to me if there's a square man left on the ranch! Go down to the bunk-house and tell the cook I'm here and I'm hungry as a wild-cat. Tell him and any of the boys that are down there that I've come to stay and that Trevors is fired. They take orders from me and no one else. And hurry, if you know how. Goodness knows, you look as though it would take you half an hour to turn around!"

"Thank you, ma'am," said Bud Lee. "But you see I had just told Trevors here he could count me out. I'm not working for the Blue Lake any more. As I go down to the corral, shall I send up one of the boys to take your orders?"

There was a little smile under the last words, just as there was a little smile in Bud Lee's heart at the thought of the boys taking orders from a little slip of a girl. Inside he was chuckling, vastly delighted with the comedy of the morning.

"She's a sure-enough little wonder-bird, all right," he mused. "But, say, what does she want to butt in on a man's-size job for, I want to know?"

"Lee," called Trevors, "you take orders from me or no one on this ranch. You can go now. And just keep your mouth shut."

Bud Lee stood there in the doorway, his hat spinning upon a brown forefinger, his thoughts his own. He was turning to go out and down to his horse when he saw the look in Trevors's eyes, a look of consuming rage. The general manager's voice had been hoarse.

"I guess," said Lee quietly, "that I'll stick around until you two get through quarrelling. I might come in handy somehow."

"Damn you," shouted Trevors, "get out!"

"Cut out the swear-words, Trevors," said Lee with quiet sternness. "There's a lady here."

"Lady!" scoffed Trevors. He laughed contemptuously. "Where's your lady? That?" and he levelled a scornful finger at the girl. "A ranting tough of a female who brings a breath of the stables with her and scolds like a fishwife. . . ."

"Shut up!" said Lee, crossing the room with quick strides, his face thrust forward a little.

"You shut up!" It was Judith's voice as Judith's hand fell upon Bud Lee's shoulder, pushing him aside. "If I couldn't take care of myself do you think I'd be fool enough to take over a job like running the Blue Lake? Now--" and with blazing eyes she confronted Trevors--"if you've got any more nice little things to say, suppose you say them to me!"

Trevors's temper had had ample provocation and now stood naked and hot in his hard eyes. In a blind instant he laid his tongue to a word which would have sent Bud Lee at his throat. But Judith stood between them and, like an echo to the word, came the resounding slap as Judith's open palm smote Trevors's cheek.

"You wildcat!" he cried. And his two big hands flew out, seeking her shoulders.

"Stand back!" called Judith. "Just because you are bigger than I am, don't make any mistake! Stand back, I tell you!"

Bud Lee marvelled at the swiftness with which her hand had gone into her blouse and out again, a small-caliber revolver in the steady fingers now. He had never known a man--himself possibly excepted--quicker at the draw.

But Bayne Trevors, from whose make-up cowardice had been omitted, laughed sneeringly at her and did not stand back. His two hands out before him, his face crimson, he came on.

"Fool!" cried the girl. "Fool!"

Still he came on. Lee gathered himself to spring.

Judith fired. Once, and Trevors's right arm fell to his side. A second time, and Trevors's left arm hung limp like the other. The crimson was gone from his face now. It was dead white. Little beads of sweat began to form on his brow.

Lee turned astonished eyes to Judith.

"Now you know who's running this outfit, don't you?" she said coolly. "Lee, have a team hitched up to carry Trevors wherever he wants to go. He's not hurt much; I just winged him. And then tell the cook about my breakfast."

But Lee stood and looked at her. He had no remark to offer. Then he turned to go upon her bidding. As he went down to the bunk-house he said softly under his breath: "Well, I'm damned. I most certainly am!"

III
AND RIDES AN OUTLAW

Wrinkled, grizzled old half-breed Jose, his hands trembling with eagerness, stood in the smaller rose-garden culling the perfect buds, a joyous tear running its zigzag way down each cheek.

"La senorita ees come home!" he announced triumphantly as Lee drew near on his way to the bunk-house. "Jesus Maria! Een my heart it is like the singing of leetle birdies. *Mira, senor*. My flowers bloomin' the brighter, already--no?"

Bud Lee paused. "So you know Miss Sanford then?" he asked.

Jose threw out his hands and opened his night-black eyes to their most enormous extent. "Do I know God?" he demanded.

"Well," smiled Bud, "as to that. . . ."

"But, senor," cried the devout Jose, "like on holy days I feel that Dios comes to sit down in the corner of my heart, so without seeing *la senorita* I know she ees come home! She ees in the air like the light of sun, like the sweetness of my roses!"

"You've known her a long time, Joe?"

"Seence she ees born!" and Jose, unashamed, wiped away a tear upon the back of a leathery hand. "Senor Sanford and me, senor, we teach her when she ees so leetle!" Jose's shaking hand was lowered until it marked the stature of a twelve-inch pigmy. In all things must the old fellow gain his emphasis by exaggeration which more often than not took the form of plain lying. "Never at all unteel one year ago does she leave us and the *rancho*. We, us two who love her, senor, learn her to walk and to ride and to shoot and to talk. You shall hear her say, 'Buenos dias, Jose, mi amigo!' You shall see her kees the cheek of old Jose."

Again his leathery hand was put in requisition, this time to wipe clean the cheek to be honored. "And one theeng I tell you, senor," he added confidentially. "Her papa was a wild devil before her. Her mama ees grow up on the ranch; and when she marry *el senor* Sanford was like a wild boy. And *mi senorita*, she ees the cross be tween a wild devil and a sweet saint, senor *Madre de Dios*! I would go down to hell for her to bring back fire to warm her leetle feet een weenter!'

Lee went thoughtfully on his way to the bunk-house. The cook, an importation of Bayne Trevors, a big, upstanding fellow with bare arms covered with flour, was putting on the breakfast to which a dozen rough-garbed men were sitting down.

"I've got orders for you fellows," said Lee from the doorway. "The boss of the outfit, the real owner, you know, just blew in. Up at the house. Says you boys are to stick around to take orders straight from headquarters. You, Benny," to the cook, "are to have a man's-size breakfast ready in a jiffy."

Naturally Benny led the clamor with a string of oaths. What in blazes did the owner of the ranch have to show up for anyway?--he wanted to know. He accepted the fact as a personal affront. Who was this owner?--demanded Ward Hannon, the foreman of the lower ranch, where the alfalfa-fields were.

Bud Lee explained gravely that the newcomer was some sort of relative of old Luke Sanford, who had recently acquired a controlling interest in the ranch. Ward Hannon grunted contemptuously. "The Lord deliver us!" he moaned. "Eastern jasper! One of the know-all-about-it brand, huh, Bud? I'll bet he combs his hair in the middle and smokes cigareets out'n a box! The putty-headed loons can't even roll their own smokes."

"Don't believe," hazarded Lee indifferently, "from the looks of our visitor that--that the owner smokes anything!"

"Listen to that!" grunted Ward Hannon.

"Softy, huh?"

"Well," Bud admitted slowly, "looks sort of like a girl, you know!"

"Wouldn't that choke you?" demanded Carson, the cow foreman, a thin, awkward little man, gray in the service of "real men." "Taking orders off'n a fool Easterner's bad enough. But old man or young, Bud?"

"Just a kid," was Lee's further dampening news. And as he nonchalantly buttered his hotcakes he added carelessly: "Something of a scrapper, though. Just put two thirty-two calibers into Trevors."

They stared at him incredulously. Then Carson's dry cackle led the laughter.

"You're the biggest liar, Bud Lee," said the old man good-naturedly, "I ever focussed my two eyes on. I'll lay an even bet there ain't nobody showed a-tall up this morning."

"You, Tommy," said Lee to the boy at his side, "shovel your grub down lively and go hitch Molly and old Pie-face to the buckboard. That's orders from headquarters," he grinned. "Trevors is to be hauled away first thing."

Tommy looked curiously at his superior. "On the level, Bud?" he asked doubtingly.

"On the level, laddie," was the quiet response.

And young Burkitt, wondering, but doubting no longer, hastened with his breakfast.

The others, looking at Lee's sober face questioningly, fired a broadside of inquiries at him. But they got no further information.

"I've told you boys all the news," he announced positively. "Lordy! Isn't that an earful for this time of day? The real boss is on the job: Trevors is winged; you are to stick around for orders from headquarters. If you want to know any more'n that, why--just go up to the house and ask your blamed questions."

Out of the tail of his eye he saw the swift approach of Bayne Trevors. The general manager's face was black with rage and through that dark wrath showed a dull red flush of shame. He walked with his two arms lax at his sides.

"Give me a cup of coffee, Ben," he commanded curtly, slumping into a chair. "Hurry!"

Benny, looking at him curiously, brought a steaming cup and offered it. Trevors moved to lift a hand; then sank back a little farther in his chair, his face twisting in his pain.

"Put some milk in it," he snarled. "Then hold it to my mouth. For the love of Heaven, hurry, man!"

Then no man there doubted longer the mad tale Bud Lee had brought them. Down from Trevors's sleeves, staining each hand, there had come a broadening trickle of blood. Trevors set his teeth and waited. Benny at last cooled the coffee and held it to his lips. Trevors drank swiftly, draining the cup.

"Get this coat off me," he commanded. "Curse you, don't tear my arms off! Slit the sleeves."

Benny's big, razor-edged butcher-knife cut away coat and shirt sleeves. And at last, to the eager gaze of the men in the bunk-house, there appeared the two wounds, one upon the outer right shoulder, the other upon the left forearm.

It was Lee who, pushing the clumsy cook aside, silently made the two bandages from strips of Trevors's shirt. It was Lee who brought a flask of brandy from which Trevors drank deep.

And then came Judith.

They stared at her as they might have done had the heavens opened and an angel come down, or the earth split and a devil sprung up. She looked in upon them with quick, keen eyes which sought to take every man's measure. They returned her regard with a variety of amazed expressions. Never since these men had come to work for Bayne Trevors had a woman so much as ridden by the door. And to have her stand there, composed, utterly at her ease, her air vaguely authoritative, a vitally vivid being who might, suddenly, have taken tangible form from the dawn, bewildered them. Bud Lee had told of the coming of the Blue Lake owner; he had not mentioned that that owner had brought his daughter with him.

"I am Judith Sanford," she said in her abrupt fashion, quite as she had made the announcement to Lee and Trevors. "This outfit belongs to me. I have fired Trevors. You take your orders straight from me from now on. Cookie, give me some coffee."

She came in without ceremony and sat down at the head of the table. Benny gasped, stood for a moment rooted to the floor, and then, Judith's eyes hard upon him, hastily brought the coffee. From some emotion certainly not clear to him he went a violent red. Perhaps the emotion was just sheer embarrassment. He brought hot cakes with one hand while with the other he buttoned his gaping shirt-collar over a bulging, hairy chest.

Men who had finished their breakfasts rose hastily with a marked awkwardness and ill-concealed haste and went outside, whence their low voices came back in a confused consultation. Men who had not finished followed them. In an amazingly short time there were but the girl, Lee, Trevors and the cook in the room. Then

Trevors went out, Benny at his heels. Bud Lee, moving with his usual leisureliness, was following when Judith's cool voice said quietly:

"You, Lee, wait a moment. I want to talk with you."

Lee hesitated. Then he came back and waited.

The men outside naturally grouped about the general manager. His angry voice, lifted clearly, reached the two in the room.

"I'm fired," said Trevors harshly. "As soon as I can get going I am leaving for the Western Lumber camp. Every one of you boys holds his job here because I gave it to him. Do you want to hold it now, with a fool girl telling you what to do? Do you want men up and down the State to laugh at you and jeer at you for a pack of softies and imbeciles? Or do you want to roll your blankets and quit? To every man that jumps the job here and follows me to-day I promise a job with the Western. You fellows know the sort of boss I've been to you. You can guess the sort of boss that chicken in there would be. Now I'm going. It's up to you. Stick to a white man or fuss around for a woman?"

He had said what he had to say and, cursing when his shoulder struck a form near him, made his way down to the stables. Burkitt was ahead of him, going for the team.

"Well, Lee," said Judith sharply, "where do you get off? Do you want to stick? Or shall I count you out?"

"I guess," said Bud very gently, "you'd better count me out."

"You're going with that crook?"

"No. I'm going on my own."

"Why? You're getting good money here. If you're square I'll keep you at the same figure."

But Bud shook his head.

"I'm game to play square," he said slowly. "I'll stick a week, giving you the chance to get a man in my place. That's all."

"What's the matter with you?" she cried hotly. "Why won't you stay with your job? Is it because you don't want to take orders from me?"

Then Lee lifted his grave eyes to hers and answered simply: "That's it. I'm not saying you're not all right. But I got it figured out, there's just two kinds of ladies. If you want to know, I don't see that you've got any call to tie into a man's job."

"Oh, scat!" cried the girl angrily. "You men make me tired. Two kinds of ladies! And ten thousand kinds of men! You want me to dress like a doll, I suppose, and keep my hands soft and white and go around like a brainless, simpering fool! There *are* two kinds of **ladies**, my fine friend: the kind that can and the kind that can't! Thank God I'm none of your precious, sighing, hothouse little fools!"

Gulping down a last mouthful of coffee, she was on her feet and passed swiftly out among the men.

"You men!" she cried, and they turned sober eyes upon her, "listen to me! You've heard that big stiff rant; now hear me! I'm here because I belong here. My dad was Luke Sanford and he made this ranch. I was raised here. It's two-thirds mine right now. Trevors there is a crook and I told him so. He's been trying to sell me out, to make such a failure of the outfit that I'd have to let it go for a comic song. He got gay and I fired him. He tried to manhandle me and I plugged him. And now I am going to run my own outfit! What have you got to say about it, you grumbling old grouch with the crooked face! Put up or shut up! I'm calling you!"

The men turned from her to Ward Hannon, the field foreman, who had been Trevors's right-hand man and who now was sneering openly.

"I'm saying it's no work for a kid of a girl," grumbled Hannon. "You run an outfit like this?" He laughed derisively. "It can't be did."

"It can't, can't it?" cried Judith. "Tell me why, old smarty. Spit it out lively."

Jake Carson's shrill cackle cut through a low rumble of laughter. "That's passing it to him straight," said the old cattleman. "What's the word, Ward?"

Ward Hannon shrugged his shoulders and spat impudently. "I ain't saying nothing," he growled, "only this: I got a right to quit, ain't I? Well, I'm quitting. Any time you ketch me working for a female girl that can't ride a horse 'thout falling off, that can't see a pig stuck 'thout fainting, that can't walk a mile 'thout getting laid up, that can't. . . ."

"Slow up there!" called Judith. "Didn't I stick a pig already this morning, and have I keeled over yet? Didn't I ride the forty miles from Rocky Bend last night and get here before sun-up? Listen to me, chief kicker: If you've got a horse on the ranch I can't ride I'll quit right now and give you my job! How's that strike you? I tell you the word on this ranch is going to be: 'Put up or shut up!' Which is it, Growly?"

Again the men laughed and Hannon's face showed his anger.

"Mean that, lady?" he demanded briefly.

"You can just bet your eyes I mean it!"

Hannon turned toward the stable. "All right. We'll see who's going to put or shut up!" he jeered over his shoulder. "You ride the Prince just two little minutes and I'll stay and work for you!"

Bud Lee from the doorway interfered. He was a man who loved fair play and he knew the Prince. "None of that, Ward," he called sternly. "Not the Prince!"

But Judith, her eyes aflame, whirled upon Lee, her voice like a whip as she said: "Lee, you keep out of this. The sooner you learn who's running things here the better for you."

"Maybe so," said Lee quietly. "But don't you fool yourself you can ride Prince. There's not a man on the job except me that can ride him." It was not boastfully said, but with calm assurance. "He's an outlaw, Miss Judith. He's the horse that killed Jimmy Carpenter last spring, and Jimmy----"

"Go ahead, Ward," ordered Judith. "You don't have to stop every time the wind blows, do you?"

Even Bud Lee smiled. But old Carson spoke up, saying: "Bud's right, miss. And if Ward wants to know, he's a low-down dawg to try to turn a trick like this. . . ."

"Go ahead, Ward," Judith repeated. "I've got something to do to-day besides play pussy-wants-a-corner with you boys."

Ward went, his eyes filled with malice. Two or three of the other men joined their voices to Bud's and Carson's, expostulating, telling of that fearful thing, an outlaw horse. Judith maintained a scornful silence.

In due time Ward came back. He was leading a saddled horse, a great, wild-eyed roan that snapped viciously as he came on, walking with the wide, spreading stride of a horse little used to the saddle. Judith measured him with her eyes as she had measured the men in the bunk-house.

"He's an ugly devil," she said, and Lee, at her side, smiled again. But the girl had not altered her intention. She stepped closer, looking to cinch, bit, and reins. She commanded Ward to draw the latigo tighter, and Ward did so, dodging back as the big brute snapped at him.

Judith laughed. "Look out, Ward," she taunted him. "He's after your hair!"

Two men held the Prince. At Judith's command they shortened the stirrups and then blinded him with a bandanna handkerchief. Then, moving with almost incredible swiftness, she was in the saddle, the reins firmly gripped. The Prince, a sudden trembling thrilling through him, stood with his four feet planted. The girl leaned forward and whipped the blind from his red-rimmed eyes.

"There's a good boy!" said Judith coolly. "Buck a little for the lady, Prince!"

Slowly the great muscles of Prince's leg and shoulder and flank corded. The trembling passed; he was like a horse carven in bluish granite. He shook his head a little. Judith, her hand tightening upon the reins, held his head well up, the severe bit thwarting the attempt to get his nose down between his forelegs.

Then suddenly, without sign of warning, the horse whirled, leaping far out to the left, striking with hard hoofs bunched, gathering himself as he landed, swerving with the quickness of light, plunging again to the right. And again he stood still. Judith, sitting securely on his rebellious back, laughed. Her laughter, cool and unafraid, sent a strange little thrill through Bud Lee--who, with fear in his heart, was watching her.

"Look out for him now!" he called warningly.

In truth the Prince had not yet begun. He had tried a trick which would have unseated any but one who rode well. He knew that he had to do with something more than a rank amateur.

Now he plunged toward the corral, his purpose plain, the one desire in his heart to crush his rider against the high fence. But Judith's spurs answered him, and the bit, savage in his jaws, brought him about, whirling, sidling, striking, bucking as only a strong, fearless, devil-hearted horse knows how to buck. He doubled up under her; he rose and fell in a quick series of short jumps which tore and jerked at her body, which strove to tear her knees away from his sides and break the grip of her hand on the reins. But it seemed to the men watching that the girl knew before the horse which way he would jump, that she knew how to sway her body with his so that she and he were not two separate beings but just one, moving together in some mad devil's dance. The Prince, in the midst of the vicious bucking, tried to rear, seeking to throw himself backward; a quick, sharp blow of a loaded quirt between his ears brought his forefeet back to earth.

"Can she ride!" whispered Bud Lee. "I want to know!"

Again the maddened Prince reared and again she brought him to earth. Again he resumed the terribly tearing series of short, sharp bucks. And still, her hair tumbling, blown about her shoulders, she rode him.

Old Carson was muttering and pulling at his lip nervously. Out of the corner of his mouth in a voice that was almost a whimper, he kept cursing and saying to Ward Hannon: "You skunk! You ornery skunk! Hunt your hole after this!"

Suddenly, with a quick, concerted action of spur, whip, and rein, Judith swung the Prince about so that he was headed for the open valley, running toward the west, giving him his head only a little, driving him. He broke into a thundering run, snorting as, with mane and tail flying, he dashed through the men who fell away from his furious rush. And as he ran, Judith spurred him so that his only thought lay in running away from the menace upon his back.

"She ain't giving him time to buck!" laughed old Carson hysterically. "Mama! Ain't she sure enough--God! She's goin' to get a fall."

For horse and rider had come to the wide irrigating ditch which, since Judith Sanford had lived here, had been constructed to carry the water of Blue Lake River down to the alfalfa-fields. She saw it when she was too close to swerve.

The men watching saw her lean forward in the saddle, gather her reins, lift her whip. Then the lifted whip came down, the spurs touched the Prince's sweating sides, the big horse leaped far and clear of the ditch and there floated back Judith's laughter.

Three minutes later she rode back to the bunkhouse and slipped from the saddle. Bud Lee, going to her, had his hat in his hand.

"Now, Ward," she said quickly, her breathing hurried, her cheeks red, "what do you say?"

"I said I'd stick if you rode him," muttered Ward. "And----"

"And," cried the girl with quick passion, "I'll tell you something. You're a great big lumbering coward! Stick with me?" She laughed again, a new laugh, ringing with her scorn. "Here's your outlaw; I've gentled him a bit. You ride him!"

His fellows laughed at Ward; for the field foreman was no horseman and the timorous way in which he had brought out this snapping, vicious animal had testified to the fact. He drew back now, muttering.

"Ride him!" cried Judith, her voice stinging him. "Ride him or get off the ranch! Which is it?"

Ward Hannon, glad of the opening, answered surlily: "Aw! think I want to take orders off'n a woman? You're right, I'll get off'n the ranch!"

"That's two down," said Judith. "Now, take this horse back to the stable; I'm going up to the office. You men come there in five minutes. If you want to stay, and are worth your salt, you can. Or I'll give you your time. It's up to you: it's a free country. But--" and she said it slowly, confronting them--"if you all throw me down and leave me short-handed without giving me time to take on another set of men, you are a pretty low-lived bunch!"

Then, without turning, she went swiftly to the ranch-house. Old man Carson wiped the sweat from his forehead.

"I remember hearing about Luke Sanford's girl," he said simply. "This is her, all right."

IV
JUDITH PUTS IT STRAIGHT

"Old man" Carson--so-called through lack of courtesy and because of the sprinkling of gray through his black hair, a man of perhaps forty-five--filled an unthinkably disreputable pipe with his own conception of "real tobacco" and chuckled so that the second match was required; before he was ready to say his say.

"You just listen to me, you boys!" he said. "I worked with the Down River outfit a year before Trevors sent me word he had a job open here at better pay. That's only seventy-five miles, and news does percolate, give it time. None of you fellers ever saw old Luke Sanford?"

"I'd been working here close to two weeks when he got killed," Bud said as Carson's twinkling eyes went from face to face. "I got my job straight from him, not Trevors."

"That's so," said Carson. "Well, Bud knows the sort Luke Sanford was. He was dead and buried when I come to the Blue Lake, but I'd saw him twice and I'd heard of him more times than that. Quiet man that 'tended to his own business and didn't say so all-fired much 'less he was stirred up. And then--!" He whistled his meaning. "A fighter. All he ever got he fought for. All he ever held on to he fought for. He bucked Western Lumber for a dozen years, first and last. And, by cripes, he nailed their durned hides on his stable-door, too!

"Well, I heard tell about this same Luke Sanford ten years ago and more--about him and his little girl. From what folks said I guess there never was a man wanted a boy-baby worse'n Luke Sanford before Judith come. And I guess there never was a man put more stock in his own flesh and blood than Luke did in her as soon as he got used to her being a she. I don't know just exactly how old she was ten years ago, women folks being so damn' tricky in the looks of their ages, but I'd say she was eight or nine or ten or eleven years old. Anyhow, Luke had took her in hand already."

"Taught her to ride, huh?" asked one of the men.

"You're shouting, Poker Face," nodded Carson with vehemence. "He sure did! Why, that girl's rid real horses since she was the size of a pair of boots. Luke took her everywhere he went, up in the mountains, over the Big Ridge, down valley-ways, into town when he went off on his yearly. And they say Luke wasn't no poky rider, either. You've rode his string, Bud? What are those for horses, huh?"

"I'm a little particular when it comes to a saddle-horse," Bud admitted. "But I never asked any better than old Sanford's string."

"You hear him!" said Carson. "Well, that Judy girl has rid horses like them for a dozen years. And her dad--anyway, folks say so down on the river--showed her his way to ride and his way to shoot and his way to play cards! I guess," and he spoke with slow thoughtfulness, "that she's a real chip off'n the old block. It's my guess number two that she ain't just shooting off her face promiscuous when she says there's something crooked in the deal Trevors has been handing her. And, third bet, there's most likely going to be seven kinds of hell popping around this end of the woods for a spell."

"What are you doing about it, Carson?" asked the man whose unusually vacuous expression gave him his name of Poker Face. "Stick on the job or quit?"

"Me?" Carson sought a match, and when he had found it, held it long in his grimy fingers, staring at it thoughtfully. "Me stay an' let a she-girl boss me? Well, it ain't the play a man might look to me to make, an' I ain't saying it's the trick I'd do every day in the week. But here there's some things to set a man scratching his head: she's a winner, all right, an' I'm the first man to up an' say so. She's got the sand an' she's got the savvy. Take 'em together an' they make what you call gumption. Sure it ain't no woman's job to step in an' run an outfit like this one; a woman ain't nacherally cut out for that sort of thing any more'n a man is to darn socks an' drink tea with lemon in it. Again, tipping it over so's you can look at the other side, like a fair man ought to, what's she going to do? She lands here sudden, striking all four feet in a mess of trouble. She grabs holt of things, seeing they belong to her in a way, an' seeing she's fed Trevors his time. I might go trailing my luck some other-where, if I did the first fool thing that plopped into my nut. But playing fair, I'm going to stick an' do my damnedest to see Luke Sanford's girl put up her scrap. Yes, sir."

"What did she want to fire Trevors for?" asked Benny, the cook.

Carson, looking at him contemptuously, spoke in contemptuous answer about the stem of his pipe. "Any man on the job can answer you that, Cookie. It's been open an' shut the last month Trevors is either crazy or crooked. I said, didn't I, Western Lumber's itching to get its devil-fish legs wropped aroun' Blue Lake timber? They've busted more than one rancher up in the mountains. Trevors is in with 'em. Any man on the ranch that don't know that, don't want to know it!" He removed his pipe at last, and his look upon Benny was full of meaning. "Roll that in your dough, Cookie, an' make biscuits out'n it."

"Go easy there, grandfather," growled Benny.

"That's something I ain't learned," was old Carson's ready answer, lightly given. "I've told you before, if you don't want your name printed plain don't come around asking me to spell it."

Benny growled an answer but did not take up the quarrel. He knew Carson well enough to know that there was no man living readier for a fight or abler to conduct his own part of it. Carson, smaller than Benny, was wiry, quick-footed, hard-eyed. There was something about him that caused a man of Benny's sort to stop and think.

"Que hay, Bud?" called a voice, and old Jose, his face shining with his joy--Bud was certain that Judith had actually kissed the leathery cheek and wondered how she could do it!--came down the knoll. "La senorita wants you!"

"Haw!" gurgled Bandy O'Neil facetiously. "It's your manly beauty, Bud! You ol' son-of-a-gun of a lady-killer!"

Bud Lee swung about upon his heel to glare at Bandy. But suddenly conscious of a flush creeping up hotly under his tan, he turned his back and strode away to the house. Bandy's "haw, haw!" followed him. Lee's face was flaming when he entered the office.

"What do you want with me?" he said shortly, angered at Bandy, Judith Sanford and himself.

"Bow, wow!" retorted Judith, looking up from Trevors's table. "Whose dog art thou? Do you want me to think you are as fierce as you look?"

"You sent for me?" he said coolly.

She looked up at him critically. "What's come over you, Lee? I took you for a cool head--Heaven knows I need a few cool heads around me right now!--and here you show up with red in your eye, barking at me."

"Let's pass up what I look like," said Lee stiffly. "What can I do for you. Miss Sanford?"

"Hm," said Judith. "On your high horse, are you? All right, stay there. What I want is some information. How long have you been on the Blue Lake pay-roll?"

"A little over six months," he answered colorlessly.

"Over six months?" A quick look of interest came into her eyes. "Trevors hired you? Or dad?"

"Your father."

"Then"--and a sudden, swift smile came for the first time that morning into the girl's eyes--"you're square! Thank God for one man to be sure of."

She had risen with a quick impetuosity and put out her hand. Lee took it into his own, and felt it shut hard, like a man's.

"Just how do you know I'm square?" he asked slowly.

"Dad was human," she replied softly. "He made some mistakes. But he never made a mistake in a horse foreman yet. He has said to me a dozen times: 'Judy, watch the way a man treats his horse if you want to size him up! And never put your horses into the care of a man who isn't white, clean through.' Dad knew, Bud Lee!"

Lee made no answer. For a little Judith, back at the long table and looking strangely small in the big, bare room before this massive piece of furniture, stared into vacancy with reminiscent eyes. Then, with a little shrug of her shoulders, she turned again to the tall foreman.

"Why did you tell Trevors this morning that you were going to quit work?" she asked with abrupt directness.

"Because," he answered, and by now his flush had subsided and his grave good-humor had come back to him with his customary serenity, "I felt like moving on."

"Because," she insisted, "you know that there was some dirty work afoot and did not care to be messed up in it?"

Now here, most positively, Bud Lee said within himself, was a person to reckon with. How did she know all that? She was just a girl, somewhere, as old Carson put it, between eighteen and twenty-two. What business did a kid like this have knowing so blamed much?

"You've got your rope on the right pair of horns," he said after his brief pause.

"How did you know that Trevors was working the double-cross on this deal?" she demanded.

"I didn't know," he said stiffly. "I just guessed. The same as you. He was spending too much money; he was getting too little to show for it; he was selling too much stock too cheap."

"What's the matter with you?" cried the girl, surprising him with the heat of her words and the sudden darkening of her eyes. "Why do you insist on being so downright stand-offish and stiff and aloof? What have I done to you that you can't be decent? Here I am only putting foot on my own land and you make me feel like an intruder."

"I am answering your questions."

"Like a half-animated trained iceberg, yes. Can't you act like a human being? Oh, I've got your number, Bud Lee, and you are just as narrow between the horns as the rest of the outfit. You are narrow and prejudiced and blindly unreasonable! I know as much about ranching as any man of you; I know more about this outfit because the best man that ever set foot on it, and that's Luke Sanford, taught me every crook, and bend of it; and now, just because I'm a girl and not a boy, you stand off like I had the smallpox; just when I need loyalty and understanding and when, the Lord knows, I've already got a double handful of trouble, I can't count for a minute on men that have been taking my pay for months! Get some of the mildew and cobwebs out of your head and tell me this: What reason in the world is there why you choose to think I haven't any business wearing my own shoes?"

"That's sure putting it straight," said Lee slowly.

"You just bet it's putting it straight!" she announced vigorously. "And you'll find that it's a way I have, putting things straight. I was trained to the business by a better man than you'll ever be, Bud Lee."

"Maybe so," he admitted without heat. "I'll take off my hat to Luke Sanford for a man. And I'll take off my hat to you, if you want to know. But, training or no training, this is no job for a lady, and shooting up Trevors and riding the Prince isn't going to make it so. Sure enough it's none of my butt-in what sort of thing you do. But at the same time there's no call for me to say you're doing fine when I don't see it that way."

"What you're looking for," sniffed Judith contemptuously, "is a female being extinct this one hundred years! You'd have every girl wear tails to her gowns, and duck and dodge behind fans and faint every time she jabbed her thumb with a pin!"

"I can't see that a woman's place is riding bucking broncos and rampsing around. . . ."

"A woman's place!" she scoffed. "Her place where a blunder-headed man puts her! How do you know what her place is? Do you suppose the blood in a healthy-bodied, healthy-minded woman is any different from your blood? How would you like to be told just what your place is? To be jammed, for instance, into a little bungalow in a city; to be squeezed into a dress-suit and told 'Stay there and look sweet'; to be commanded not to get up a natural sweat, nor to kick over the traces with which some woman had hitched you to the cart of convention. How'd *you* like it, Bud Lee?"

Bud Lee grinned and a new look crept into his eyes. "Being Bud Lee," he answered frankly, "I wouldn't stand it for one little tick of the clock! If you want me to swap talk with you; all day at ninety bucks a month, all right. I'd say there's two kinds of men, too. There's my kind; there's the Dave Burril Lee kind. You see, he s a sort of relation of mine, is Dave Burril Lee, and I'm not exactly proud of him. He's the kind that wears dress-suits and sticks in a bungalow. He's proud of his name Burril and Lee, both, because big men down South wore 'em before he did, and they were relations. He's swelled up over the way he can dance and ride after a fox, and over the coin he's got in the bank. Then there's Bud Lee who ducks out of that sort of a scrap-heap and beats it for the open."

"I get you!" broke in Judith, her eyes very bright. "And you men here, my men, want me to be the sort of woman that your precious cousin, Dave Burril, is a man? Is that it? Where's your logic this morning?"

"Meaning horse sense?" he smiled. "It's in these few little words: 'What's right for a man may be dead wrong for a woman.'"

"Oh, scat!" she cried impatiently. "What am I wasting time with you for? You're right when you say that if I am paying you ninety dollars a month and grub and blankets I'd better get something out of you besides talk." She swung back to her table. "What was Trevors's latest excuse for selling at a sacrifice?" she asked, her tone dry and businesslike. "Why was he selling those horses at fifty dollars a head?"

"Told me he just had a wire last night from Young Hampton, asking for three thousand," he explained in a similar tone, though his eyes were twinkling at her.

"Pollock Hampton has his nerve!" she snapped. She took up the telephone instrument at her elbow and demanded the Western Union at Rocky Bend. "Judith Sanford speaking," she said crisply. "Repeat the message of last night for the general manager, Blue Lake Ranch."

In a moment she had it. "So Trevors wasn't lying about that part of it," she said reluctantly. And to the Western Union agent, "Take this message:

POLLOCK HAMPTON, Hotel Glennlyn, San Francisco:

Impossible send money now or for some time. Have fired Trevors. Running outfit myself. Need every cent we can raise to pay interest on loans, men's salaries and keep going. This is final.

JUDITH SANFORD, *General Manager*.

"That may start his gray matter working," she ended as she clicked up the receiver. "Now, Lee, will you stick with me ten days or so and give me time to get a man in your place?"

"Yes, I'll do that, Miss Sanford."

"You will help me in every way you can while you are with me?"

"When I work for a man--or a woman," he added gravely, "I don't hold back anything."

"All right. Then start in right now and tell me about the gang Trevors has taken on. Are they all crooks?"

"I wouldn't say so. I wouldn't put it that strong."

"That little gray, quick-spoken man with the smelly pipe--he's straight, isn't he?"

"That would be old Carson? Yes; he's a good man. You won't find a better."

"Is he going to quit, too? Just because I've come?"

Lee shook his head. "If you work him right Carson will stick right along. Being white clean through, being broader-minded than I am"--and the twinkle came again into his eyes--"Carson'll show you a square deal."

"Has he any love for Bayne Trevors?"

"Maybe you'd better ask Carson."

In a flash she was on her feet and had gone to the door. "Carson!" she called loudly. "Come here, will you?"

There was a little silence, a low sound of laughter, then Carson's sharp voice answering: "I'm coming!"

Judith went back to her chair. She did not speak until Carson's wiry form slipped through the doorway. Then with the old cattleman's shrewd, hard eyes upon her she turned from a clip full of papers she had been looking through and spoke to him quietly:

"You used to work for the Granite Canyon crowd, didn't you, Carson?"

"Yes'm," he answered.

"Cattle foreman there for several years?"

"Yes'm."

"Helped clean out the Roaring Creek gang didn't you, Carson?"

Carson shifted a bit, colored under her fixed eyes, and finally admitted:

"Yes'm."

"Haven't had a real first-class fight for quite a bit, have you, Carson? Not since that gash on your jaw healed? Not since you and Scotty Webb mixed with the Roaring Creekers?"

Carson rubbed his jaw, flashed a quick look at Bud Lee as though for moral support, looked still further embarrassed, and finally choked over his brief:

"No'm."

Judith sat smiling brightly up at his hard features. "I've heard dad talk about that," she said thoughtfully. "I guess I've got at least one real man on the ranch, Carson. Oh, don't dodge like that! I'm not going to put my arms around you and kiss you on the top of your head. But I do love a man that loves a fair fight. . . . Lee, here, has given me his promise to stick on the job for ten days or so, to give me time to get some one else to look after my horses."

"Yes'm," said Carson, fingering his pipe and looking down.

For a few moments the girl sat still, now and then flashing a quick, keen look from one to the other of her two foremen. Then, abruptly, her eyes on Carson, she snapped: "You've found out, more or less recently, haven't you, that Bayne Trevors is a crook? You've perhaps even guessed that he's been taking money from me with one hand and from the Western Lumber with the other?"

"Yes'm," said Carson. "I doped it up like that."

"Why," cried the girl, "he's fired all of the old men and Heaven knows how many of his sort he's put in their places! Help me clean 'em out, Carson! Where will we begin? I've chucked Trevors and Ward Hannon. Who goes next, Carson?"

"Benny the cook," said Carson gently. "An' I'd be obliged, ma'am, if you'd let me go boot him off'n the ranch."

"That's talking," she said enthusiastically. "You can attend to him. Any one else?"

Carson shook his head. "I got my suspicions," he said. "But that's all I'm dead sure on."

"The others can wait then. Now, I'm taking a gamble on you and Lee. You have all kinds of chances to double-cross me. But I've got to take a chance now and then. I'm going to tell you something: Trevors is trying to sell me out to the Western Lumber people. He is one of their crowd and has been since they bought him up six months ago. They want our timber tract over the north ridge but they don't think they will have to pay the price. They want the lake; they want the water-power of Blue Lake River! They want pretty well all we've got. The ranch outside the stock we've got running on it, is worth a clean million dollars if it is worth a nickel. Well, the Western Lumber Company has offered us exactly two hundred and fifty thousand! Only quarter of what it's worth! They know we're mortgaged; they know the interest we have to pay is heavy; they know Pollock Hampton, for one, is a spender who knows nothing about big business; they think that I, because I'm a girl, am a fool. It looks to them like a melon easy to cut and ripe for the slicing."

She paused a moment, frowning thoughtfully at the floor. Then suddenly she lifted her eyes to Carson's, saying crisply: "Trevors took time at the end to tell me something. That something was that he was going to make me sell. He was excited a bit, I'll admit, or he wouldn't have spoken quite so plainly. And he counted upon the fact of my sex, of course, to feel confident that he could throw a scare into me.

He even threatened, if I hadn't come to my senses before the ranch was dry in the summer, to burn me out!"

Carson blinked at her. "How's that?" he asked.

She told him again, coolly indifferent, it seemed to Carson.

"The durned polecat!" whispered the cattle foreman.

"Now then," cried Judith, "you've got your first job cut out for you. Let Bayne Trevors or one of his gang set foot on Blue Lake land, and I'll tell you what I think of you, Carson! Or is the job going to be too big for you?"

Carson smiled deprecatingly. "I'd like to see 'em try it," he said in that soft, whispering voice which upon occasions was characteristic of him. "I sure would, Miss Judy!"

"That's all this morning, Carson," she said quietly. "On your way don't forget to look in on your friend Benny."

Carson went hastily down the knoll, his eyes bright. Judith laughed softly.

"I've got his number, Bud Lee! All that's needed to keep that old mountain-lion on the job is to show him a real fight ahead! And by golly, Mr. Man, there's going to be scrap enough from the very jump to make Carson forget whether he's working for a woman or John W. Satan, Esquire!"

V
THE BIGNESS OF THE VENTURE

And now," said Judith Sanford to the stillness about her--she was alone in the big ranch-house--"not being constructed of iron, I'm going to take a snooze."

She yawned, stretched her supple young body luxuriously, and passed slowly through the empty rooms which, at her command, Jose had opened to the sweet morning air. Through the great living-room, library, and music-room, where the grand piano stood dejectedly in its mantle of dust, she came to her own chambers at the southwest corner of the building. Her bed was made, the sheets clean and fresh and inviting, dressing-gown and slippers were upon the window-seat, and from her table a vase of glorious roses sent out a welcoming perfume.

"Good old Jose," she smiled.

Vivid blossom that she was upon the tough, hardy stalk of her pioneer ancestry, creature of ardent flame and passion which her blood and her life in the open had made her, she was not devoid of the understanding of the limit of physical endurance. Last night, through the late moonlight and later starlight, through the thick darkness which lay across the mountain trails before the coming of day, on into the dawn, she had ridden the forty miles from the railroad at Rocky Bend. Certain of treachery on the part of Bayne Trevors, she had arrived only to find him plotting another blow at her interests. She had ridden a mad brute of a horse whose rebellious struggle against her authority had taxed her to the last ounce of her strength. She had shot a man in the right shoulder and the left forearm. . . . And now, with no one to see her, she was pale and shaking a little, suddenly faint from the heavy beating of her own heart. She had had virtually no sleep last night. She was glad of it. For now she would sleep, sleep.

"I am not to be called, no matter what happens," she said to Jose who came trotting to the tinkle of her bell. "Thank you for the roses, Jose."

Slipping out of her clothes, she drew the sheet up to her throat--and tossed for a wretched hour before sleep came to her. A restless sleep, filled with broken bits of unpleasant dreams.

At two o'clock, swiftly dressing after a leisurely bath, she went out into the courtyard, where she found Jose making a pretense of gardening, whereas in truth for a matter of hours he had done little but watch for her coming.

"Jose," she said, as he swept off his wide hat and made her the bow reserved for *la senorita* and *la senorita* alone, "you will have to be lady's maid and errand-boy for me until I get things running right. I am going to telephone into town this minute for a woman to do my cooking and housekeeping and be a nuisance around generally. While I do that, will you scare up something for me to eat and then saddle a horse for me? And don't make a fire, either; just something cold out of a can, you know."

She went to the office, arranged over the wire with Mrs. Simpson of Rocky Bend to come out on the following day, and then spent fifteen minutes studying the pay-roll taken from the safe, which, fortunately, Trevors had left open. As Jose came in with a big tray she was running through a file of reports made at the month-end, two weeks ago, by certain of the ranch foremen.

"Put it down on the table, Jose. Thank you," and she found time for a smile at her devoted servitor; "Now, have a horse ready, will you?" And without waiting for Jose's answer, taking up the telephone, she asked for the office at the Lower End, as the rich valley land of the western portion of the ranch was commonly known.

Briefly making herself known to the owner of the boyish voice which answered, she asked, for "Doc" Tripp and was informed that the ranch veterinarian was no longer with the outfit. Judith frowned.

"Where is he?"

"Rocky Bend, I think."

"When did he leave us?"

"Three days ago."

"Why?"

"Fired. Mr. Trevors let him go."

"Hm!" said Judith. "Who has taken his place?"

"Bill Crowdy is sort of acting vet, right now."

"Thanks," she said. Clicking off, she put in a call for "Doc" Tripp in Rocky Bend. "Get him for me as quick as you can, will you, please?" she asked of the operator in town.

For five minutes she munched at a sandwich and pored over the papers before her, dealing with this or that of the many interests of the big ranch. When at last her telephone-bell rang she found that it was Tripp.

"Hello, Doc," she said cordially. "I haven't seen you for so long I almost have forgotten how you comb your hair!" Tripp laughed with her at that; across the miles she could picture him running his big hand through the rebellious shock. "Yes, I'm back to stay, and from the looks of it I didn't come any too soon. Yes, Doc, we do miss him," and her voice softened wonderfully to Tripp's mention of the man who had been more than father to her, more than friend to him. "But we are going to buck up and show folks that he *knew*. He would have made a go of the thing; we are going to do it. What was the trouble with you and Trevors?"

Tripp explained succinctly. He and the general manager had disagreed openly and frequently about that part of the work in which, until the coming of Trevors, the veterinarian had been entirely unhampered. Two months ago Trevors had reduced Tripp's wages and had threatened another cut.

"Just to make me quit, you know," he added. "And I would have quit if it had been any other outfit in the world."

"I know," she said, and she did understand. "Go on. What was the excuse for canning you?"

"Case of lung-worms," he told her. "Some of the calves, I don't know just how many yet. He insisted on my treating them the old way."

"Slaked lime? Or sulphur fumes?" she said quickly. "And you insisted on chloroform?"

"You've hit it!" he exclaimed wonderingly. "How'd you know?"

"I haven't been loafing on the job the last six months," she laughed. "I've been at the school at Davis and hobnobbing with some of the university men at Berkeley. They're doing some great work there. Doc, I'll want to talk to you about it. You're going down there, expenses paid, to brush up with a course or two this year.

Now, how soon can you get back here?--Trevors? Oh, Trevors is fired. I'm running the ranch myself. And, Doc, I need a few men like you! Can you come early to-morrow?--To-night? You're a God-blessed brick! Yes, I'll stop that murderous sulphur treatment if it isn't too late. Good-by."

She lost no time in calling for Bill Crowdy, the man whom Trevors had put into Tripp's place.

"By the way," she said when the man with the voice which had sounded so boyish in her ears answered again, "who are you?"

"Ed Masters," he told her. "Electrician, you know."

A glance at the pay-roll in front of her showed that Edward Masters, general electrician, was a new man and was drawing eighty-five dollars monthly.

"What are you doing this afternoon?" she demanded sharply--"just hanging around the office? Is that the way you earn your eighty-five dollars?"

"Not always. But Trevors told me to be on hand to-day to take some orders."

"What work?"

"Don't know," he said frankly. "He didn't say."

"Well," said Judith, "I'll tell you one thing, Ed Masters. If you are one of the loaf-around kind you'd better call for your time to-night. If there's anything for you to do, go do it. Don't wait for Trevors. He's gone. Yes, for good. You can report to me here the first thing in the morning. Now send me Crowdy."

"He's down in the hospital and the hospital phone is out of order."

"And you're an electrician, hanging around for orders! That's your first job. Send the first man you can get your hands on to tell Crowdy I say not to touch one of those calves with the lung-worm. And not to do anything else but get ready to talk with me. I'll be down in half an hour."

She clicked up the receiver, drank a cup of lukewarm coffee, noting subconsciously that Jose must have had a fire ready against the time of her awakening, and again consulted the files before her. Then again she used the telephone, ringing the Lower End office. This time it was another voice answering her.

"Where's Masters?" she asked.

"Gone down to the cow hospital," was the answer.

"Where's Johnson, the irrigation foreman?"

"Out in the south fields."

"And Dennings?"

"Went to look the olives over."

"Send out for both of them. I'm coming right down as fast as a horse will carry me and I want to talk with them. Wait a minute--I'll tell you when I'm through with you. Who are you, anyway?"

"Williams, the ranch carpenter."

"What *are* you doing to-day? Repairs needed at the office where you are?"

"No. You see----"

"You bet I see!" she cried warmly. "The first thing I see is that I've got more men on this job than I need. If there's no work for you to do, call tonight for your time. If you've got anything to do, go do it."

She clicked off again, waited a brief second and rang three for the dairy. After she had rung several times and got no answer, she murmured to herself:

"There's some one too busy on the ranch to be just hanging round after all, it seems."

And she went out to Jose and the waiting horse.

As she rode the five miles down to the office at the Lower End, her thoughts were constantly charged with an appreciation of the wonders which had been worked about her everywhere since that day, ten years ago, when she had first come with Luke Sanford to the original Blue Lake ranch. Then there had been only a wild cattle-range, ten thousand acres of brush, timber, and uncultivated open spaces. Nowhere would one find rougher, wilder stock-land in California. But Luke Sanford had seen possibilities and had bought the whole ten thousand acres, counting, from the first sight of it, upon acquiring as soon as might be those other thousands of acres which now made Blue Lake ranch one of the biggest of Western ventures.

It was late May, and the afternoon air was sweet and warm with the passing of spring. The girl's eager eyes travelled the length of the sky-seeking cliff almost at the back door of the ranch-house, which stood like some mighty barricade thrown up in that mythical day given over to the colossal struggle of a contending race of giants, and she found that there, alone, time had shown no change. Elsewhere, improvements at every turn were living monuments to the tireless brain of her father. Stock-corrals, sturdily built, out-houses spotless in their gleaming whitewash, monster barns, fenced-off fields, bridges across the narrow chasm of the frothing river, telephone-poles with their wires binding into one sheaf the numerous activities of the ranch, a broad, graded road over which she and her father had come here the last time together in the big touring-car.

Here the valley was only a mile across, shut in on both sides by cliff and steep, rocky mountain, walled by cliffs at the upper end, where the river from three-mile distant Blue Lake came down in flashing waterfalls.

But, as she rode, the valley widened, changed in character. At first, wandering herds of beef-cattle, with now and then a riding cowboy turning in his saddle to wonder at her; then a gate to be opened as she stooped forward from her own saddle, and wide fields where the grass stood tall and untrodden and blooded Jersey cows looked up in mild interest; yonder a small pasture in which were five Guernseys, kept in religious seclusion, under ideal conditions, to further certain investigations into the ratios of five different kinds of fodder to the amount of butter-fat produced; across a green meadow a pure-blooded Jersey bull, whose mellow bellowings drew Judith's eyes to the clean line of his perfect back, over which, with pawing hoofs, he was throwing much trampled earth; in a more distant pen, accepting the trumpeted challenge and challenging back, a beautiful specimen of careful breeding in Ayrshire.

The road wound on, following generally the line of the river, which began a generous broadening, flowing more evenly through level fields. Looking down the valley, Judith could see the whitewashed clump of buildings where were the second office, the store and the blacksmith's shop, the tiny cottages. And beyond, the barns, the dairy, the tall silos standing like lookout towers, the alfalfa-fields criss-crossed with irrigating ditches, and still farther on, the pasture-lands where the big herd of cows was grazing.

Here the valley was spread out until from side to side it measured something more than four miles. The bordering mountains, like the river, had grown into a softer mood; rolling hills scantily timbered, rich in grass, were dotted with herds, cattle and horses, or fenced off here and there, reserved for later pasturage.

Across the river, to the south, Judith marked the wandering calves, offspring of the herd; to the north, along the foothills, the subdued green of the olive-orchards.

"It's a big, big thing!" she whispered, and her eyes were very bright with it all, her cheeks flushed. "Big!"

Passing one of the great barns, she heard the trumpet call of a stallion and, turning, saw in the corral one of those glorious brutes which Bud Lee had spoken of to Trevors as "clean spirit." From the instant her eyes filled to the massive beauty of him, she knew who he was: Night Shade, sprung from the union of Mountain King and Black Empress; regal-blooded, ebon-black from silken fetlock to flowing mane; a splendid four-year-old destined to tread his proud way to a first prize at the coming State fair at Sacramento, a horse many stock-fanciers had coveted.

She stopped and marvelled afresh at him, paid him his due of unstinted admiration, and then spurred on to the little clump of buildings marking the lower ranch headquarters. At the store, where a ten-by-ten room was partitioned off to serve as office, she swung down from the saddle and, leaving her horse with dragging reins, went in.

"Hello, Charlie. You're still left to us, are you?" she said, as she stepped forward to shake hands with Miller, the storekeeper and general utility man of the settlement. "I'm glad to see you.

"So'm I, Miss Judy," grinned Charlie, looking the part. "Howdy."

"I wanted to see Johnson and Dennings. Are they here yet?"

"No," answered Miller. "Johnson, the ditch man, you mean? He's somewhere at the Upper End. Has got a crew of men up there making a new dam or somethin' or other. Been at it purty near a week, now, I guess. They camp up there."

"How many men are with him?" she asked quickly.

"About a dozen," and he looked hard at her. Judith frowned. But instead of saying what she might be thinking, she inquired where Dennings was.

"Out in the olive-orchards, I guess." He paused, filled a pipe he had neither desire nor intention of smoking, and said abruptly: "What's this I hear about Trevors? Canned him?"

"Yes."

"Um!" said Miller. "Well, Miss Judy, I ain't sayin' it wasn't purty near time he got the hooks. But, lemme tell you something. While you're riding around this afternoon, if I was you I'd pike over to the milking corrals."

She looked at him sharply.

"What is it, Charlie?"

"You just ride over," said Miller. "It ain't more'n a step an' I'll just shet up store an' mosey along after you."

Vaguely uneasy because of Charlie Miller's manner, Judith galloped down toward the four corrals where the cows were milked. From a distance she saw that there were a number of men, ten or twelve of them, standing in a close-packed group. She wondered what it was that had drawn them from their work at this time of day; what that big, bull-voiced man was saying to them. She heard the muttering rumble of his words before the words themselves meant anything to her. A quick glance over her shoulder showed her Charlie Miller hastening behind her, pick-handle in hand.

Her way carried her by a long, narrow building standing out like a great capital E, the cow hospital. She thought of Bill Crowdy and the sick calves as she drew near, but was passing on to the men at the milk corrals, when the breeze, blowing lightly from the west, brought to her nostrils a whiff of sulphur.

A quick tide of red ran into her cheeks; that fool, Ed Masters, had not told Crowdy to refrain from the old-fashioned, deadly treatment! Almost before her horse had set his four feet at the command of a quick touch upon the reins, the girl was down and hurrying into the middle door of the three, calling out as she went:

"Crowdy! Oh, Crowdy!"

She came into a small whitewashed room where were a table, two chairs, and a telephone; passed through this into the calf-yard. Here were several compartments with doors which allowed of making them almost air-tight. And here she was met by a stronger smell of sulphur fumes.

"Crowdy!" she called again. "Where are you?"

Bill Crowdy, a heavy, squat figure of a man, shifty-eyed, with hard mouth and a nervous, restless air, came down a long hallway, smoking a cigarette. His eyes rested with no uncertain dislike upon Judith's eager face.

"I'm Crowdy," he said. "Want me?"

"I told Masters to tell you to stop the sulphur treatment for the lung-worm calves. Hasn't he told you?"

"Mr. Trevors said I was to give it to them," said Crowdy. "I can't be taking orders off'n every hop-o'-my-thumb like that college kid."

"Then Masters did tell you?"

"Sure, he told me," said Crowdy in surly defiance. "But if I was to listen to everything the likes of him says----"

Judith's eyes were fairly snapping.

"You'll listen to the likes of me, Bill Crowdy!" she cried passionately, a small fist clinched. "You get those calves out into some fresh air just as quick as the Lord will let you! Into a pen by themselves. Doc Tripp will attend to them in the morning."

"Tripp's gone."

"He's on his way back, right now. And you're on your way off the ranch. Understand? You can come to the office for your pay to-night."

Crowdy shrugged his shoulders and turned away.

"If I'm fired," he growled in that ugly voice which was so fitting a companion to that ugly mouth of his, "I quit right now. Get some of your other Willies to turn your calves out."

For a moment, in the heat of her anger, Judith's quirt was lifted as though she would strike him. Then she turned instead and ran to do her own bidding. A moment later Miller was with her. The two of them got the calves--there were seven of them--out of the sulphur-laden air and into the corral. The poor brutes, coughing softly in paroxysms, some of them frothing at the mouth, two of them falling repeatedly and rising slowly upon trembling legs, filed by in a pitiful string. One of the youngest lay still in the hospital, dead.

"He would have killed them all," said Judith, her teeth set as she looked at the living calves in the corral where, with necks thrust far out, they fought for each breath. "And Bayne Trevors ordered a treatment that he knows has gone into the discard! Charlie, that man has gone further than I thought he had the nerve to go."

"Crowdy did something else that don't look just right," said Miller, gazing with eyes of longing after the burly, departing figure. "I saw him do it just after Masters carried him your message. He drove three of the sick calves--there's a dozen or more got the worms, you know--out into the pasture with the well calves."

Judith didn't answer. She looked at Miller a moment as though she thought this must be some wretched jest of his. And when she read in his eyes the earnestness in his heart, there rose within her the question: "How far has Bayne Trevors gone?"

"Charlie," she said finally, "I want you to close store for the rest of the day. Get some one to help you and cut the sick calves out from the bunch. Haze them back here into the detention corral. Tripp will attend to them all in the morning. Now, tell me--what's wrong down at the milk corrals? What are all of those men up to?"

"We're going to see, me an' you," answered Miller. "I don't just know. But I do know there's a big guy down there that come onto the ranch a couple of hours ago an' that don't belong here. He's that guy talking. Name of Nelson. He ain't done any talking to me, but from a word or two I picked up from one of the milkers I got a hunch he's been sent over by Trevors."

Nelson, the big emissary for Trevors--for he admitted the fact openly and pleasantly--took off his hat to Judith and said he guessed he'd be going. And the men with whom he had been talking, including all of the milkers and all of the other workmen upon whom Nelson could get his meddlesome hands at short notice, all men whom Trevors had placed here, made known in hesitant speech or awkward silence that they were going with Nelson. There were good jobs open with the lumber company, it seemed. Nelson even expressed the hope that the quitting of these men wouldn't work any hardship to the Blue Lake ranch.

Judith, her eyes flashing, asked no man of them to remain, seeing that thus she would but humiliate herself fruitlessly, and turned away. And yet, with the herds of cows with bursting bags soon ready for the nightly milking, she watched the men move away, her heart bitter with anger.

"They've got to be milked, Charlie," was all that she said. "Who will milk them until I can get a new crew?"

"I'll tuck in an' help," answered Miller ruefully. "I hate it worse'n poison, an' I can't milk more'n ten cows, workin twenty-four-hour shifts. I'll try an' scare up some of the other boys that can milk." But he shook his head and looked regretfully at the pick-handle. "Good milkers is scarce as gold eggs," he muttered. "And the separator men has quit with the rest."

"Get Masters, the electrician, on the job. Get anybody you can. I'm going back to the ranchhouse pretty soon and I'll try to send some one from there."

"Cowboys can't milk," said Miller positively. "An' besides, they won't. But somehow we'll make out for a day or so."

"We've got to make out!" exclaimed Judith. "We've got to beat that man Trevors, Charlie, and do it quick. If he'll try to keep us short-handed, if he'll spend money to do it, if he'll do a trick like giving sulphur for lung-worm and then send infected stock out into the herds, I don't know just where he will stop--unless we stop him."

In spite of her intentions, it was nearing the time of dusk when she returned to the ranchhouse. As she came up the knoll from the barn, she saw for the first time a thin line of bluish smoke rising from the north ridge. Saw and understood the new menace.

For that way had Benny, the discharged cook, gone.

VI
YOUNG HAMPTON REGISTERS A PROTEST

It was after eight o'clock when Tripp rode in on a sweat-wet horse Judith met him in the courtyard, giving him her two hands impulsively.

"I'm so glad you've come, Doc!" she cried softly. "Oh, you don't know how glad--yet."

She called Jose to take Tripp's mount and then led the way into the great living-room where deep cushions and leather chairs made for comfort.

"I'll give you time to draw a second breath," she told him, forcing into her tone a lightness which she did not quite feel, even though a surge of satisfaction had warmed her at the first thud of his horse's hoofs. "Then we'll talk."

She switched on the lights and turned to look at Tripp. He was the same little old Doc Tripp, she noted. His wiry body scarcely bigger than a boy's of fourteen, he was a man of fifty whose face, like his body, suggested the boy with bright, eager eyes and a frank, friendly smile.

"Prettier than ever, eh, Judy?" Tripp cocked his head to one side and gave his unqualified approval of the slim, supple body, and superb carriage of this girl of the mountains, warming to the vivid, vital beauty of the rosy face. "Been driving those cow-college boys down at Berkeley plumb crazy, I'll bet a prize colt!"

Judith laughed at him, watched his slight form disappear in the wide arms of a chair which seemed fairly to smother him in its embrace. Then from her own nook by the fireplace she opened her heart to him:

"It's not just that Trevors has crippled me by taking all of my milkers away; not just that he has come near doing I don't know how much harm in having Crowdy turn those calves with the lung-worm out into the fields with the others; not just that during the last few months, he has lost money for us right and left; not just that

Benny, the cook, has tried to fire the range."

"What's that last?" said Tripp quickly. "Tried to smoke you out, huh?"

She told him briefly. How she had first seen the smoke as she came back to the ranch-house; how she had sent Jose on the run to get some of the other hands to see that the fire did not spread; how, a little while ago, Carson, the cattle foreman, had come in and assured her that the damage was negligible.

"It was just a brush fire," said Judith. "Thank Heaven, things are pretty green yet. Carson says it might have been lighted by Benny, who, it seems, is one of Trevors's hirelings and not above this sort of thing; or it might have been accidentally started by some careless hunter. Anyway, and that's enough for me, the fire broke out close to the trail that Benny travelled on his way to the Western Lumber camp. But it isn't just these things which have set me to wondering, Doc. What I want to know is this: in how many other, still undiscovered ways, has Trevors been knifing us? And what else will he have ready to spring on us now?"

"Just what do you mean?" Tripp looked a her keenly.

"This case of lung-worm, to begin with: where did it come from?"

"Imported," said Tripp. "Trevors bought those calves, or at least four of the sick ones, last month. Brought them in from somewhere down the river. Smuggled 'em in, so far as I am concerned. Never gave me a chance to look them over." He paused a second. "Specially imported, I might say."

"I knew it!" cried Judith. "That's the sort of thing I am afraid of. If he has gone to the limit of introducing one disease among our cattle, what other plagues has he brought to the ranch? Has he imported any other outside stock?"

"No. He's been busier selling at a sacrifice than buying, just as I wrote you. Never another head has he bought lately--unless," and Tripp's eyes twinkled at her, "you count pigeons!"

"Pigeons!" repeated Judith.

Tripp nodded.

"Funny, isn't it," he went on lightly--"that a man like Bayne Trevors, hard as nails and as free of sentiment as a mule, should fancy little cooing, innocent-like pigeons? You'll hear them in the morning."

But Judith was not to be distracted by Tripp's talk. She smiled at him, however, to show him that she had understood and appreciated the purpose back of his light words.

"We're all going to have our hands full for a spell, Doc," was what she said. "To Trevors, with a free swing here, it must have appeared rather a simple matter to make so complete a failure as to force us, encumbered as we are, into selling out to the highest bidder inside the year. Especially when he counted young Pollock Hampton as a man without business experience and Judith Sanford as a girl without brains! But, Doc, he must have known, too, that at any time there might occur the very thing which has happened--that he'd lose his job. He strikes me as a rather long-headed man, doesn't he you? Now, a man who saw ahead, figuring on this very contingency, would have more than one trick up his sleeve. We've caught him, luckily, at the sick-calf game, before it is too late. I think that the obvious thing for you to do is to make certain that all the rest of the stock are in shape. Will you begin to-morrow making a thorough investigation?"

"Yes," he answered. "You're right there, Judith. There's nothing like making sure."

"He's not through with us," continued the girl thoughtfully; "you could read that in the look of his jaw and eye when he left. Just what he stands to make on his play, I don't know. But I do know that the Western Lumber crowd is offering us only a quarter of what they'd be willing to pay if they had to. That means that they could afford to bribe Bayne Trevors pretty heavily and still save half a million on the deal if he succeeded in the thing he has begun."

"In his way," admitted Tripp thoughtfully, "Trevors is a big man. Big men cost big money. And, besides, it looks to me as though he were a heavy stockholder in the Western Lumber. He'd stand to win two ways."

"Another thing I want you to do," Judith went on, "is to try to locate all of dad's old men whom Trevors let go. Johnny Hodge and Kelley and Harper and Tod Bruce. We'll need them. We've got to have men that crooked money can't buy."

"Aren't you magnifying things, Judith?" asked Tripp quietly. "There's such a thing as law in this country, you know."

But she shook her head.

"Maybe I am seeing the dangers too big. But I don't think so. And it will be a lot better for Blue Lake ranch if I see them that way at the beginning. And as for the law, it costs money. I'm not sure that Trevors or the lumber people would be averse to getting us involved in a lot of legal intricacies. Oh, he has been careful not to leave any definite proof behind him."

"You hit the bell that time!" laughed Tripp, and Judith smiled with him as there came to their ears the faint tinkle of the telephone-bell in the office.

Judith excused herself and hastened to answer the summons. Hastened because she wanted to be back with Tripp as soon as might be. So, knowing her way so well about the big house, she went quickly through the dark hall-way without turning aside to switch on the lights and came into the office, dimly lighted by the stars shining in through the windows.

"Doc!" Her voice rang out suddenly and Tripp sprang to his feet, wondering what had put that note into her exclamation. "Doc! Come here, quick!"

He ran into the hall that was suddenly illuminated as at last Judith's groping hand found the office switch. He saw Judith running ahead of him, out of the door opening on to the veranda and down into the courtyard.

"What is it?" he asked sharply.

"There was some one here," she told him quickly. "He went out that way, I think. Look through the lilacs."

She ran on one way, Tripp hurrying the other, wondering. They saw the lilacs standing still in the starlight, saw the thick shadows thrown by the columns and grape-covered trellises, heard the murmuring of the fountain.

"Jose, perhaps," suggested Tripp, coming at last to her side.

"No!" cried Judith. "It wasn't. It was somebody in his stocking feet, standing in the hallway, listening to us. I heard him run before me; I saw him for a second, framed against the square of the window as he slipped through and out on the veranda. Who could it have been, Doc?"

But a close search through the shrubbery showed them nothing. It was clear that if a man had been listening at the door he could have had ample opportunity to slip away into the darkness. He would not be loitering here now.

The telephone-bell was still insistently ringing and they turned back to the office.

"Judy," said Tripp solicitously, "don't you go and get nerves, now."

"You think I imagined the whole thing!" She looked at him with clear, confident eyes. "Don't you fool yourself for one little minute, Doc Tripp. I'm not the imagining kind--yet!"

She snatched up the telephone instrument.

"Hello," said Judith. "Who is it?"

It was the telegraph operator in Rocky Bend. A message for Miss Judith Sanford from Pollock Hampton, San Francisco. And the message ran:

What were you thinking of to chuck Trevors? Thoroughly excellent man. You should have consulted me. Don't do anything more until I come. Send conveyance to meet Saturday train. Bringing five guests with me.

POLLOCK HAMPTON.

Judith turned frowning to Tripp.

"As if I didn't have enough on my hands already," she exclaimed bitterly, "without Hampton dragging his fool guests into the mix-up! I could slap his face."

"Do it!" chuckled Tripp. "Good idea!"

VII
THE HAPPENING IN SQUAW CREEK CANON

Busy days followed for Judith Sanford and for every man remaining upon Blue Lake ranch. A score of men, including the milkers, Johnson, the irrigation foreman and his crew of laborers, had quit work, going over openly to Bayne Trevors at the Western Lumber camp. He had work there for every man of them, and Judith was not the only one upon the ranch who came to wonder how much money Trevors--or the lumber company--was prepared to spend in fighting her. From the first day she found the outfit short-handed.

Almost her first answer to Trevors's *coup* was to telegraph San Francisco for a Firth milking-machine, together with an expert sent out by the Firth Company to install and superintend its working for the first few days. At the same time she hired from one of the Sacramento dairies a man who was to be foreman of her own dairy industry, a capable fellow with an intimate practical knowledge of automatic milkers. He, with a couple of strippers paid overtime wages managed until the dairy crew could be builded up again. Her new foreman from the first took the greater part of this burden off her shoulders.

Mrs. Simpson, the matron from Rocky Bend, arrived, true to her promise and, motherly soul that she was, took a keen interest in Judith's comforts and in caring for the big house, of which she immediately waxed proud with an air of semiproprietorship. Jose, from the first, bestowed upon the cheerful, bustling woman a black hatred born of his thoroughgoing Latin jealousy. From this or that corner, appearing unexpectedly, glaring darkly at her in a manner which ruffled her placidity and suggested to her lively imagination terrible visions of knives in one's back, he brought an actual thrill into Mrs. Simpson's long days of routine.

Busy days also for Bud Lee, who had already begun the education of a string of colts. Busy days for Doc Tripp who, unhampered, trusted, aided at every turn by his employer, was from dawn until dark among the ranch live stock, all but feeling pulse and taking temperature of horses, cows, colts, calves, hogs, and mules. He stopped the calf sickness; effected cures in every case excepting one. And the rest of the stock he finally gave a clean bill of health.

Busy days for Carson. Painstakingly he estimated, to the head, the number of cattle the pastures should be carrying, counting from long experience upon the hard months to come from August until December; estimating values; appearing at the week's end to suggest the purchase of a herd of calves from the John Peters Dairy Company, to be had now at a very attractive figure. And suggesting, almost insistently, upon buying a certain Shorthorn bull worth twice the twelve hundred dollars asked for him. Busy days for the foremen who had held over from the management of Trevors or who had been taken on since. The first crop of alfalfa, shot through with foxtails, must be cut without delay and fed into the silos before the beards of the interloping growth could harden. Busy days for the short-handed milking crew; busy days of installing the new milking-machines.

Judith and Doc Tripp had sought to find some trace of the man who, Judith insisted, had listened at the door in the hall. They had found nothing. So that episode, as well as Trevors himself, was shoved aside in their minds, in the stress of activity demanding attention everywhere.

With Saturday came Pollock Hampton and his guests. Trevors had misnamed him a fool, sweepingly mistaking youth, business inexperience and a careless way, for lack of brains. Just a breezy young fellow, likable, gay-hearted, keen for the joy of life, scarcely more than a boy after all. One of those rare beings whose attitude toward his fellow mortals was one of generous faith, who sought to see the best in people, who had an outspoken admiration for efficiency in any form. He came to the ranch prepared to like everything and everybody.

"Look here!" he exclaimed to Judith, before she had had time for more than a sweeping appraisal of his friends. "Why didn't you tell me you were up to a thing like this? Great Scott, Judith, you don't know what you are tackling, do you? It's ripping of you; you're a sheer wonder to tie into it; you've got no end of nerve. But running a ranch like this--why, it's a big proposition for a thunderingly big man to swing."

"Is it?" smiled Judith.

Beyond that, the only answer he got from this brief conference was the timely suggestion that his chief concern for the immediate present lay in making his guests comfortable.

Accompanying young Hampton were "Major" Langworthy, a little short, fat, bald gentleman, who, so far as the knowledge of his club members went, had never been connected with any part of the army or navy, unless one counted his congenial brigades of cocktail drinkers; Mrs. Langworthy, his supercilious, uninteresting wife; Marcia, his languidly graceful daughter, in whom Hampton gave certain signs of being considerably interested; Marshal Rogers, the Oakland lawyer, and Frank Farris, the artist. Also Marcia's maid and Hampton's Japanese valet, Fujioki. In due course of time this representative of the Flowery Kingdom grew to be great friends with Jose, the two forthwith suspected by Mrs. Simpson of all sorts of dark plots and of a racial sympathy which must be watched lest it produce "something terrible."

Pollock Hampton, holding a third of the shares of the big venture, with his legitimate claim upon a third of the income, was of course a factor which must be taken into account. Judith, knowing little of him, sought to know more, watched him when he was talking, got his views upon many matters that came up haphazard, and found that, while she liked him, she would have been more than glad if he had not come to still further complicate matters for her. For it was open and shut that his interest and enthusiasm would demand a voice. She asked frankly how long he planned to stay?

"I'm here for good," he answered cheerfully. His explanation followed with a grin, quite as though he were telling her of some rare good news: "Money's all gone, creditors are nuisances, there's no prospect with you here of having you send me anything. What is left for me but to stay?"

Judith suggested a monthly allowance. Hampton laughed good-humoredly.

"Pay me to keep me out of the way? There's nothing stirring, Judith. Absolutely. I'm here to give a hand."

Judith had hopes, even yet, that a couple or weeks or a month at the most, of life as it runs forty miles from a railroad would dampen and finally extinguish his bright enthusiasm. But swiftly those hopes died. This was his first visit to the mountains, and for a man sick of the city's social round, every inch of the ranch, river and cliffs and rolling hills had its compelling interest. Perhaps the thing which Judith overlooked was the blood of his fathers. For before Pollock Hampton, Sr., had made his money, he and his wife had been, like Luke Sanford, pioneers. Now something in the mountains here called vaguely to the soul of young Hampton and made him restless and stirred his heart. He looked up at the sheer and mighty fall of rock behind the ranchhouse and his face glowed; he leaned over the rail of a rustic bridge and forgot Marcia, who was with him, as he watched the beauty of the foam-flecked water. As he stood stock-still, looking on while Bud Lee rode a bucking bronco, his eyes were bright and eager.

"Glory to be!" he exclaimed to the major, who had been coaxed away from the buffet for a brief half-hour. "Watch that man ride! While I've been learning to dance and play the piano these men have been doing real things."

"Let's go have something," said the major hurriedly. For it did not fit in with his and Mrs. Langworthy's plans to have Hampton risk his neck at such pastimes--at least not yet.

It soon became obvious that long ago Hampton had given freely of his admiration to Bayne Trevors. For Trevors had taken the time, his own purpose in mind, to look in upon Hampton some months ago in San Francisco. Further, he had created the impression which he sought to make. An impression, by the way, not entirely erroneous.

"A great man!" cried Hampton warmly. "The only man I know big enough to swing a job like this."

To himself he said that the chief good he could do at the outset was to work to get Trevors back. With this in his mind and having had no full account of Judith's manner of ejecting the general manager, he went straight to her.

"Trevors is a friend of mine," he said lightly. "I'm going to ask him over to meet my guests. No objection, is there?"

She looked at him keenly.

"Do as you please," was her cool answer. "I imagine he won't care to come."

Launched upon his first business venture, Hampton went to the telephone. That evening at table he surprised Judith not a little when he said casually that Trevors had said he'd run over in a day or so, as soon as he could find time.

"What's that?" he asked, breaking off.

For certainly Judith had started to speak. But now she merely shrugged her shoulders and sat in silent thoughtfulness.

Mrs. Langworthy had no liking to bestow upon such as Judith. The girl, she confided every night to the major, was unladylike, unwomanly, **outre**, horsy, unthinkable, an insult to any woman into whose presence she came. The major agreed monosyllabically or with silent nods for the sake of peace. Personally he was rather inclined to fancy Judith's uncorseted figure, to admire her red-blooded beauty, and he always touched up the ends of his mustaches in her presence.

Judith, having early taken Mrs. Langworthy's measure, found an impish joy in murdering the proprieties for her especial benefit. She said "Damn" upon occasions when Mrs. Langworthy was there to hear; she rode her horse at a gallop into the yard and right up to the veranda when Mrs. Langworthy was there to see, swinging down as her mount jerked to standstill, as "ladylike" about it all as a wild Comanche; at table she talked of prize boars and sick calves and other kindred vulgar matters.

But the major admired her; Marcia, as days went by, proved to be a sweet-tempered, somewhat timid, but highly good-natured, affectionate creature generously offering her good-will; and Rogers, the lawyer, and Farris, the artist, both of the sophisticated, self-sufficient type, were little behind the major in interest.

During the last week of May, a rumor came to Judith's ears of which, at first, she thought little. Carson, coming to her upon a bit of ranch business, remarked dryly before taking his departure, that a report had got around among his men--Poker Face had mentioned it to him--that Blue Lake ranch was on its last legs; that it was even to be doubted, if the men ever saw another pay-day before the whole affair went into a receiver's hands. Judith laughed at him and told him not to worry.

"Me?" said Carson. "I'm not the worrying kind. But idees like that ain't good to have floating around. A man won't do more'n half work when he's wondering all the time if he's going to get his mazuma for it."

But, when again the rumor came, this time telephoned up to her from the Lower End by Doc Tripp, she frowned and wondered. And she was careful, upon the thirtieth of May, to send Charlie Miller, the storekeeper, into Rocky Bend for the monthly pay-roll money. She gave him her check for one thousand dollars which, with what was in Charlie's safe at the store and in her own here, would more than pay the monthly wages. Charlie left for Rocky Bend in the afternoon, spending the night in town to get the customary morning start for the ranch. The men were to be paid at six o'clock.

Upon this same day Pollock Hampton told Judith that Bayne Trevors was coming to the ranch to have dinner, spend the night and the following day. Judith made no reply beyond favoring him with a quick look of question. She had not believed that the man would come. What next?

The last day of May came, and true to his premise, Trevors was a guest at the house from which, so short a time ago, he had been evicted. He dined there that night, cool and self-confident, casually polite to Judith, civil and courteous to the other guests, especially to Major and Mrs. Langworthy and Marcia, leading conversations unobtrusively, making himself liked. He watched a game of billiards, but refused to play, saying carelessly that he had a stiff shoulder. He and Hampton strolled out into the starlight and for some two or three hours walked up and down, talking quietly.

"A gentleman!" cried Mrs. Langworthy with spirit. "It just shows that a person can do out-doors work and not sink back into the barbarian!"

The morning after Trevors's arrival, Judith was up betimes and breakfasted alone. Lunching early, noon found her in the office expecting Charlie Miller. She was at work on the pay-roll book when her telephone rang. It was Doc Tripp and there was suppressed excitement in his voice.

"Bad news, Judy," he began. "It sure looks as though you were getting your share."

"What is it, Doc?" she broke in sharply. "Tell me!"

"It's Charlie Miller. Hurt. No, not bad. Thrown off his horse, back in Squaw Creek canon. And--robbed."

Quickly he told all that had happened. Miller, hastening back with the wage money, was riding through the narrow gorge when a man had sprung out suddenly in front of him. Miller's horse, shying, swerving unexpectedly, had thrown him. Before he could get to his feet the bag of gold under his coat had been torn off, his revolver wrenched away and the highwayman, his face masked with a red bandana handkerchief, had run into the thick timber.

"Charlie just walked in, reeling like a drunken man," Tripp concluded. "His fall and a rap over the head with a gun-butt have made him pretty sick. I am sending out a posse of men from this end to try and get the stick-up man. You'd better do the same up there."

For a moment Judith sat staring at the telephone dully. Robbed of a thousand dollars, and in broad daylight! A thing like this had not occurred on the Blue Lake for a dozen years.

"Bayne Trevors!" she gasped. For, suddenly, she thought that she understood the significance of the rumor which had twice in a week come to her. Perhaps, as Tripp himself had said, she was getting nerves. Trevors himself was on the ranch right now. . . . Her two fists clinched. Yes, Trevors was here with triple purpose: To curry favor with Hampton against a possible need of it, to establish an alibi for himself, to witness Judith's discomfiture, when at six o'clock she must turn the men away with an excuse.

VIII
RIFLE SHOTS FROM THE CLIFFS

Thank Heaven it was just noon! Judith sprang to her feet, her eyes bright and hard, and ran down to the men's quarters. Coming up from the corral were Carson and Bud Lee.

"Miller with the pay-roll money has been held up and robbed at Squaw Creek," she told them swiftly. "Get some men together, Carson, and try to head the robber off."

The two men, having glanced quickly at each other, stood a moment looking at her curiously.

"That's on the level, is it, Miss Judith?" demanded Carson slowly.

"Of course it's on the level!" she cried impatiently. "Oh, I know what you're thinking. I'm going to phone immediately to the bank at Rocky Bend and have another man sent out with more money. You can count upon getting your pay at six o'clock!"

"I told you, didn't I," muttered Carson, "that I wasn't worrying none personal? But if I was you I'd sure have the money on tap!"

With that he left her, going hastily to round up what men he could find and get them into their saddles. Bud Lee, his eyes still on her, stood where he was.

"Well," demanded the girl, "aren't you going, too?" Suddenly angered by his leisurely air, she added cuttingly: "Not afraid, are you?"

"I was thinking," Lee answered coolly, "that the stick-up gent will most probably figure on a play like that. If he was real wise he'd mosey along toward Rocky Bend and pop off your second man. Two thousand bucks a day would make a real nice little draw."

Judith paused, frowning. There was truth in that. If Trevors really were behind this, he would have chosen his man carefully; he would have planned ahead.

"If you'll do my way," continued Lee thoughtfully, "I'll have just enough time to roll a smoke and saddle little old Climax. He's in the stable now. You're not afraid of my double-crossing you? Even if a smart-headed man had planned the hold-up he wouldn't figure on a play like this. He'd think we'd have a Rocky Bender bring it out or else wait until to-morrow."

"It won't do," she decided quickly. "I want that money here at six o'clock."

"Eighty miles," mused the horse foreman. "Six hours. That's riding right along, but do it my way and I'll gamble you my own string of horses--and they're worth considerable more than a thousand--that I'll be back, heeled, at six."

Judith, quick at decisions, looked him hard in the eye, heard his plan, and three minutes later Bud Lee, a revolver in his shirt, rode away from the ranch-house, headed toward Rocky Bend. Judith already had called up Tripp, and the veterinarian himself, leading the fastest saddle-horse he could get his hands on at brief notice, was also riding toward Rocky Bend, from the Lower End, five miles in advance of Lee at the start. He went at a gentle trot, consulting his watch now and then.

So Bud Lee, riding as once those hard, dare-devil riders rode who carried across the land the mail-bag of the Pony Express, overtook Doc Tripp and changed to a fresh horse at the end of the first fifteen miles. He swung out of his saddle, stretched his long legs, remarked lightly that it was a real fine day, and was gone again upon a fresh mount with twenty-five miles between him and Rocky Bend. The clock at the bank marked forty-three minutes after two as Lee, leaving a sweating horse at the door on Main Street, presented his check at the paying teller's window. The money, in a small canvas bag, was ready.

"Hello, Bud," and "Hello, Dan'l," was the beginning and end of the conversation which ensued. Lee did not stop to count the money. He drew his belt up a hole as he went back to the door, found a fresh horse there fighting its bit and all but lifting the stable-boy off his feet, mounted and sped back along Main Street.

Judith was to send out another man leading still another fresh horse for him so that he could not fail to be back at the ranch-house by six o'clock. As Bud Lee, riding hard but never without thought for the horse which carried him, began the return trip, he drew the heavy caliber revolver from his shirt and thrust it into his belt. When he had left Rocky Bend half a dozen miles behind him and was hurrying on into the outskirts of that country of rolling hills and pine forests, his hand was never six inches from the gun-butt.

The road wound in and out among the pines, always climbing. Lee raced on, his eyes bright and keen, watchful and suspicious of every still shadow or stirring branch. Coming up the two-mile-long Cuesta Grade, he saved his horse a little. From the top of the mountain, before he again followed a winding road back to the river's side, he saw a horseman riding a distant ridge; the glinted upon the rider's rifle.

"Old Carson himself," thought Lee. "Looking for the hold-up man. Shucks! They'll never find him this trip."

Letting his own animal out into its swinging stride as he got down to more level going, he hammered on at his clip of fifteen miles an hour. In the thick shade of the forest, three miles before he came to the line fence of the Blue Lake ranch, he saw another horseman, this one Ed Masters, the "college kid." The young fellow's flushed, eager face passed in a blur as Lee shot by.

Another mile, and Bud Lee was riding through a clearing, with the tall cliffs of Squaw Creek canon looming high on his left, when suddenly and absolutely without warning, his horse screamed, gathered itself for a wild plunge, staggered, stood a moment trembling terribly, then with a low moan collapsed under him.

Lee swung out and to one side, landing clear as the big brute fell. He did not understand. He had ridden the animal hard but certainly not hard enough for this. And then he saw and his eyes blazed with anger. He had heard no shot, nothing beyond the metallic pounding of the shod hoofs on flinty road, but there from an ugly hole in the neck the saddle-horse was pouring out its blood.

"Smokeless powder and a Maxim silencer!" muttered Lee, his eyes taking note of the ten thousand possible hiding-places on the cliffs.

In his ears there was a little whine as a second bullet sang its way by his head. Again he sought to locate the marksman, again saw nothing but crag and precipice and brushy clump. He took time for that thing which came so hard to him, sent a bullet from his own revolver into his horse's brain, and then slipped out of the clearing into the shelter of the pines.

"Two miles left to the border line," he estimated it. "Afoot."

Stiff from the saddle, he moved on slowly for a little. But as his muscles responded and warmed to the effort, he broke into a trotting run. Only a little now could he keep under cover; if he went on with any degree of speed he must keep to the road and the open. The thought came to him that he might lie under cover until dark. The second thought came to him that he had assured Judith that he would be back on time, and he forged ahead.

For the second time that day he heard the whine of a bullet. He thought that the shot came from the cliffs just at the head of Squaw Creek canon. But he could not be sure. There was ample protection there for a man hiding, tall brush in a hollow and three or four stunted trees, wind-twisted. He'd make the climb to-morrow and see about it. Now he'd keep right on moving. Little used to travelling save on a horse's back he was shot through with odd little pains when at last he came to the border-line fenced and the waiting horse. Tommy Burkitt held it for him while Lee mounted.

"Somebody up on the cliffs, head of the canon," panted Lee at Tommy's amazed expression when Lee came running into sight. "Killed my horse. Go after him, Tommy. Tell the other boys." And on he went, pounding out the last fifteen miles, the canvas bag beating safely against his side.

Judith, in the courtyard, watched him ride in. She looked swiftly at him from the watch on her wrist. Her eyes brightened. It lacked seven minutes to six. As Bud dropped the canvas bag into her hands she flashed at him the most wonderful, radiant smile that the long horseman had ever seen. She gripped his lean, brown hand hard in hers.

"Bud, you're a brick!" she cried.

Mrs. Langworthy had just come out with Hampton, Trevors, and the major.

Judith turned from Lee to Trevors but managed to keep half an eye on Mrs. Langworthy.

"You see, it's pay-day with us, Mr. Trevors," she said quietly. "And when pay-day comes we pay our men at six o'clock in spite of hell and high water!"

Bud Lee, leading his horse away, turned for a word. "A man killed a horse for me to-day," he said very gently, and his eyes rested steadily upon Trevors. "If I ever get him, or the man who put him up to it, I'm going to get him right."

IX
THE OLD TRAIL

On the Blue Lake Ranch there was more than one man ready to scoff at the idea of a robbery like this one, frank enough to voice the suspicion: "It's just a stall for time!" So much had last week's rumor done for them, preparing them to expect something that would set aside the customary monthly pay-day. But when they had seen Charlie Miller's bruised head and heard his story; when they had sat on their horses and looked down at the animal which had been shot under Bud Lee, they were silent. And, besides, when long after dark they came in behind Carson from a fruitless quest, their pay was ready for them as formerly, in gold and silver.

Major Langworthy imbibed an unusually large number of cocktails and long before noon of the following day had suggested that the ranch be put immediately under military law, hinting that a military-mustached gentleman be appointed commanding general of the Blue Lake forces, and forming within his own mind the picture of himself in the office, revolver on table, cocktail at elbow, directing the manoeuvres from this point of vantage, not to say safety. Mrs. Langworthy ruffled her feathers and sniffed when Judith's name was mentioned. It was perfectly clear to her that all the ruffians of the West would be quick to take the advantage arising from the ridiculous condition of a rowdy girl assuming men's pantaloons.

"I am rather inclined to think, mama," said Marcia, "that you don't do Judith justice."

Trevors, with little to say to any one, took his departure in the forenoon, extracting from Hampton the promise to ride over and see the lumber-camp some day soon.

Judith, held at the office by a lot of first-of-the-month details, did not get away until close to eleven o'clock that morning. Then she rode swiftly down the river, a purpose of her own in mind. At the store she stopped for a sympathetic word with Charlie Miller who had long ago forgotten his own hurt in his grief and anger that he had lost her thousand dollars for her.

"What's a thousand dollars, Charlie?" she laughed at him. "We'll lose and make many a thousand before the year dies."

Just below the Lower End settlement she came upon Doc Tripp. He was in one of the quarantine hog-corrals, his sleeves rolled up, a puzzled look of worry puckering his boyish face.

"What's up, Doc?" asked Judith.

"Don't know, Judy. That's what gets my mad up. Just performed an autopsy on one of your Poland-China gilts."

"Found it dead?" asked Judith.

"Killed it," grunted Tripp. "Sick. Half dozen more are off their feed and don't look right. A man's always afraid of the cholera. And," stubbornly, "I won't believe it! There's been no chance of infection; why, there's not an infected herd this side of the Bagley ranch, sixty miles the other side of Rocky Bend, a clean hundred miles from here. But, just the same, I'm taking temperatures this morning and having my herders cut out all the dull-looking ones and break the herds up."

"Not getting nerves? Are you, Doc?" And Judith spurred on down the valley.

Before she came to the spot where Bud Lee's horse had been shot she came upon Lee himself. A rifle across his arm, he was looking up at the cliffs of Squaw Creek canon.

"Well, Lee," she said, "what do you make of it?"

He showed no surprise at seeing her and answered slowly, that far-away look in his eyes as though he were alone still and speaking simply to Bud Lee.

"Using smokeless powder nowadays is a handy thing for a man shooting under cover," he said. "Then rig up your gun with a silencer and get off at fair range, half a mile and up, with a telescope sight, and it's real nice fun picking folks off!"

"All of that spells preparation," suggested Judith.

He nodded. When he offered no further remark but sat staring up at the cliffs, Judith asked:

"What else have you learned by coming back down here? Anything?"

"There were two men, anyway. I'd guess, three. The one who stuck up Charlie and then drifted while the drifting was good. Then the two other jaspers that tried to wing me."

"How do you know that?"

"My horse that was shot," he explained, "got it in the left side of the neck. Now, look at that hole in the little fir-tree yonder."

Judith saw what he meant now. At this point Lee yesterday had heard the second bullet singing dangerously near. It had struck the fir, and plainly had been fired from some point off to the right of the canon. Her eyes went swiftly, after his up the cliff walls.

"I doped it out while I was running," he went on. "Look at the way the trees grow here. If a man was on the cliffs shooting at me, and coming that close to winging me, why, he'd have to be off to the right. These big pines would shunt him off from the other side. It's open and shut there were two of them. And darn good shots," he added dryly.

Briefly he went on to give her the rest of the results of his two-hour seeking for something definite. If she'd ride on a little she'd come to the spot where his horse had been killed; she would see in the road the signs where, at Tripp's, orders, the carcass had been dragged away. From there, looking off to the left, up the cliffs, she would see the spot which Lee believed had harbored one of the riflemen. High above the canon rose the rocky pinnacle he had marked yesterday, with brush standing tall in a little depression.

"Indian Head," broke in Judith, gazing upward. "Bud Lee, I'll bet a horse you're right. . . ."

"And," said Lee, swinging from the saddle, "I'm going up there to have a little look around."

In an instant the girl was at his side.

"I am going with you," she said simply.

He looked at her curiously. Then he shrugged his shoulders. An angry flush came to the girl's cheeks, but she went on with him. Not a word passed between them during the entire hour required to climb the steep side of the mountain and come under Indian Head cliffs. Here they stood together upon a narrow ledge panting, resting. Again Judith saw Lee glance at her curiously. He had not sought to accommodate his swift climbing to a girl's gait and yet he had not distanced her in the ascent. But in Lee's glance there was nothing of approval. There were two kinds of women, as he had said, and . . .

"Pretty steep climb from here up," he remarked bluntly.

"For a valley man or a cobble-pounder, maybe," was Judith's curt rejoinder.

Thereafter they did not speak again until, after nearly another hour, they at last came to the crest of Indian Head. And here, in the eagerness of their search, rewarded by the signs which they found, they forgot, both of them, to maintain their reserve.

In the clump of brush, close to the outer fringe, behind a low, broad boulder, a man had lain on his belly no longer ago than yesterday. Broken twigs showed it, a small bush crushed down told of it, the marks of his toes in some of the softer soil proclaimed it eloquently. And, had other signs been required, there they were: two empty brass cartridges where the automatic ejector had thrown them several feet away. Lee picked up one of the shells.

"Latest thing in an up-to-the-minute Savage," he told her. "That gun is good for twice the distance he used it for. I'm in tolerable luck to be mountain-climbing to-day, I guess!"

While Judith visualized just what had occurred, saw the tall man--he must have been tall for his boot toes to scratch the earth yonder while his rifle-barrel lay for support across the boulder in front--resting his gun and firing down into the canon--Lee was back at her side, saying shortly:

"What do you think? There's a plain trail up here, old as the hills, but tip-top for speedy going."

"And," said Judith without looking up, "it runs down into the next saddle, to the north of that ridge, curves up again and with monuments all along the way, runs straight to the Upper End and comes down from the northeast to the lake."

Lee looked at her, wondering.

"You knew about it all the time, then?"

"If we hadn't been on our high horses," she told him quietly, "I should have told you about it. It's the old Indian Trail. If the man we want turned east, then he went right on to the lake before he stopped putting one foot in front of the other. Unless he hid out all night, which I don't believe."

"What makes you think he went that far?"

"There's no other trail up here that gets anywhere. If he left this one for a short cut he'd know, if he knows anything, that he'd have to take a chance every ten steps of breaking his neck in the dark. Now," and she rose swiftly, confronting him, "the thing for you to do, Bud Lee, is to get back to your horse, take the road, make time getting to the Upper End and see what you can see there!"

Hurrying back to their horses, they rode to the ranch-house where Judith, with no word of adieu, left Lee to go to the house. Lee made a late lunch, saddled another horse, and when the bunk-house clock stood at a quarter of four, started for the Upper End.

"That girl's got the savvy," was his one remark to himself.

X
UNDER FIRE

Blue Lake, while but three miles farther eastward, flashed its jewelled waters into the sun from a plane fully five hundred feet higher than the tall chimneys of the ranch-house. About it stood the most precipitous granite cliffs to be found hereabouts. They rose, sheer and majestic, still another five hundred feet, here and there eight hundred and a thousand. The lake, half a mile in diameter, circular like some polished mirror presented by an ancient giant to his lady-love, was shut in everywhere by these crags and cliffs save at the west, where the overflowing water, going to swell the turbulent river, poured like molten crystal through a wide gorge. The farther cliffs marked the eastern boundary-line of the ranch. Beyond them lay a small plateau rimmed about on three sides by still other steep precipices.

Lee, coming to the water's edge sought to guess where the old Indian Trail came down. And again, startling him for a second time, Judith rode up.

She, too, had a fresh horse; she too now carried a rifle across her arm. Bud Lee frowned.

"What makes you so certain, Bud Lee," was her abrupt word of greeting, "that Bayne Trevors is back of this deal?"

"When did I say that?" he countered.

"Yesterday, when I told you Charlie Miller had been held up, you intimated that a long-headed man had planned the whole thing. That means Trevors, doesn't it?"

"One of us," said Lee calmly, ignoring her question and looking her straight in the eyes, "is going back. Which one?"

"Neither!" she retorted promptly. She even smiled confidently at him. "For I won't. And you won't."

"Do you need to be told," he asked her coolly, "that this is no sort of job for a girl? You'd only be in the way."

"If you want glittering generalities," she jeered at him, "then listen to this: A man's job, first, last, and all the time, is to be chivalrous to a woman! And not a bumptious boor!"

With that she spurred by him, taking the trail which led off to the right and so under the cliffs and to the mouth of a great, ragged chasm. In spite of him, Bud Lee grinned after her. And, seeing that she was not to be turned back, he followed.

They left their horses and followed the old footpath, made their way into the chasm deeper and deeper and little by little climbed upward. The climb was less difficult than it looked, and fifteen minutes brought them to the upland plateau and to the door of an old cabin, made of logs, set back in a tiny grove of cedars.

"I haven't been here for a year," cried the girl, forgetful of the constraint which had held them until now. "It's like getting back home for the first time! I love it."

"So do I," Lee said within himself.

"Look!" exclaimed Judith. "Some one has been repairing the old cabin! He's made a bench yonder under the big tree, too. And he has walled in the spring with rocks, and . . . Who in the world can it be? There's even a little garden of wild flowers!"

Bud Lee, for no reason clear to himself, flushed. He offered no explanation at first. Here he spent many an hour when the time was his for idling, lying on the grass, looking out over the immensity of the wilderness; here he came many a night to sleep under the stars, far from the other boys, when his soul craved solitude; here upon many a Sunday, when work was slack, did he come to smoke alone, loaf alone, read from the few books on the cabin's shelves.

"Maybe," he suggested at last, when it was clear that Judith was going straight to the door, "this is where our stick-up gents hang out. Choice place for a cutthroat to hibernate, huh?"

"I don't believe it," answered Judith positively. "The man who made his hermitage here has a soul!"

Behind her back Lee smiled.

"We've got something to do," he said hastily, "without wasting time poking into old shacks. Where's the Indian Trail you talked about?"

"Shack!" cried Judith indignantly. "You make me sick. Bud Lee! I'd rather own this cabin and live here, than have a palace on Fifth Avenue!"

She knocked at the door, knowing that silence would answer her, but hoping to have a man, calm-eyed, gentle-voiced, a romantic hermit in all of his pictur-esqueness, come to the door.

"Going in?" asked Lee in well-simulated carelessness.

"No," she told him freezingly. "Why should I? Would you want people pok-ing about into your home just because it was in the heart of the wilderness and you weren't there to drive them out?"

"No," answered Bud gravely. "Now that you ask me, I wouldn't! Let's go find that trail."

"But," continued Judith, "not being a fool, and realizing that one of the men we want might possibly be in hiding in here, I am going to peek in."

"Not being a fool," he repeated after her, adding gently, "and being a girl, which means filled with curiosity."

A disdainful shoulder gave him his answer. The door was unlocked, after im-memorial Western custom, and Judith opened it. Lee heard her little gasp of pure delight.

"He's a dear, the man who lives here!" she announced positively. "You can just tell by looking at his home."

Looking in over her shoulder, Bud Lee wondered just what in his one-room shanty had caught her enthusiasm. He was secretly pleased that it had done so, though that "it" was somewhat vague in his masculine mind. There was the rock fireplace with an iron hook protruding from each side for coffee-pot and stew-pot; a bunk with a blanket smoothed over cedar-boughs; a shelf with a dozen books; little else, so far as he could see or remember, to catch at Judith's delight. Yet she, look-ing through woman's eyes, read in one quick "peek" the character of the dweller in this abode. One who was content with little, who loved a clean, outdoor life, and who was tranquilly above the pettiness of humanity. Judith closed the door softly.

"I'd like to look inside his books!" she confessed. "But I won't."

The lean horse foreman chuckled. Judith sniffed at him.

"You haven't any curiosity about such things as books," she retorted. "To be sure, why should you have?"

Again, leaving the cabin, she went before him. Going straight across the plateau, she showed him where one could clamber up a steep way to the ridge. Once up there, it was but ten minutes until, in a hollow, they found the monument marking a trail, a stone set upon a boulder.

It was after five o'clock. When, following the trail back and forth in its winding along the side of the ridge, they found the signs they sought, it was fast growing dark. But there, in a narrow defile where loose soil had filtered down, were tracks left by a large boot. Lee went down on his hands and knees to study them in the dusk. He got up with a little grunt and moved down the trail. Again he found tracks, this time more clearly defined. So dark was it now that they had lighted several matches.

"Two men," he announced wonderingly. "Fresh tracks, too. Made this morning or last night, I'll bet. One coming east from Indian Head. The other coming west from the plateau behind us. Who's *he*? Where'd he come from?"

"He's the second of the two men who shot at you," said Judith quickly. "Don't I know every trail in this neck of the woods, Bud Lee? He followed another old, worn-out trail on the south side of the ranch. They met here just as I knew they would!"

"What for?" Lee frowned through the darkness at her eager face. "What would they want to get together for? If they had any sense they would scatter and clean out of the country."

"Unless," Judith reminded him, "they don't intend to clean out at all! Unless they mean to stick to the cliffs and try their hands again at their sort of game. They'll figure that we will expect them to be a long way from here by now, won't they? Then where would they be safer than right here in these mountains? Give me a rifle and something to eat and I'll defy an army getting me out there. And think of it: If this is Trevors's work, if he means business, think what two gunmen on these heights could do to us. They could pick off a three-thousand-dollar stallion down in the pens; they could drop more than one prize bull or cow; and," she added sharply, "if they thought about girls as some men think, they could take a chance on scaring Judith Sanford out of the country."

Lee stared at her a long time in silence.

"I wouldn't have said," he offered finally, "that Bayne Trevors would make quite so strong a play as that."

"You wouldn't! Then look him in the eye! And where's his risk, if he's picked the right men, if he sees them through, keeping the back door open when they want to run for it? You just gamble your boots, Bud Lee, that Bayne Trevors . . ."

Without warning, without a sound of explosion came a wiry whine into the still air, a little venomous ping, and a bullet sped by just over their heads. But, through the gloom, they both saw the flash of the gun as it spat fire and lead, and, as though one impulse commanded them, Judith's rifle and Bud Lee's went to their shoulders and two reverberating reports rang out in answer.

"Lie down, damn it!" cried Bud Lee to the girl at his side, as again there came the flash from the cliffs off to the right and as again he answered it with his rifle.

"Lie down yourself!" snapped Judith. And once more her rifle spoke with his.

For one instant, framed against the darkening sky along the cliff edge five hundred yards away to the right, they saw the silhouette of a man, leaping from one boulder to another, a man who looked gigantically big in the uncertain light. They fired; he jumped again and passed out of sight.

"Got his nerve," grunted Lee as he pumped lead at the running figure.

As an answer there came the third flash, the bullet striking the trail in front of them. And then the fourth flash, from a point a hundred yards to the left of the other.

"That's Number Two," muttered Lee. "They've got us in the open, Judith. Let's beat it back to the cabin."

"I'm with you," said Judith, between shots. "It's just foolishness" . . . *bang*! . . . "sticking out here" . . . *bang*! . . . "for them to pop us off." *Bang*! *Bang*!

They ran then, Bud slipping in front of her, his tall body looming darkly between her and the cliffs whence the shots came. He slid along the sharp slope to the plateau, putting out his arms toward her. And as she came down, Bud Lee grunted and cursed under his breath. For there had been another flash out of the thickening night, this one from the refuge toward which they were running. A third man was shooting from the shelter of the cabin walls. And Lee had felt a stinging pain as though a hot iron had scorched its way along the side of his leg.

"Hurt much?" asked Judith quickly. Without waiting for an answer, she pumped two shots at the flash by the cabin.

"No," grunted Lee. "Just scared. And now what? I want to know."

XI
IN THE OLD CABIN

Bud Lee, in the thicker darkness lying along the edge of the plateau, sat with his back against the rocks while he gave swift first aid to his wound. He brought into requisition the knotted handkerchief from about his throat, bound it tightly around the calf of his leg, and said lightly to Judith:

"Just a fool scratch, you know. But I've no hankering to dribble out a lot of blood from it."

Judith made no answer. Lee took up his rifle and turned to the spot where she had been standing a moment ago. She was not there.

"Gone!" he grunted, frowning into the blackness hemming him in. "Now, what do you suppose she's up to? Fainted, most likely."

He got up and moved along the low rock wall, seeking her. A spurt of flame from the east corner of the cabin drew his eyes away from his search and he pumped three quick shots in answer.

"Little chance of hitting anything," he muttered. "Too blamed dark. Just fool's luck that I got mine in the leg."

Again he sought Judith, calling softly. There was no answer. Once more came the spurt of flame from the shelter of the cabin wall. Then fifty yards off to Lee's right, some fifty yards nearer the cabin, another shot.

The first suspicion that one of the men from the cliffs had made his way down to join issue at close quarters, was gone in a clear understanding. That was the bark of Judith's rifle; she had slipped away from him without an instant's delay and was creeping closer and closer to the cabin.

"Damn the girl!" cried Lee angrily. "She'll get her fool self killed!"

But as he ran forward to join her, he realized that she was doing the right thing--the only thing if they did not want to lie out here all night for the men on the cliffs to pick off in the morning light. He knew that she could shoot; it seemed that she could do everything that was a man's work and which a woman should know nothing about.

A fresh thought locked his hand like steel about his gun-stock. Suppose that Judith, in the mad thing she was attempting, should actually succeed in it, that she should bring down the man she was attacking? How would Bud Lee feel about it when the boys came to know? What would Bud Lee answer when they asked what he was doing about that time? "Nursin' a scratched leg? Mos' likely! Huh!" He could hear old Carson's dry cackle.

Frowning into the night, he thought that he could make out the dim blur of Judith's form. The girl was standing erect; shooting, too, for again the duel of red spurts of flame told where she and her quarry stood.

Meantime Lee ran on, changing his original purpose, swerving out from where Judith was moving forward, turning to the left, hopeful to come to close quarters with their assailant before she could go down under that sharp rifle-fire or could bring down the other. For certainly, if she kept on that way, the time would come when some one would stop hot lead.

Lee shifted his rifle to his left hand, taking his revolver into his right. From the cliffs came a shot and he grunted at it contemptuously. It could do nothing but assure those below that there was still some one up there.

"Three of them to our two," he estimated, "counting the two jaspers on the cliff. Two of us to their one, counting what's down here. And that's all that counts right this minute."

A shot from Judith; a shot from the cabin; two shots from the cliffs. The two shots from above brought fresh news; not only were they closer together, but they indicated the men up yonder were coming down. Lee hurried.

Then, at last, his narrowed eyes made out the faint outline of that which he sought. Close to the cabin, low down, evidently upon his knees, was the most important factor to be considered, now. Still Lee was too far away to be certain of a hit and he meant with all of the grim determination in him to hit something at last. He ran on drawing the fire away from Judith. A rifle-ball sang close to his side, another and an other. He lost the dim shape of the kneeling man, who, he thought, had risen from his knees and was standing, his body tight-pressed to the cabin.

"Why the devil doesn't he run for it?" wondered Lee.

But evidently, be the reason what it might, the man had no intention of running. A bullet cut through Lee's sleeve. At last Lee answered. He ran in closer as he fired and, running, emptied his revolver, jammed it into his waistband, clubbed his rifle . . . and realized with something of a shock that there were but the two rifles on the cliffs to take into consideration. That other rifle, at the cabin, was still. Out of ammunition? Or plugged? Or playing 'possum? Which?

"Stop shooting!" he shouted to Judith.

"I'm coming!" she cried back to him.

Almost at the same instant, their two rifles ready, they came to the cabin. Between them on the ground a man lay at the corner, moving helplessly, groping for his fallen gun, falling back.

"Open the door," said Bud. "I'll get him inside and we'll see who he is. Hurry, Judith; those other jaspers are working down this way as fast as they know how."

Judith, taking time to snatch up the fallen rifle, ran around to the door. Lee slipped his hands under the armpits of the wounded man and dragged him in Judith's wake. In the cabin, the door shut, Lee struck a match and went to a little shelf where there was a candle.

"Bill Crowdy!" gasped Judith.

Almost before Lee saw the man's face he saw the canvas bag tied to his belt, a bag identical with the one he himself had brought from the bank at Rocky Bend.

"The man that stuck up Charlie Miller," he said slowly. "And there's your thousand bucks, or I'm a liar. I get something of their play now: those two fellows up there were waiting to meet him and split the swag three ways. And I've got the guess they'll be asking a look-in yet!"

He dropped a heavy bar into its place across the door and then went to the two small windows and fastened the heavy oaken shutters. When he came back to Judith she was bending over the wounded man. Crowdy's eyes were closed; he looked to be on the verge of death. The girl's face was almost as white as Crowdy's.

Lee knelt and with quick fingers sought the wound. There was a hole in Crowdy's chest, high up near the throat, that was bleeding profusely. At first that seemed the only wound. But in a second Lee had found another. This was in the leg, and this, like Lee's, was bound tightly with a handkerchief.

"Got that, first rattle out of the box!" commented Lee. "See it? That's why he stuck on the job and didn't try to run for it. Looks like a rifle-ball had smashed the bone."

He didn't look up. His fingers, busy with the string at Crowdy's belt, brought away the canvas bag. There was blood on it; it was heavy and gave forth the mellow jangle of gold.

"You win back your thousand on to-night's play," he said, holding up the bag to Judith, lifting his eyes to her face.

But Judith shrank back, her eyes wide with horror.

"I don't want it! I can never touch it!" she whispered.

Suddenly she was shaking from head to foot, her eyes fixed in terrible fascination upon Crowdy's face. Lee tossed the bag to the bunk across the room, whence it fell clanking to the floor.

"Now she's going to faint," was his thought. "Well, I won't blame her so damn much. Poor little kid!"

But he did not look at her again. He tore away Crowdy's shirt to discover just how serious the wound in the chest was. The collar-bone had been broken; the ball had ploughed its way through the upper chest, well above the heart, and could be felt under the skin of the shoulder. Unless Bill Crowdy bled to death, he stood an excellent chance of doing time in the penitentiary. Lee stanched the flow of blood, made a rude bandage, and then, lifting the body gently, carried it to the bunk. Crowdy's lax arm, extended downward at the side of the bunk, seemed to be reaching again for the canvas bag; the red fingers touched it with their tips.

"Now," said Lee, speaking bluntly, afraid that a tone of sympathy might merely aid the girl to "shake to pieces," "we've got a chance to be on our way before Number Two and Number Three get into the game. Let's run for it, Judith."

Judith went to the bench by the fireplace and sank down upon it. For a moment she made no reply. Then she shook her head.

"We'll stay here until morning," she said finally, her voice surprising Lee, who had looked for a sign of weakening to accord with her sudden pallor and visible trembling.

"What for?" he wanted to know. "We'll have another fight on our hands if we do. Those fellows, this deep in it, are not going to quit while they know that there's all that money in the shack!"

"I don't care," said Judith firmly. "I won't run from them or anybody else I know! And, besides, Bud Lee, I am not going to give them the chance to get Crowdy away. . . . Do you think he is going to die?"

"No, I don't. Doc Tripp will fix him up."

"Then here I stay, for one. When I go, Bill Crowdy goes with me! He's going to talk, and he's going to help me send Bayne Trevors to the pen."

Bud Lee expressed all he had to say in a silent whistle. He'd made another mistake, that was all. Judith wasn't going to faint for him to-night.

"Then," he said presently, setting her the example, "slip some fresh cartridges into your rifle and get ready for more shooting. I'll put out the light and we'll wait for what's next."

Judith replenished the magazine of her rifle. Lee, watching from under the low-drawn brim of his hat, noted that her fingers were steady now. Crowdy moved on his bunk, lifted a hand weakly, groaned, and grew still. Presently he stirred again, asking weakly for water.

Lee went to the water-bucket standing in a corner. It happened to be half full. He filled a cup, and lifting Crowdy's head, held it to the fevered lips.

"Not exactly what you'd call fresh, is it, Crowdy?" he said lightly. "But the spring's outside and I'm scared to go out in the dark."

Crowdy drank thirstily and lay back, his eyes closed again. Lee rearranged his bandage.

"Put out the light now?" he asked Judith.

"No," she answered. "What's the use, Bud? There are no holes in the walls they could stick a gun-barrel through, are there?"

No one knew better than he that there were not.

"You see," said Judith, with a half-smile, heroically assumed, "I'm a little afraid of the dark, too! Anyway, since we've got to spend the night with a man in Crowdy's shape, it will be more cosey, won't it, with the light on?"

She even put out her hand to one of the books on the shelves which she could reach from her bench.

"And now," she added, "I'm sure that our hermit won't mind if we peep into his library, will he?"

"No," answered Lee gravely. "Most likely he'll be proud."

Lee found time to muse that life is made of incongruities, woman of inconsistencies. Here with a badly hurt man lying ten feet from her, with every likelihood of the night stillness being ripped in two by a rifle-shot, Judith sat and turned the pages of a book. It was a volume on the breeding and care of pure-blooded horses. Odd sort of thing for her hermit to have brought here with him! Her hand took down another volume. Horses again; a treatise by an eminent authority upon a newly imported line from Arabia. A third book; this, a volume of Elizabethan lyrics. Bud Lee flushed as he watched her. She turned the pages slowly, came back to the fly-leaf page, read the name scrawled there and, turning swiftly to Lee, said accusingly:

"David Burrill Lee, you are a humbug!"

"Wrong again," grinned Lee. "A hermit, you mean! 'A man with a soul.' . . ."

"Scat!" answered Judith. But, under Bud Lee's teasing eyes, the color began to come back into her cheeks. She *had* been a wee bit enthusiastic over her hermit, making of him a picturesque ideal. She had visioned him, even to the calm eyes, gentle voice. A quick little frown touched her brows as she realized that the eyes and voice which her fancy had bestowed upon the hermit were in actuality the eyes and voice of Bud Lee. But she had called him a dear. And Lee had been laughing at her all the time--had not told her, would never have told her. The thought came to her that she would like to slap Bud Lee's face for him. And she had told Tripp she would like to slap Pollock Hampton's. Good and hard!

XII
PARDNERS

From without came the low murmur of men's voices. Judith laid her book aside and drew her rifle across her knees, her eyes bright and eager. At infrequent intervals for perhaps three or four minutes the two voices came indistinctly to those in the cabin. Then silence for as long a time. And then a voice again, this time quite near the door, calling out clearly:

"Hey, you in there! Pitch the money out the window and we'll let you go."

"There's a voice," said Judith quietly, "to remember! I'll be able to swear to it in court."

Certainly a voice to remember, just as one remembers an unusual face for years, though it be but a chance one seen in a crowd. A voice markedly individual, not merely because it was somewhat high-pitched for a man's, but rather for a quality not easily defined, which gave to it a certain vibrant, unpleasant harshness, sounding metallic almost, rasping, as though with the hiss of steel surfaces rubbing. Altogether impossible to describe adequately, yet, as Judith said, not to be forgotten.

Judith noticed a puzzled look on Bud's face. He called out: "What did you say out there?"

Word for word came the command again:

"Pitch the money out of the window and we'll let you go."

Lee turned triumphantly to Judith.

"I've got his tag!" he whispered to her. "I played poker with that voice one night not four months ago in Rocky Bend!"

"Who is he?" Judith whispered back. "With Crowdy down, if we know who one of these men is, the rest will be easy. Who is he?"

"A bad egg," Lee told her gravely. "He's done time in the State pen. He's been out less than a year. Gunman, stick-up man, convicted once already for manslaughter . . ."

"Not Chris Quinnion, Bud Lee!" she cried excitedly. "Not Chris Quinnion!"

"Sh!" he commanded softly. "There's no use tipping our hand off to him. Yes; it's crooked Chris Quinnion. You don't know him, do you?"

He had never seen her eyes look as they looked now. They were as hard and bright as steel; no true woman's eyes, he thought swiftly. Rather the eyes of a man with murder in his heart.

"Then, thank God!" whispered Judith, her voice tense. "Can you keep a secret with me, Bud Lee? Were it not for the man calling to us now, Luke Sanford would be here in our stead. Crooked Chris Quinnion served his time in San Quentin because my father sent him there. And he had not been free six months before he kept his oath and murdered my poor old dad!"

"Well?" came the interrupting snarl of Quinnion's voice, like the ominous whine of an enraged animal. "What's the word?"

"Give us five minutes to think it over," returned Lee coolly. And, incredulous eyes on Judith's set face, he said gently: "I was on the ranch when the accident happened. He must have driven that heavy car a little too close to the edge of the grade. The bank just naturally gave way."

Judith, her lips tightly compressed, shook her head.

"You didn't find him under the car, did you? And the blow that killed him might have been dealt with some heavy weapon in the hands of a man standing behind him, mightn't it? I know, Bud Lee, I know!"

"How do you know?" he demanded intently. "You weren't here even."

"No. I was in San Francisco. But the day before I had a letter from father. He expected me home very soon. He was going out, he said in his letter, to look at the road over the mountain. He wrote that the grade was dangerous, especially at the very place where the car went over! He wanted me to know so that in case he could not get the work done on it before I came, I would be careful. On top of that would he go and run his car into such danger as that? Oh, I know!" she cried again, her hands hard upon her rifle. "I know, I tell you! From the first I suspected. I knew that Chris Quinnion had threatened a dozen times to 'get' father; I knew that soon or late he would try. I wrote Emmet Sawyer, our county sheriff, and told him what

I believed, asked him to go to the spot and see what the signs told. A square man is Emmet Sawyer and as sharp as tacks."

"And he told you that you were mistaken?"

"He did nothing of the kind! He reported that the tracks of the car showed that it had kept well away from the bank, that evidently it had stopped there, that again it had gone on, swerving so as to run close to the edge! I know what happened: Father got out to look at the dangerous spot and to put up the sign he had brought with him and that was found in the road. Chris Quinnion had followed him, perhaps to shoot him down from behind, Chris Quinnion's way! Then he saw a safer way. He came up behind poor old dad and struck him in the head with something, rifle-barrel or revolver. He started the car up and let it run over the bank. He--"

She broke off then. Bud Lee felt that he knew what she would say if she could bring herself to go on; that she would tell how crooked Chris Quinnion had thrown the unconscious man down over the bank to lie, bruised and broken, by the wrecked car.

"You've got to be almighty sure before you make a charge like that," he reminded her. "If Quinnion had done it, why didn't Emmet Sawyer get the deadwood on him?"

"Because," she whispered quickly, "a man fooled Sawyer! Yes, and fooled me! Quinnion established an alibi. A man whose word there was no reason to doubt said that Quinnion was with him at the time of the murder. And that man was-- Bayne Trevors!"

"Trevors?" muttered Lee. He shook his head. "Trevors is a hard man, Judith. And he's a scoundrel, if you want to know! But frame up a murder deal--plan to murder Luke Sanford--No. I don't believe it!"

"Is he the man to miss a chance that lay at his hand? The main chance for him? The chance to hold a man like Chris Quinnion in the hollow of his hand, to make him do his bidding, to set him just such work as he is doing now? Answer me! Is Bayne Trevors above a deal like that?"

Bud Lee's answer was silence.

"And there is one other thing," went on Judith swiftly, "known to no one but Emmet Sawyer, whom I told, and me and Chris Quinnion: In father's letter he told me that a man had paid him some money the day before, and that he was going to drive to Rocky Bend to bank it. 'There are some tough customers in the country,' he wrote, 'and it's foolhardy to have too much money in our old safe.' That money, several hundred dollars, was never banked. It was not found on his body. Where did it go?"

"Even that doesn't incriminate Quinnion, you know."

"No. The rest is pure guesswork on my part. Guesswork based on what I know. Not enough to hang Chris Quinnion, Bud Lee. But enough to make me sure. He's working at Trevor's game right now. If we can prove that it is Trevors's game, it will go to show how worthless his alibi was."

"Well?" called Quinnion, the third time. "What about it? We ain't goin' to wait all night."

"Tell him," whispered Judith, her hand on Lee's arm, "to come and get it if he wants it! One of us can hold the cabin against the two of them while the other slips out in the dark and rides back to the ranch-house for help. If we're in luck, Bud Lee, we'll corner the bunch of them before daylight!"

Lee stood a moment looking down into her face, his mind filled with uncertainties. With all his soul he wished that Judith had not come with him to-night, that he had only himself to think of now. Quinnion, not to be further put off, called again, the snarl of his voice rising into ugly threat. Still Lee, thinking of Judith, hesitated.

"It's the only way," she insisted. "If we gave them the money they'd want Bill Crowdy next. If they got Crowdy away with them into the mountains I am not sure that they could not hide until they got him safe in Trevors's hands. Then we'd have the whole fight still to make, sooner or later. It's our one bet, Lee!"

And Bud Lee, seeing no better way ahead for them, blew out the candle, forced Judith to stand close to the rock chimney of the fireplace, took his station near her, and answered Quinnion, saying shortly:

"Come ahead when you're ready. We're waiting."

Quinnion's curse, the crack of his rifle, the flying splinters from the cabin door, came together like one implacable menace.

"And now, Bud Lee," cried Judith quickly, "I don't mind telling you, not seeing the end of the string we are playing, that you are a man to my liking!"

"My hat's off," said Lee, with grave simplicity. "And in any old kind of a fight a man wouldn't want a better pardner than I can reach now, putting out my hand. He'd want--just a thoroughbred! And now, little pardner, let's give them--fits!"

Judith, even as Quinnion's second shot tore into the door, laughed softly.

"Finish it as you began it, Bud Lee! Even George Washington swore at Monmouth, you know!"

So Bud Lee amended his words and spoke his thought:

"Then, pardner, let's give 'em hell!"

Crouching in the dark, reserving their own fire while they waited for something more definite than the bark of a rifle to shoot at, their hand met.

XIII
THE CAPTURE OF SHORTY

It came about, quite as matters often do, that at the three-mile-distant ranch headquarters it was one who knew comparatively little of the ways of this part of the world who was first to suspect that all was not well with Judith Sanford. To Pollock Hampton her failure to appear at dinner was significant.

Together with the other newcomers to the ranch from the city he had been deeply moved by yesterday's outlawry. Drawing upon a vivid imagination, he peopled the woods with desperate characters. When after dinner an hour passed without bringing Judith, he began to show signs of nervous anxiety. Without making his fears known to his friends, he went to the office and telephoned to Doc Tripp. All that Tripp could tell him was that he didn't know where Judith was and didn't care; she could take care of herself. Though the veterinarian didn't say as much, he was at the moment puzzled by the new sickness among the hogs and his irritable concern in this matter allowed him scant interest in other people's affairs.

Hampton learned from Mrs. Simpson that in the afternoon Judith after a hurried lunch had taken her rifle and ridden away. Where? Mrs. Simpson did not know. But she grasped the opportunity to confide in Hampton a certain suspicion which she held in connection with the robbery and killing of Bud Lee's horse under him--a suspicion which was growing rapidly into positive certainty. She didn't like to mention the matter to him, since Fujioki was his servant. But had he noted Fujioki and that other black Spanish, Jose? They had a community of interest which must extend far beyond racial kinship; they were, even at this very second, out in the courtyard together talking in subdued voices. Mrs. Simpson had been raised a lady, Mr. Hampton, sir; and she knew that in the best families one was not supposed to eavesdrop. But at a time like this. . . . Well, she *had* crept up behind the lilac-bushes and they *were* speaking guardedly about the hold-up! Almost in whispers, with every sign of guilt----

"Hurried lunch?" said Hampton. "Took her rifle, did she?"

His eyes had grown very serious as he stared down into Mrs. Simpson's concerned face.

"Send Jose to me," was what he said next.

"Aren't you afraid, Mr. Hampton?" she exclaimed, picturing to herself this pleasant young gentleman at death-grips with the sombre Jose. However, she obeyed and called Jose whom Hampton merely sent to the men's quarters with word for Carson and Lee to come to the house. Mrs. Simpson, witnessing the bloodless meeting from the hallway, was a little relieved and very much disappointed.

Hampton strode up and down the office, the frown gathering upon his usually smooth brows. Plainly if something had happened to Judith the present responsibility lay upon his shoulders as next in authority.

"Here I am," announced Carson briefly. "What is it?"

"I am a little worried, Carson," said Hampton, "about Miss Sanford."

"Huh?" grunted the old cattleman.

"Judith hasn't put in an appearance and it's growing late," continued Hampton hastily "I'm afraid----"

"Afraid? Afraid of what? You don't think she eloped with your Jap or stole the spoons, do you?" snapped Carson. He had been interrupted at the crucial point in a game of cribbage with Poker Face and the cattleman's weak spot was cribbage. He glared at Hampton belligerently.

"Where is Lee?" questioned Hampton sharply. "I told Jose I wanted the two of you. Why didn't he come?"

"Dunno," answered Carson, still without interest. "I ain't seen him. Wasn't in for supper----"

"I tell you," cried Hampton, angry at Carson's quiet acceptance of facts which to him were darkly significant, "he, too, was out with his rifle to-day; I saw him myself. Now *he* fails to show up! Don't you see what all this points to?"

Carson, who seldom lost his poise with one-half of his brain still given over to the hand he meant to play with Poker Face, merely sighed and shook his head.

"I'm real busy down at the bunk-house, Mr. Hampton," at last came his quiet answer, "where me an' Poker Face is figuring out something important. As for worrying about a man like Bud Lee or a girl like Judy, why, I just ain't going to do it a-tall. Most likely if you'll call up the Lower End----"

"I've done it!" Whirling in his impatient stride across the room, Hampton came swiftly to Carson's side. "They're not there. They left the Lower End this afternoon and came on here. Then, both armed, they rode away again at four or five o'clock. I tell you, man, something has happened to them."

"Don't believe it," retorted Carson. "Not for one little half-minute, I don't. What's to happen? Huh?"

"You know as well as I do what sort of characters are about. The man who robbed Charlie Miller--who shot at Bud Lee----"

"Whoa!" grinned Carson. "Don't you go and fool yourself. That stick-up gent is a clean hundred miles from here right now an' still going, real lively. If any other jasper lent him a hand, why, he's on his way, too. Not stopping to pick flowers. It's the way them kind plays the game."

Carson was so cheerfully certain, so amused at the thought of Bud Lee and Judith Sanford requiring anybody's assistance, so confident concerning the methods of outlaws, that finally Hampton sent him away, half assured, and went himself to his friends in the living-room. Here he found the major and Mrs. Langworthy reading and yawning. Marcia laughed at a jest of Farris's, while Rogers sought to interest her in himself. The every-day, homelike atmosphere had its effect in allaying his picturesque fears. Hampton noted how her handful of days in the country had done Marcia a world of good, putting fresh, warm color in her rather pale cheeks, breeding a new sparkle in her eyes. She was good to look upon.

He let half an hour slip by in restless inactivity. For, no matter what Carson might say or these people in here do, Judith had not yet come in. When Marcia addressed a bright remark to him, he started and stammered: "I *beg* your pardon!" They laughed at him, saying that Pollock Hampton was growing absent-minded in his old age. But their banter failed to reach him; he was telling himself that some accident might have befallen one or both of two persons whom he frankly admired for their efficiency.

By half past eight they had caught his uneasiness. At every little sound they turned expectantly. Still no Judith. Mrs. Simpson, comfortable woman that she was, came in, bustling with apprehension. Mrs. Langworthy shook off for a little her listlessness and recounted how she had watched "that girl" riding like a wild Indian toward the Upper End. Perhaps her gun had gone off accidentally.

"Or," she concluded with a touch of venom, "it wouldn't be above her to run off with that long horse foreman."

"Eh?" said the major. "Don't believe it. A fine fig--ahem. Where should she run to? And why run at all?"

Marcia looked a quick distress to Mr. Hampton.

"It *is* late," she said timidly, "Oh, Pollock! Do you think----"

No longer to be restrained, Hampton left them and went to his room for a rifle and cartridge-belt. He intended to slip out quietly, feeling that he would get from Farris and Rogers only the sort of disbelief he had gotten from Carson. Marcia met him in the hall; she had heard his quick steps and guessed that he was going out. Now clearly, though she was frightened, she was delighted with him. He had never thrilled her like this before. She had never guessed that Pollock Hampton could be so stern-faced, so purposeful. She whispered an entreaty that he be careful, then as he went out, ran back to the others, her eyes shining.

"Pollock is going to see what is the matter," she announced excitedly. Whereat Mrs. Langworthy stared at her and then indicated facially her supreme disgust. The major suggested taking something, the occasion so plainly demanding it.

Hampton passed swiftly through the courtyard. He saw the light of the bunk-house gleaming brightly. On his way down the knoll he came upon Tommy Burkitt.

"Is it Mr. Hampton?" asked Tommy, coming close in the darkness to peer at him.

"Yes. What is it? Who are you?"

"I'm Burkitt, Tommy Burkitt, you know--Bud Lee's helper. I--I am afraid something has happened. Lee hasn't come in yet; they tried to pick him off once already, you know----"

"Neither has Miss Sanford come in," said Hampton quickly, sensing here at last a fear that was fellow to his own. "They rode toward the Upper End. You know the way, Burkitt?"

He moved on toward the corral; Burkitt turned and came with him.

"Sure I know the trail," muttered Tommy. "You're goin' to see what's wrong with 'em! Miss Judy, too! My God----"

"Bring out a couple of horses," Hampton commanded crisply. "We've lost time enough already."

"I'll go tell Carson an' the boys----"

"I have already told Carson. He says it's all nonsense. Leave him alone."

Tommy, boy that he was, asked no further questions, but ran ahead and brought out two horses. In a twinkling he had saddled them, and the two riders, each with a rifle across his arm, were hurrying over the mountain trail.

In the blackness which lay along the upper river Hampton gave his horse a free rein and let it follow at Tommy's heels. The roar of the lashing water, the pounding of shod hoofs, the whining creak of saddle-leather were the only sounds coming to them out of the night. When, finally, they drew rein under the cliffs at the lake's edge all was silent save for the faint distant booming of the river below them.

"Now which way?" whispered Hampton, his voice eloquent of suppressed excitement and eagerness.

Tommy was shaking his head in uncertainty when suddenly from above there came to them the sharp report of a rifle. Then, like a bundle of firecrackers, a volley of half a dozen staccato shots.

"Listen to that, Burkitt," muttered Hampton. "They're at it now--we're on time----"

Tommy slipped from the saddle wordlessly, came to Hampton's side and tugged gently at his leg, whispering for him to get down. Leaving their horses there, they slipped into the utter darkness of the narrow chasm in the rocks which gave access to the plateau above.

"Now," cautioned Tommy guardedly, as they came to the top, "keep close to me if you don't want to take a header about a thousan' feet. Look!" He nudged Hampton and pointed. "There are two horses across yonder; Bud's an' Miss Judy's, most likely."

Hampton did not see them, did not seek to see them. Something new, vital, big, had swept suddenly into his life. He was at grips first-hand with unmasked, pulsing forces. A tremor went through him and he was not ashamed of it; for it was not the quaking of fear, but the thrill in the blood of a man who, plucked from a round of social artificialities, finds himself with the smell of burnt powder in his nostrils and who feels a swift eagerness for what may lie just yonder waiting for him. "They're at it now!" he whispered to Burkitt. Men--yes, and a girl--were shooting, not at just wooden and paper targets, but at other men! At men who shot back, and shot to kill.

"Listen," said Burkitt. "Somebody's in the old cabin; somebody's outside. Which is which? We got to be awful careful."

They began a slow, cautious approach, slipping from bush to bush, from tree to tree, standing motionless now and then to frown into the folds of the night's curtains. Abruptly the firing ceased. They made out vaguely the two forms of the attackers, having located them a moment ago by the spurting flames from their guns. Then, "Got enough in there?" came the snarling voice of Quinnion. "If you haven't, I'm going to burn you out an' be damned to you!"

He got an answer he little expected. For Hampton, running out into the open, now that he knew that Bud and Judith must be in the cabin, was firing as he came. Burkitt's rifle spoke with his.

"Run for it, Shorty!" yelled Quinnion. "You know where. We're up against the Blue Lake boys."

"Bud!" shouted Tommy. "Oh, Bud!"

"In the cabin," came Bud's ringing answer. "Give 'em hell, Tommy! Coming!"

With his words came the sound of the door snapping back against the wall, the reports of Tommy's rifle and Hampton's pumping hot lead after two racing forms.

"They'll get away!" shouted Hampton, a sudden red rage upon him. "Curse it! It's too dark----"

Then Tommy gave over shooting and yelled to Lee to hold his fire. For instead of two there were three flying forms, three fast-racing, blurring, shadowy shapes merging with the night. Pollock Hampton, his rifle clubbed in his hand, was running with a college sprinter's speed after Quinnion and Shorty, calling breathlessly:

"Look out, they'll get away!"

Once Quinnion stopped to shoot back. The hissing lead went wide of the pursuer and he gave over firing and settled down to good, hard running, disappearing from Hampton's staring eyes. But Shorty was still to be seen, running heavily.

"Don't shoot, Bud!" cried Tommy again as two figures ran out of the cabin. "Hampton's out there--the crazy fool----"

"Hampton, come back!" shouted Lee, running after him.

But Hampton was gaining on the heavy-set Shorty and had no thought of coming back. Nor a thought of anything in all the wide world just then but overtaking the flying figure in front of him. Shorty stumbled over a fallen log and rose, cursing and calling:

"Chris! Lend a hand."

That little chance of an uprooted tree saved Hampton's life that night. Shorty, falling, had dropped his gun and hurt his knee. For a moment he groped wildly for the lost rifle, then ran on without it. Hampton cleared the log, and with a yell rather befitting a victorious savage than the young man whom Mrs. Langworthy hoped to call her son, threw his long arms about Shorty's neck.

"I got him!" shouted Hampton. "By glory----"

Shorty drove a big brutal fist smashing into his captor's face. But Hampton merely lowered his head, hiding it against Shorty's heaving shoulder, and tightened his grip. Shorty struggled to his feet, shaking at him, tearing at him, driving one fist after the other into Hampton's body. But with a grimness of purpose as new to him as was the whole of to-night's adventure Hampton held on.

Judith and Lee and Burkitt came to them as they were falling again. Now suddenly, with other hard hands upon him, Shorty relaxed, and Hampton, his face bloody, his body sore, sank back. He had done a mad thing--but triumph lay in that he had done it.

"A man never can tell," muttered Bud Lee, with less thought of the captive than of the captor--"never can tell."

"I am thinking," said Judith wonderingly, "that I never quite did you justice, Pollock Hampton!"

XIV
SPRINGTIME AND A VISION

Hampton's captive, known to them only as Shorty, a heavy, surly man whose small, close-set eyes burned evilly under his pale brows, rode that night between Hampton and Judith down to the ranch-house. He maintained a stubborn silence after the first outburst of rage. His hands tied behind his back, a rope run round his waist and down on each side through a cinch-ring, he sat idly humped forward, making no protest.

Burkitt and Lee, despite Judith's objections because of Lee's wounded leg, remained at the cabin with Bill Crowdy. Crowdy had lost a deal of blood, and though he complained of little pain, was clearly in sore need of medical attention. Judith, coming to the bunk-side just before she left, assured him very gently that she would send Doc Tripp to him immediately and, further, that she would telephone into Rocky Bend for a physician. Crowdy, like Shorty, refused to talk.

"Aw, hell," he grunted as Lee demanded what influence had brought him with Shorty and Quinnion into this mad project, "let me alone, can't you?"

And Lee let him alone. He and Burkitt sat and smoked and so passed the remaining hours of a long night. The folly of seeking Quinnion in this thick darkness was so obvious that they gave no thought to it, impatiently awaiting the dawn and the coming of the men whom Judith would send.

The events of the rest of the night and of the morrow may be briefly told: Shorty's modest request of a glass of whiskey was granted him. Then, his hands still bound securely by Carson, he was put in the small grain-house, a windowless, ten-by-ten house of logs. An admirable jail this, with its heavy padlock snapped into a deeply embedded staple and the great hasp in place. The key safely in Judith's possession, Shorty was left to his own thoughts while Judith, and Hampton went to the house.

In answer to Judith's call, Doc Tripp came without delay, left brief, disconcerting word that without the shadow of a doubt the hogs were stricken with cholera, and went on with his little bag to see what his skill could do for Bill Crowdy.

"Ought to give him sulphur fumes," grunted Tripp. But his hands were very gentle with the wounded man for all that.

Pollock Hampton had no thought of sleep that night; didn't so much as go to bed. He lay on a couch in the living-room and Marcia Langworthy, tremendously moved at the recital Judith gave of Hampton's heroism, fluttered about him, playing nurse to her heart's delight. The major suggested that Hampton have something and Hampton was glad to accept. Mrs. Langworthy complacently looked into the future and to the maturity of her own plans. In truth, good had come out of evil, and Marcia and Hampton held hands quite unblushingly.

Before daylight Carson, with half a dozen men, had breakfasted, saddled and was ready to ride to the Upper End to begin the search for Quinnion. But before he rode, Carson made the discovery that during the night the staple and hasp on the grain-house door had been wrenched away and that Shorty was gone, leaving behind him no sign of the way of his going. Carson's face was a dull, brick red. Not yet had he brought himself to accept the full significance of events A hold-up, such as Charlie Miller had experienced, is one thing; a continued series of incidents like these happening upon the confines of the Blue Lake Ranch, was quite another. Hampton, knowing nothing of conditions in the mountains, had been quick to imagine the predicament in which he had found Judith and Bud Lee. To Carson that had been a thing not to be thought of. Now, only too plainly he realized that Shorty had had an accomplice at the ranch headquarters who had come to his assistance.

Carson blamed himself for the escape. And yet, he growled to himself, in a mingling of shame and anger, it would have looked like plumb foolishness to sit out in front of that heavy door all night, when he himself had tied Shorty's hands.

"Quinnion might have let him loose," he mused as he went slowly to the house to tell Judith what had happened. "An' then he mightn't. If he, didn't, then who the devil did?"

Judith received the news sleepily and much more quietly than Carson had expected.

"We'll have to keep our eyes open after this, Carson," was her criticism. Remembering the night when she had been so certain that there had been some one listening to her talk with Tripp she added thoughtfully: "We've got to keep an eye on our own men, Carson. Some one of our crowd, taking my pay, is double-crossing us. Now, get your men on the jump and we won't bother about the milk-spilling. If we are in luck we'll get Shorty yet. And Quinnion, Carson! Don't forget Quinnion. And we've still got Bill Crowdy; we'll get everything out of him that he knows."

The cattleman rode away in heavy silence, headed toward the cabin at the Upper End, his men riding with him, an eager, watchful crowd. But Carson had his doubts about getting Quinnion, his fears that it would be a long time before he ever put a rope again to Shorty's thick wrists.

During the day Emmet Sawyer, the Rocky Bend sheriff, came, and with him Doctor Brannan. Sawyer assured Judith that he would be followed shortly by a posse led by a deputy and that they would hunt through the mountains until they got the outlaws. He listened to all that she had to tell him and then looked up Bud Lee.

"You didn't see Quinnion?" he asked. "Could you swear to him if we ever bring him in? Just by his voice?"

"Yes," answered Lee. "I can. But see if you can't get Crowdy to squeal. We're shy Shorty's real name, too, you know."

To all questions put him, Bill Crowdy answered with stubborn denial of knowledge or not at all. He had been alone; he didn't know any man named Quinnion; he didn't know anything about Shorty. And he hadn't robbed Miller. That canvas bag, then, with the thousand dollars in it? He had found it; picked it up in a gully.

"I won't do any talking," he grunted in final word, "until I get a lawyer to talk to. I know that much, Sawyer, if I don't know a hell of a lot. An' you can get it out'n your head that I'm the kind to snitch on a pal--even if I had one, which I didn't."

Crowdy, at Doctor Brannan's orders, was taken to Rocky Bend where Sawyer promised him a speedy trial, conviction and heavy sentence unless he changed his mind and turned state's evidence. And--to be done with Bill Crowdy for good and all--he never came to stand trial. A mad attempt at escape a week later, another bullet-hole given him in his struggle with his jailer, and with lips still stubbornly locked, he died without "snitching on a pal."

Under fire in the dark cabin with life grown suddenly tense for them, Bud Lee and Judith Sanford had touched hands lingeringly. No one who knew them guessed it; certainly one of them, perhaps both, sought to forget it. There had been that strange thrill which comes sometimes when a man's hand and a woman's meet. Bud Lee grunted at the memory of it; Judith, remembering, blushed scarlet. For, at that moment of deep, sympathetic understanding touched with the romance which young life will draw even from a dark night fraught with danger, there had been in Bud Lee's heart but an acceptance, eager as it was, of a "pardner." For the time being he thought of her--or, rather, he thought that he thought of her, as a man would think of a companion of his own sex. He approved of her. But he did not approve of her as a girl, as a woman.

He had said: "There are two kinds of women." And Judith, knowing that his ideal was an impossible but poetic She, rich in subtle feminine graces, steeped in that vague charm of her sex like a rose in its own perfume, had accepted his friendship during a dark hour, allowing herself to forget that upon the morrow, if morrow came to them at all, he would hold her in that gentle scorn of his.

"A narrow-minded, bigoted fool!" she cried in the seclusion of her bedroom. "I'll show you where you get off, Mr. Bud Lee! Just you wait."

When she and Lee met, she looked him straight in the eye with marked coolness, oddly aloof, and Lee, lifting his hat, was stiff and short-worded.

In the long, quiet hours which came during the few days following the end of a fruitless search for Quinnion and Shorty, he had ample time to analyze his own emotion. He liked her; from the bottom of his heart he liked her. But she was not the lady of his dreams. She rode like a man, she shot like a man, she gave her orders like a man. She was efficient. She was as square as a die; under fire she was a pardner for any man. But she was not a little lady to be thought of sentimentally. He wondered what she would look like if she shed boots and broad hat and riding-habit and appeared before a man in an evening gown--"all lacy and ribbony, you know." He couldn't picture her that way; he couldn't imagine her dallying, as the lady of his dreams dallied, in an atmosphere of rose-leaves, perhaps a volume of Tennyson on her knee.

"Shucks!" he grinned to himself, a trifle shame-facedly. "It's just the springtime in the air."

In such a mood there appeared to Bud Lee a vision. Nothing less. He was in the little meadow hidden from the ranch-house by gentle hills still green with young June. He had been working Lovelady, a newly broken saddle-mare. Standing with his back to a tree, a cigarette in the making in his hands, his black hat far back upon his head, he smilingly watched Lovelady as with regained freedom she galloped back across the meadow to her herd. Then a shadow on the grass drew Lee's eyes swiftly away from the mare and to the vision.

Over the verdant flooring of the meadow, stepping daintily in and out among the big golden buttercups, came one who might well have been that lady of his dreams. A milk-white hand held up a pale-pink skirt, disclosing the lacy flounce of a fine underskirt, pale-pink stockings and mincing little slippers; a pink parasol cast the most delicate of tints upon a pretty face from which big blue eyes looked out a little timorously upon the tall horse foreman.

He knew that this was Marcia Langworthy. He had never known until now just how pretty she was, how like a flower.

Marcia paused, seemed to hesitate, dodged suddenly as a noisy bumblebee sailed down the air. Then the bee buzzed on and Marcia smiled. Still stepping daintily she came on until, with her parasol twirling over her shoulder, she stood in the shade with Lee.

"You're Mr. Lee, aren't you?" asked Marcia. She was still smiling and looked cool and fresh and very alluring.

Lee dropped the makings of his cigarette, ground the paper into the sod with his heel and removed his hat with a gallantry little short of reverence.

"Yes," he answered, his gravity touched with the hint of a responsive smile. "Is there something I can do for you, Miss Langworthy?"

"Oh!" cried Marcia. "So you know who I am? Yet I have never seen you, I think."

"The star doesn't always see the moth, you know," offered Lee, a little intoxicated by the first "vision" of this kind he had seen in many years.

"Oh!" cried Marcia again, and then stopped, looking at him, frankly puzzled. She knew little first-hand of horse foremen. But she had seen Carson, even talked with him. And she had seen other workmen. She would, until now, have summed them all up as illiterate, awkward, and impossibly backward and shy. A second long, curious glance at Lee failed to show that he was embarrassed, though in truth he had had time to be a bit ashamed of that moth-and-star observation of his. Instead, he appeared quite self-possessed. And he was good-looking, remarkably good-looking. And he didn't seem illiterate; quite the contrary, Marcia thought. In an instant she catalogued this tall, dark, calm-eyed man as interesting.

She twirled her parasol at him and laughed softly. A strand of blond hair that was very becoming where it was, against her delicate cheek, she tucked back where it evidently belonged, since there it looked even more becoming.

"Mr. Hampton isn't here, is he?" she asked.

"No. Come to think of it, he did say this morning that he would be out right after lunch to help me break Lovelady. But I haven't seen him."

"He wanted me to stroll out here with him," Marcia explained. "And I wouldn't. It was too hot. Didn't you find it terribly hot about an hour ago, Mr. Lee?"

As a matter of fact Bud Lee had been altogether too busy an hour ago with the capers of Lovelady to note whether it was hot or cold. But he courteously agreed with Miss Langworthy.

"Then," she ran on brightly, "it got cool all of a sudden. Or at least I did. And I thought that Polly had come out here, so I walked out to surprise him. And now, he isn't here!"

Marcia looked up at Lee helplessly, smilingly, fascinatingly. It was quite as though she had added: "Oh, dear! What **shall** I do?"

Pollock Hampton had fully meant to come. But by now he had forgotten all about Bud Lee and horses to ride and to be bucked off by. A telegram had come from a nasty little tailor in San Francisco who had discovered Hampton's retreat and who was devilishly insistent upon a small matter--oh, some suits and things, you know. The whole thing totalled scarcely seven hundred dollars. He went to find Judith, to beg an advance against his wages or allowance or dividends or whatever you call it. Judith was out somewhere at the Lower End, Mrs. Simpson thought. Hampton saddled his own horse and went to find her. All this Marcia was to learn that evening.

After the swift passing of a few bright minutes, Marcia and Bud Lee strolled together across the meadow to the spring. Marcia, it seemed, was interested in everything. Lee told her much of the ways of horses, of breaking them, of a score of little ranch matters, not without their color. Marcia noted that he spoke rather slowly, and guessed that he was choosing his words with particular care.

She was delighted when they came to the bank under the willows where a pipe sent forth a clear, cold stream of water from a shady recess in the hillside. Here, at Lee's solicitous suggestion, she rested after her long walk--it was nearly a half-mile to the ranch-house--disposing her skirts fluffily about her, taking her seat upon a convenient log from which, with his hat, Lee had swept the loose dust.

"I'm dreadfully improper, am I not?" said Marcia. "But I am tired, and it is hot, isn't it? Out there in the fields, I mean. Here it's just lovely. And I do so love to hear about all the things you know which are so wonderful to me. Isn't life narrow in the cities? Don't you think so, Mr. Lee?"

The breeze playing gently with the ribbons of her sunshade brought to him the faintest of violet perfumes. He lay at her feet, obeying her tardy command to have the smoke which she had interrupted. His eyes were full of her.

"I'd so love," went on Marcia dreamily, "to live always out-of-doors. Out here I feel so sorry for the people I know in town. Here women must grow up so sweet and pure and innocent; men must be so fine and manly and strong!"

And she meant it. It was perfectly clear that she spoke in utter sincerity. For this long, summer day, no matter how she would feel to-morrow, Marcia was in tune with the open, yearned for the life blown clean with the air of the mountains. In the morning her mood had been one of rebellion, for her mother had said things which both hurt and shocked the girl. Her mother was so mercenary, so unromantic. Now, as a bit of reaction, the rebellious spirit had grown tender; opposition had been followed by listlessness; and into the mood of tender listlessness there had come a man. A man whom Marcia had never noted until now and who was an anomaly, almost a mystery.

Fate, in the form of old Carson, turned a herd of bellowing steers out into the fields lying between the meadow and the ranch-house that afternoon just as Marcia, making a late concession to propriety, was shaking her skirts and lifting her parasol. It was scarcely to be wondered at that the steers seemed to Marcia a great herd of bloodthirsty beasts. Then there were her pink gown and sunshade. . . .

"Oh, dear, oh, dear!" cried Marcia.

So it was under Lee's protection that she went back through the meadows and to the house. At first she was frightened by the strange noises his led horse made, little snorts which made her jump. But in the end she put out a timid hand and stroked the velvet nose. When finally Bud Lee lifted his hat to her at the base of the knoll upon which the house stood Marcia thanked him for his kindness.

"I've been terribly unconventional, haven't I?" she smiled at him. "But I mustn't again. Next time we meet, Mr. Lee, I am not even going to speak to you. Unless," relenting brightly, "you come up to the house and are properly introduced!"

As she went through the lilacs Lee saw her wave her parasol to him.

XV
JUST A GIRL, AFTER ALL

Three days later Bud Lee learned that Judith Sanford was, after all, "just a girl, you know"; that at least for once in her life she had slipped away to be by herself and to cry. He stopped dead in his tracks when he came unexpectedly upon her, become suddenly awkward, embarrassed, a moment uncertain, but yielding swiftly to an impulse to run for it.

"Come here, Bud Lee!" commanded Judith sharply, dabbing at her eyes. "I want to talk with you."

He was at the Upper End where he had ridden for half a dozen young horses which were to be taken down into the meadow for their education. And here she was, on a bench outside the old cabin, indulging herself in a hearty cry.

"I--I didn't know you were here," he stammered. "I was going to make some coffee and have lunch here. I do, sometimes. It's a real fine day, isn't it, Miss Sanford? Nice and warm and--" His voice trailed off indistinctly.

"Oh, scat!" cried Judith at him, half laughing, still half crying. She had wiped her eyes but still two big tears, untouched, trembled on her cheeks. In spite of him Lee couldn't keep his eyes off of them.

"I'm just crying," Judith told him then, with a sudden assumption of cool dignity which had in it something of defiance. "I've got a right to, if I want to, haven't I? What do you look at me like that for?"

"Sure," he answered hastily. "It does you good to cry; I know. Great thing. All ladies do, sometimes----"

Judith sniffed.

"You know all that there is to be known about 'ladies,' don't you? In your vast wisdom all you've got to do is lump 'em in one of your brilliant generalities. That's the man of you!"

"Maybe I'd better go make the coffee?" he suggested hurriedly. "It's after twelve. And it'll do you good. A nice hot cup."

"Maybe you had," said Judith icily. "Perhaps I can postpone my conversation with you until the water boils."

Lee went into the cabin without looking back. Judith, watching him, saw that he ran his hand across his forehead. She sniffed at him again. But when Lee had the coffee ready she had washed her face at the spring, had tucked her tumbled hair back under her hat, and, looking remarkably cool, came into the cabin. Lee thought of his meeting with Marcia, of her repeated assurance that she knew she had violated the conventions.

"You *can* make coffee," Judith nodded her approval as she sipped at the black beverage, cooled a little by condensed milk. Lee was busied with a tin containing potted meat. "Now, have you got over your shock so that I can talk with you?"

He smiled at her across the little oil-cloth-covered table, and answered lightly and with his old assurance that he guessed he had steadied his nerve. Hadn't he told her a cup of coffee would do wonders?

"Would it go to your head," began the girl abruptly, "if I were to tell you that I size you up as the best man I've got on my pay-roll?"

"I'd try to keep both feet on the ground," he said gravely, though he wondered what was coming.

"I'll explain," she continued, her tone impersonally businesslike. "Next to you, I count on Doc Tripp; next to Tripp, on Carson. They are good men; they are trustworthy; they understand ranch conditions and they know what loyalty to the home-range means. But Tripp is just a veterinarian; simply that and nothing more. His horizon isn't very wide. Neither is Carson's."

"And mine?" he grinned at her. "Read me my horoscope, Miss Sanford!"

"You have taken the trouble to be something more than just a horse foreman," she told him quietly. "I don't know what your advantages have been; if you haven't gone through high school, then at least you have been ambitious enough to get books, to read, to educate yourself. You have developed further than Carson; you have broadened more than Tripp."

"Thanks," he offered dryly.

"Oh, I'm not seeking to intrude into your private affairs, Mr. Bud Lee!" she cried warmly at his tone. "I have no desire to do so, having no interest in them. First of all, I want one thing clear: You said when I first came that you'd stay a few days, long enough for me to get a man in your place. We have both been rather too busy to think of your leaving or my seeking a substitute. Now what? The job is yours as long as you want it--if you'll stay. I don't want you leaving me in the lurch. Do you want to go? Or do you want to stick?"

What did he want? He had anticipated an interference from the girl in his management of the duty allotted him and no such interference had come. She left him unhampered, even as she did Tripp and Carson. He had his interest in his horses. It was pleasant here. This cabin was a sort of home to him. Besides, he had the idea that Quinnion and Shorty might again be heard from--that if Trevors was backing their play, there would be other threats offered the Blue Lake outfit from which he had no desire to run. There was such a thing as loyalty to the home-range, and in the half-year he had worked here it had become a part of him.

"I'll stick," he said quietly.

"I'm glad of that," replied Judith. "Oh, you'll have your work cut out for you, Bud Lee, and, that you may be the better fitted to do it, I want you to know just what I am up against."

She paused a moment, stirring her coffee with one of Lee's tin spoons, gathering her thoughts. Then, speaking thoughtfully, she explained:

"It's a gamble, with us bucking the long odds. Dad left me a third interest, clear, valued, counting stock, at a good deal more than four hundred thousand dollars. He left me no cash. Dad never had any cash. Just so soon as he got his hands on it he put it to work. I knew he had planned taking over another one-third interest, and I went on with his plans. I mortgaged my share for two hundred thousand dollars, which I got at five per cent. That means I have to dig up each year, just interest, ten thousand dollars. That's a pretty big lump, you know."

"Yes," he admitted slowly. "That's big; mighty big."

"With the money I raised," Judith continued, "I bought out the third owner, Timothy Gray. He let his holding go for three hundred and fifty thousand. It was a bargain for me--if I can make a go of it. I still owe, on the principal, one hundred and fifty thousand dollars. I owe on my mortgage two hundred thousand. Total of my indebtedness, three hundred and fifty thousand dollars. And that's bigger, Bud Lee."

"Yes. That's bigger figures than I can quite get the hang of."

No wonder she had been crying. Even if everything went smooth on the Blue Lake she, too, had her work cut out for her.

"Now," she ran on, her voice stirring him with the ringing note in it, "I can make a go of it--if they will just let me alone! I am playing close to the table, Lee, close! I have a little money in the bank, enough to run along for two or three months, that's all. I said that dad left no cash. I didn't mention his insurance." Her eyes grew suddenly wet but she did not avert them from Lee's face, going on quietly: "That was ten thousand dollars. Close to seven thousand had to go for his current obligations. I have about two thousand to run on."

"Close hauled," grunted Lee. And to himself, he remarked as he had remarked once before: "She's got her sand."

Quite naturally Bud Lee thought swiftly of his horses. He had told Trevors that he wanted to make no sale for at least six months. Given until then--if Judith could make a go of it without forcing a sale--he'd show her the way to at least seven or eight thousand, with a good percentage of clear profit.

"To begin with," Judith's voice interrupted his musings, "I am going to have trouble with Carson. I admit that he's an exceptionally good cattle foreman; I admit, too, that he has his limitations. He is of the old school, and has got to learn something! Already he has his weather-eye cocked for the lean season; he'll be coming to me in August or September, telling me I've got to begin selling. That's the way they all do! And the result is that beef cattle drop and the market clogs with them. What I am going to do is make Carson start in buying them. Oh, he'll buck like one of his own red bay steers but he'll buy!"

"We're pretty well stocked up," Lee offered gently. "Turning the hills over to the hogs makes a difference, too. We're going to be short of feed long before September is over."

"Short of range feed, yes," she retorted warmly. "But we're going to put our trust in our silos, Lee, and make them do such work for us as they have never done before. Then, when other folks are forced to sell off for what they can get, we'll hold on and buy. We won't sell before December or January, when the market is up."

He shook his head. Though not of the old school which had produced Carson, still he put little faith in those tall towers into which alfalfa and Indian corn were fed to make lush fodder.

"I don't know a whole lot about silos," he admitted.

"Neither does Carson," said Judith. "He looks at such things as silos and milking-machines and tractors and fences even as the old Indians must have looked at the inroads of the white men. But, do you know where he has been these last few days?"

"In San Francisco? Heard him say he was going to take a few days off."

Judith laughed.

"That's Carson for you! He wouldn't admit where he was going. I sent him down to Davis where the State experimental farm and laboratories are. He's going to see silo, study silo, think silo until he gets a new idea into his head. I have ordered a big extension in our irrigated area, I have begun the construction of two more silos. When Carson gets back he's going to look around for some more shorthorns at bargain prices. I have an idea it wouldn't do you any harm either, to look over what we are doing down at the Lower End."

Again she paused. Then, her eyes suddenly darkening, she told him what, after all, lay top-most in her mind.

"I have said that if I am given the chance, I can make a go of this. It's up to you, Bud Lee, to help see that I get that chance. An attempt was made to spread the lung-worm through my calves. Now it's the hogs. Do you know what the latest news is from the pens? There's cholera among them."

"Where did it come from?" he demanded. "Tripp's been keeping the health of our stock up right along."

"Where did it come from?" Judith repeated after him. "That's what I don't know. We've been so careful. But where did the calf sickness come from? Bayne Trevors imported it."

The inference was clear. He stared at her with frowning eyes.

"I don't see how he could have done it without Tripp's getting on to it. He hasn't bought any new hogs."

"But you understand now why I wanted to talk to you? If I win out in the thing

I have taken on my shoulders, it is going to be by a close margin. I've thought it all out. We can't slip up in a single deal! But, it's up to you to give me a hand. To find out for yourself such things as where did the cholera come from! And to look out, that the next time they don't burn us out, when the range is dry. To see that nothing happens to your horses. To keep your two eyes wide open. To help me find the man, working with us right now, who is double-crossing us, who turned Shorty loose, who is watching a chance to do his knife act again somewhere else. Do you get me, Bud Lee?"

"I get you," replied Lee.

From without, gay voices, calling merrily, interrupted them. Lee went swiftly to the door while Judith finished her coffee and pulled her broad hat a little lower to throw its shadow in her eyes.

"Ahoy, there!" It was Pollock Hampton's voice. "We saw your horses and thought we'd catch you picnicking. Got a fire going, too! Say, that's bully. Come ahead, Marcia."

Marcia, a long riding-habit gathered in one hand, her cheeks flushed with her ride, her eyes bright as they rested upon the tall form in the doorway, came on behind Hampton. As the eyes of the two girls met, a sudden hot flush flooded Judith's cheeks. She hated herself for it; she wondered just how red her eyes were.

"Say, Judith," called Hampton, "I'm glad as the dickens we found you. Sawyer, the sheriff, telephoned just now. Said to tell you he'd located Quinnion. The funny part of it is that we made a mistake. It wasn't Quinnion at all that tried to shoot you and Bud up the other night."

"How's that?" demanded Lee. "Who says it wasn't?"

"Sawyer. Found Quinnion at a sheepman's place thirty or forty miles north of here. The sheepman swore Quinnion had been with him two weeks, was with him that night."

"A sheepman *can* lie," grunted Lee.

Judith's brief moment of confusion passed, she ushered Marcia into the cabin. True to her promise, Miss Langworthy, though she flashed a quick look toward Lee, did not speak to him. He found himself flushing quite as hotly as Judith had done.

"We've just finished our lunch," Judith was saying. "And we've left you half of our coffee."

"I've been simply dying to see this place!" cried Marcia impetuously. "I told Pollock that it was a sure sign he didn't love me any more if he wouldn't bring me. And you and--and one of the men," her eyes on Judith's, "actually were in here, being shot at! Judith, dear, you are just the bravest girl in the world. If I'd been here I'd have simply died. I know I would."

Perhaps she would. At any rate she shuddered delightfully. She found a bullet-hole in the door and put a pink forefinger into it, giving a second little shiver. She managed to keep her back full upon Lee.

"Oh, by the way," said Hampton, busy opening the parcel of lunch they had brought with them, "Marcia's heard all about you, Bud. You said you wanted to meet Lee, Marcia. Well, here he is, tall and handsome in a devilish reckless way, looking at the dimple at the back of your neck. Miss Langworthy, Mr. Lee. Judith, that coffee smells good!"

"You are a naughty little boy, Pollock," said Miss Langworthy coolly. Nevertheless she turned smiling to Lee and put out her hand to him. "Mr. Hampton really makes quite a hero of you," she said composedly. "I think I have seen you--from a distance, you know."

The small whiteness of her hand was swallowed up in the lean brown of his.

"Hampton's a prevaricator," he said gravely, as he looked down into the merry blue eyes turned up to him. "But he's a gentleman I have to thank for the introduction. I am very happy to know you, Miss Langworthy."

"And now," cried Marcia, slipping her hand out of Lee's and going to a chair near the table, "do tell me all about that terrible, terrible night. But do you think we are quite safe here now, Mr. Lee?"

To herself Judith was saying: "Just the type to be Bud Lee's ideal lady!"

When they left the cabin, an hour later, Judith challenged Hampton to a ride and so left Marcia and Bud Lee to follow leisurely.

XVI
POKER FACE AND A WHITE PIGEON

Mrs. Simpson had made a discovery. It was epoch-marking. It was tremendous. Nothing short of that! So, at the very least, Mrs. Simpson was prepared to maintain stoutly in the face of possible ridicule. Though, as Judith's housekeeper, she had sufficient household duties on her plump shoulders to send a less doughty woman creeping wearily to bed with the chickens, she found time before the dawn and long after nightfall to keep her eye upon that Black Spanish and his recruit and treacherous ally, Fujioki.

One morning, very early, Mrs. Simpson, from the thick curtains of the living-room, saw Jose "prowling around suspicious-like in the courtyard!" She thrilled at the sight. She always thrilled to Jose. The half-breed had gone silently, "sneaking-like," by Judith's outer door. He had paused there, listening. He had gone back to the courtyard, hesitating, pretending that he was looking at the roses! Such a ruse on the part of so black-hearted a villain inspired in the scarcely breathing Mrs. Simpson a vast disgust. As if he could fool **her** like that, pottering around among the roses!

She, too, sought to move silently in his wake, though under her ample weight the veranda creaked audibly. Still, making less noise than usual, she peered through the lilacs. She saw Jose at the base of the knoll, going swiftly toward the stables. She saw another man who, evidently, was a third of the "gang," and who, of course, had risen early to creep out of the men's bunkhouse before the others were awake, to meet Jose. Screening herself behind the lilacs, her heart throbbing as it had not done for many a long year, she watched.

Jose and the other man did meet. Jose stopped. The two exchanged a few words, too low for Mrs. Simpson to hear at that distance. But she made out that the other man had something in his hand, something white. A pigeon! For, suddenly released, it fluttered out of the man's hands and, circling high above Mrs. Simpson's head, flew to join the other birds cooing on the housetop!

"A carrier-pigeon!" gasped Mrs. Simpson. "Taking a message to the other cut-throats!"

From that instant there was no doubt in her mind. This fitted in too well with her many suspicions not to be the clew she had sought long and unceasingly.

Jose went on, the man from the bunk-house went back into it, and Mrs. Simpson fled to the house and hastened excitedly to Judith's room. Judith, rudely awakened, came hurriedly to her door in her dressing-gown, her eyelids heavy with sleep. When she heard, she laughed.

"You dear old goose!" cried Judith joyously. "I just love you to death. You put fresh interest into life."

Despite Mrs. Simpson's earnest protests, Judith hugged her and pushed her out again, saying that since she was awake now she would want her breakfast just as soon as she could get it. The housekeeper shook her head and retreated heavily.

"You've got to show some folks a man cutting their throats," she muttered to herself, "before they'll believe it. It is a carrier-pigeon and I know it. And that Black Spanish--ugh! He makes my blood curdle, just to look at him!"

"Carrier-pigeons!" laughed Judith, as she began a hurried dressing. "The dear old goosie! And poor old Jose. She'll get something on him yet. I wonder why she----"

Suddenly Judith broke off. She was standing in front of a tall mirror, still only half-dressed. As she looked into the bright face of the smiling girl in the glass, a sudden change came. Pigeons! Doc Tripp had said that Trevors had got them; had remarked on the incongruity of a man like Trevors caring for little cooing birds. It was rather odd. Carrier-pigeons--carrier----

Judith whipped on her dressing-gown again and, slipperless, her warm, bare feet pat-patting upon the cold surfaces of the polished floors, she ran to the office.

"Send Jose to me," she called to Mrs. Simpson. "In the office. I want him immediately."

A warm glow came into Mrs. Simpson's breast. With a big kitchen poker behind her broad back, she hastened out to call Jose. Judith, at the telephone, called for Doc Tripp.

"Come up immediately," she commanded, "prepared to make a test for hog-cholera germs, Doc. No, I am not sure of anything, but I think I begin to see where it came from and how. Hurry, will you?"

To Jose she said abruptly:

"Go down to the men's quarters, Jose. Tell Carson and Lee to come right up." And as Jose turned to go, she added carelessly: "Seen any of the men yet?"

"Si, senorita," answered Jose. "Poky Face is up."

"Poker Face? All right, Jose. The others will be about, then."

Jose took little more time for his errand than for his elaborate bow. Carson and Lee came promptly, Carson a score of steps in advance, for Lee had tarried just long enough to wash his face and brush his hair; Carson had not.

"Tell me," demanded Judith, looking at her cattleman with intent eagerness, "what do you know about Poker Face?"

"One of the best men I've got," answered Carson heartily.

"Square, you think?"

"Yes. If I didn't think so he'd have been on his way a long time ago."

"How long has he been here? Who took him on?"

"Trevors hired him. About the same time he hired me."

Bud Lee, entering then, wondered what new thing was afoot. He glanced down and saw a bare foot peeping out from the hem of Judith's heavy red robe; he saw the hair tumbled in a glorious brown confusion over her shoulders. She was amazingly pretty this way.

"I want you two men to just stick around until I send for you again," said Judith, her eyes upon Carson alone, a little pink, naked foot suddenly withdrawn and tucked somewhere under her in her chair. "And keep your eyes on Poker Face. Keep him here, too, Carson. By the way, did any of you boys come in late last night? Or early this morning?"

"Why, no," answered Carson slowly. "An' yes. None of the reg'lar boys, but a man from down the river, looking for a job. Heard we was short-handed. Blew in early. Just got in a few moments ago, Poker Face said."

Quick new interest flew into Judith's eyes.

"Keep him here, too!" she cried. "And I'll give you something to do while you wait: bring me all the pigeons you can get your hands on--white ones. Shoot them if you have to. And be careful you don't rub the dust off their feet."

Carson's eyes went swiftly to Bud Lee's. In Carson's mind there was a quick suspicion: The strain of life on the ranch was proving too much for a girl, after all.

Judith, reading his thought, turned up her nose at him and, seeking to keep her feet hidden as she walked by sagging a little at the knees, went to the door. Turning there, she saw in Lee's eyes the hint of a smile, a very approving, admiring smile.

"Impudent!" she cried within herself. Looking very tiny, her knees bent so that her robe might sweep the floor, she continued with all possible dignity to the hallway. Once there, she ran for her room, her gown fluttering widely about her. In her room, though she dressed hurriedly, she still took time for a long and critical examination of two rows of little pink toes.

"Just the same," she said to the flushed Judith in the mirror, "they are very nice feet--Bud Lee, I'd just like to make you squirm one of these days. You're altogether too--too--oh, scat, Judy. What's the matter with you?"

In less than half an hour Doc Tripp, showing every sign of a hurried toilet, rode into the courtyard. He came swiftly into the office, bag in hand. Judith, waiting impatiently for him, lost no words in telling him her suspicions. And Doc Tripp, hearing her out, swore softly and fluently, briefly asking her pardon when he had done.

"I'm a jackass," he said fervently. "I always knew I was a fool, but I didn't know that I was an idiot! Why, Judy, those damned pigeons have been sailing all over the ranch, billing and cooing and picking up and toting cholera germs. Any fool can see it now. I might have known something was up when Trevors bought the infernal things. It's as simple as one, two, three. Now this other jasper, pretending to look for a job, brings on some more of them, so that the disease will spread the faster. Let me get my two hands on him, Judith. For the love of God, lead me to him."

But, instead, she led him to the dozen white pigeons which Carson brought in.

Tripp, all business again, improvised his laboratory, washed the pigeons' feet, made his test, with never another curse to tell of his progress. Judith left him and went into the courtyard, where, in a moment, Carson came to her.

"You better tell me what's up," he said sharply. "I know something is. That new guy that just come in is darned hard to keep. Just as quick as I grab a shotgun an' go to shooting pigeons he moseys out to the corrals an' starts saddling his horse."

"Don't let him go!"

Carson smiled a dry, mirthless smile.

"Bud is looking out for him right now," he explained. "Don't you worry none about his going before we say so. But I want to know what the play is."

Judith told him. Carson shook his head.

"Think of that?" he muttered. "Why, a man that would do a trick like that oughtn't to be let live two seconds. Only," and he wrinkled his brows at her, "where does Poker Face come in? We ain't got no call to suspicion he's in on it."

"You watch him, just the same, Carson. We know that somebody here has been working against us. Some one who turned Shorty loose. Maybe it isn't Poker Face, and maybe it is."

"He plays a crib game like a sport an' a gentleman," muttered Carson. "He beat me seven games out'n nine last night!" And, still with that puzzled frown in his eyes, he went to watch Poker Face and the new man. To have one of the men for whom he was responsible suspected hurt old Carson sorely. And Poker Face, the man with whom he delighted to play a game of cards--it was almost as though Carson himself had come under suspicion.

"You're going to stick around just a little while, stranger," Bud Lee was saying quietly to a shifty-eyed man in the corral. "Just why, I don't know. Orders, you know."

"Orders be damned," snarled the newcomer. "I go where I please and when I please."

He set a foot to his stirrups. A lean, muscular hand fell lightly upon his shoulder and he was jerked back promptly. Lee smiled at him. And the shifty-eyed man, though he protested sharply, remained where he was.

A thin, saturnine man whose lips never seemed to move, a man with dead-looking eyes into which no light of emotion ever came, watched them expressionlessly from where he stood with Carson. It was Poker Face.

"No," Poker Face answered, to a sharp question from the persistent Carson.

"Sure, are you?"

"Yes."

At last word came from Judith. Carson and Lee were to bring both of the suspected men to the house. Doc Tripp, wiping his hands on a towel, his sleeves up, bestowed upon the two of them a look of unutterable contempt and hatred.

"You low-lived skunks!" was his greeting to them.

"Easy, Doc," continued Judith from her desk. "That won't get us anywhere. Who are you?" she demanded of the man standing at Lee's side.

"Me?" demanded the man with an assumption of jauntiness. "I'm Donley, Dick Donley, that's who I am!"

"When did you get here?"

"'Bout an hour ago."

"What did you come for?"

"Lookin' for a job."

"Did Carson say he hadn't anything for you?"

"No, he didn't. You're askin' a lot of questions, if you want to know," he added with new surliness.

"Then why are you going in such a hurry? Don't you like to see any one shoot pigeons?"

Donley stared back at her insolently.

"Because I didn't fall for the crowd," he retorted bluntly. "An', if you want to know, because I didn't hanker for the job when I found out who was runnin' it."

"Meaning me? A girl? That it?"

"You guessed it."

"Who told you that I was running the outfit?" she demanded suddenly, her eyes hard on his. "You must have found that out pretty soon! Who told you?"

Donley hesitated, his eyes running from her to the other faces about him, resting longest upon the expressionless, dead-looking eyes of Poker Face.

"What difference does it make who told me?" he snapped.

"Answer me," she commanded. "Who told you?"

"Well," said Donley, "he did. Poker Face told me."

"Who told you that his name was Poker Face?" Judith shot the question at him.

Donley moved a scuffling foot back and forth, stirring uneasily. That he was lying, no one there doubted; that he was but a poor liar after all was equally evident.

"You ain't got no call to keep me here," he said at last. "I ain't goin' to answer questions all day."

"You'll answer my questions if you don't want me to turn you over to Emmet Sawyer in Rocky Bend!" she told him coolly. "How did you know this man was called Poker Face? Did you know him before?"

Donley's eyes went again, furtive and swift, to Poker Face. But so did all other eyes. Poker Face gave no sign.

"Yes," answered Donley then, taking refuge at last upon the solid basis of truth.

"Did you know this man?" Judith asked then of Poker Face, turning suddenly on him.

"No," said Poker Face.

Donley, having guessed wrong, flushed and dropped his head. Then he looked up defiantly and with a short, forced laugh.

"Suppose I know him or don't know him," he asked with his old insolence, "whose business is it?"

But Judith was giving her attention to Poker Face now.

"Where did you get that white pigeon you turned loose this morning?" she asked crisply.

"Caught it," was the quiet answer.

"How?"

"With my han's."

"Why?"

"Jus' for fun."

"Did you know that pigeons could carry hog-cholera on their feet?"

"No. But I wouldn't have been afraid, not bein' a hawg."

Donley tittered. Poker Face looked unconcerned.

"Take that man Donley into the hall," Judith said to Lee. "See if he has got any pigeon feathers sticking to him anywhere, inside his shirt, probably. If you need any help, say so."

Very gravely Bud Lee put a hand on Donley's shoulder.

"Come ahead, stranger," he said quietly.

"You go to hell!" cried Donley, springing away.

But Bud Lee's hand was on him, and though he struggled and cursed and threatened he went with Lee into the hallway. Tripp, watching through the open door, smiled. Donley was on his back, Lee's knees on his chest.

"I'll tell you one thing, stranger," Bud Lee was saying to him softly, as his hand tore open Donley's shirt, "you open your dirty mouth to cuss just once more in Miss Sanford's presence and I'll ruin the looks of your face for you. Now lie still, will you?"

"Connect me with the Bagley ranch," Judith directed the Rocky Mountain operator. "That's right, isn't it, Doc?"

"Yes," answered Tripp. "That's the nearest case of cholera."

"Hello," said Judith when the connection had been established. "Mr. Bagley? This is Judith Sanford, Blue Lake ranch. I've got a case of hog-cholera here, too. I want some information."

She asked her questions, got her answers. Triumphantly she turned to Tripp.

The Bagley ranch, though a hundred miles away, was the nearest cholera-infected place of which Tripp had any knowledge. Bagley did have a flock of pigeons; a man, a month or so ago, had bought two dozen from him; the man wasn't Trevors. Bagley didn't know who he was. The same man, however, had shown up three days ago and had asked for another half-dozen of the birds. There had been three white pigeons among them. He was a shifty-eyed chap, Bagley said, old brown suit, hat with a rattlesnake skin around the crown. That, point for point, spelled Donley.

Lee returned with the shirt which he had ripped from his prisoner's back. Adhering to the inside of it were little, downy feathers and three or four larger feathers from a pigeon's wing.

"I guess he rode mostly at night, at that," concluded Lee. "A great little fat man you must have looked, stranger, with six of those birdies in your shirt."

Donley's face was a violet red. But a glance from Lee shut his mouth for him. Poker Face, still looking on, gave no sign of interest.

"Put him in the grain-house," said Judith, her eyes bright with anger. "And see that he doesn't go Shorty's trail. Poker Face, have you anything else to say for yourself?"

"No," answered Poker Face.

"Then," cried Judith hotly, "you can have your time right now! Donley, here, I'll prosecute. He's going to pay for this morning's work. I've got nothing on you. It's up to you to see that I don't get it! And you can tell Shorty for me--yes, and Quinnion too, and Bayne Trevors, if you like--that I am ready and waiting for your next play! And don't forget that when San Quentin is full there's still room in Folsom."

Judith telephoned Emmet Sawyer that she had a man for him. Lee and Carson conducted an expostulating Donley to the grain-house and jailed him wordlessly. Then Carson put a man on guard at the door, daylight though it was. When all was done he filled his pipe slowly and turned troubled eyes after Poker Face.

"She made a mistake there, though," he said regretfully. "A better cow-hand I never ask to see, Bud. An' you ought to see the game of crib that man plays! Nope, Judy; you're wrong there."

But Bud Lee, the man who did not approve of the sort of woman who did man's work, said with unusual warmth:

"Don't you fool yourself, Carson! She hasn't made one little misplay yet!"

XVII
"ONCE A FOOL--ALWAYS A FOOL"

Though, under the surface, life upon Blue Lake ranch was sufficiently tense, the remaining days of June frivoled by as bright and bonny as the little meadow-blues flirting with the field-flowers.

Since from the very first the ranch had been short-handed, the hours from dawn to dusk were filled with activity. Carson, who, true to Judith's expectations, had brought back some new ideas from his few days at the experimental farm-- ideas not to be admitted by Carson, however--bought a hundred young steers from a neighboring overstocked range. In the lower corrals the new milking-machines were working smoothly, only a few of the older cows refusing to have anything to do with them.

Tripp had succeeded in locating and getting back some of the men who had worked long under Luke Sanford and whom Trevors had discharged. It was a joy to see the familiar faces of Sunny Harper, Johnny Hodge, Bing Kelley, Tod Bruce. The alfalfa acreage was extended, a little more than doubled. Plans were made for an abundance of dry fodder to be fed with the lush silage during the coming lean months. Bud Lee broke his string of horses, and with Tommy Burkitt and one other dependable man began perfecting their education, with an eye turned toward a profitable sale in January.

Quinnion, perforce, was left undisturbed upon the sheep-ranch whither Emmet Sawyer had followed him. Against Bud Lee's word that he had had a hand at the trouble at the old cabin were the combined oaths of two of the sheepmen that he had been with them at the time.

Hampton's guests, who had planned for a month at the ranch, stayed on. But they would be leaving at the end of June. That is, Farris and Rogers positively; the

Langworthys, perhaps. The major was content here, and to stay always and always, would be an unbounded joy--of course, with little runs to the city for the opera season and for shopping trips, and a great, jolly house-party now and then.

The only fly in Marcia's ointment was Hampton himself. She confessed as much to Judith. She liked him, oh, ever so much! But was that love? She yearned for a man who would thrill her through and through, and Hampton didn't always do that. Just after his heroic capture of the terrible Shorty, Marcia was thrilled to her heart's content. But there were other days when Hampton was just Pollock Hampton. If it could only be arranged so that she could stay on and on, with no day of reckoning to come, no matrimonial ventures on the horizon . . .

"That's simple, my dear," Judith smiled at her. "When you get through being Pollock Hampton's guest, you can be mine for a while."

Hampton was now a great puzzle to Mrs. Langworthy, and even an object of her secret displeasure. Not that that displeasure ever went to the limit of changing Mrs. Langworthy's plans. But she longed for the right to talk to him as a mother should. For, seeking to emulate those whom he so unstintedly admired, Bud Lee and Carson and the rest of the hard-handed, quick-eyed men in the service of the ranch, Hampton was no longer the careless, frankly inefficient youth who had escorted his guests here. He went for days at a time unshaven, having other matters to think of; he came to the table bringing with him the aroma of the stables. He wore a pair of trousers as cylindrical in the leg as a stove-pipe; over them he wore a pair of cheap blue overalls, with the proper six-inch turn-up at the bottom to show the stovepipe trousers underneath. The overalls got soiled, then dirty, then disgracefully blotched with wagon grease and picturesque stains, and Hampton made no apologies for them.

Twice he left the ranch, once to be gone overnight, intending that it should be a mystery where he went. But, since he rode the north trail which led to the Western Lumber camp, no one doubted that he had gone to see Bayne Trevors, in whom he still stoutly believed.

Between the 15th and the memorable 30th of June, Bud Lee saw little of Judith Sanford. She was here, there, everywhere; busy, preoccupied. Marcia he talked with twice; once when they rode together while Hampton, racing recklessly down a rocky slope for a shot at a deer got a fall, a sore shoulder and made his debut in certain new swear-words; once when all of the guests, with the exception of Farris, who was painting the portrait of the stallion, Nightshade, and the major, who had "letters to write," came out to watch the horse-breaking. This time, introduced to Mrs. Langworthy, Lee got for his bow a remarkably cold stare. Others might forget, here in the open, the distinction between people of the better class and their servants--not Mrs. Langworthy, if you please.

Having created his imaginary woman, Lee was ripe to fall in love with her when she came. He had thrilled to the touch of Judith's hand that night in the cabin; his thoughts, many and many a day, centred about the superbly alive beauty that was Judith's. The fact disturbed him vaguely. The thought that he was very deeply interested in her in the good old way between man and maid, never entered his stubborn head. She was as far removed from his ideal woman as the furthermost star in the infinite firmament. Perhaps it was this very disquiet within him, caused by Judith, which now turned his thoughts to Marcia.

"That's the sort of woman," he told himself stoutly. "A man's woman; his other self, not just a pardner; the necessary other side of him, not just the same side in a different way."

Marcia had little, feminine ways of helplessness which turned flatteringly to the strength of the other sex. Judith asked no man to aid her in mounting her horse; Marcia coquettishly slipped a daintily slippered foot into a man's palm, rising because of his strength.

Now, when his thoughts went to Judith, Bud Lee turned them dexterously to Marcia, making his comparisons, shaping them to fit into his pet theory. When, days passing, he did not see Judith, he told himself that he was going to miss Marcia when she left. When one day he came unexpectedly upon Judith and with lips and eyes she flashed her ready smile at him, he felt that odd stir in his blood. What a pity that a girl like her, who might have been anything, elected to do a man's work! When, again unexpectedly, he came another day upon Marcia riding with Hampton, there was no quick stirring of the pulses, and he contented himself with the thought: "Now, that is the sort of woman. A man's woman! His other self . . ." and so on.

When Judith planned a little party to mark the departure of Marcia on the 30th of June--it wasn't definitely decided that the Langworthys were leaving then, but at least Farris and Rogers were--the reasons actuating her were rather more complex than Judith herself fully realized or would have admitted. She liked Marcia; she wanted to do at least this much for her. Living-room, dining-room, music-room, library--they would all be cleared of the larger pieces of furniture, the double-doors thrown open. The string band from Rocky Bend would come. Judith would send out invitations to the nicer people there and to the ranches hereabout. She would have a barbecue, there would be races and the usual holiday games, then the dance. Marcia would know nothing of it until the last day, when her eager enthusiasm would send her a-flutter to her dressing-room.

Unanalyzed, it was simplicity itself, this giving a farewell party to Marcia. Under analysis, it was a different matter. The boys at the ranch would be invited, and of course most of them would come. Bud Lee would come. Judith would see to that, even if he should hesitate.

Bud Lee had always been so self-possessed, had so coolly found her lacking, that, piqued a little, Judith longed for the opportunity to place him in an atmosphere where a little of his calm self-possession might be snatched from him. If she could embarrass him, if she could see the red rise under his tanned skin, she would be giving Mr. Lee a lesson good for his soul.

"I've got powerful little use for an affair like that," said Lee coolly, when she told him. "Thank you, Miss Sanford, but I don't think I'll come."

Judith shrugged her shoulders as though it did not in the least matter to her.

"I'm giving it for Marcia," she said. "Do you think it would be quite nice to her to stay away? I am afraid that she will be hurt."

Not Judith's words, but the look in her eyes changed Lee's intentions.

"If it's for Miss Langworthy," he said quietly, "I'll come."

The day came and Bud Lee began to regret that he had given his promise to go to Marcia's dance. All day he was taciturn, aloof, avoiding not only the visitors from Rocky Bend and the other ranches, but his own fellows as well. He took no part in the races, was missing when the blazing trenches and smell of broiling meat told that the barbecue was in progress. He worked with his horses as he had worked yesterday, as he would work to-morrow. With the dusk he went, not to the men's quarters, but to the old cabin at the Upper End.

Again and again that day he had thought of that look in Judith's eyes when she had asked him to come for Marcia's sake. What the devil did she mean by it? He didn't know exactly, but he did know that in its own vague way it irritated him. Her eyes had laughed at him, they had teased, they had told him that Judith herself wasn't wasting a single thought upon Mr. Bud Lee, but that she had noticed his obvious interest in Miss Langworthy.

"Damn it," muttered Lee. "I won't go."

But he had said that he would go, and in little things as in big ones he was scrupulous. He would go, just to dance with Marcia and show Miss Judith a thing or two. He felt unreasonably like taking Miss Judith across his knee and spanking her. And he did have a curiosity to see just what Judith would look like in a real party-dress.

"Poor little wild Indian," he grumbled. "She's got the making of a wonder in her, and she doesn't even know it. What's worse, doesn't care."

He sat with a dead cigarette between his fingers, staring at the wind-blown flame of his coal-oil lamp. Judith was doing this as she did everything that she set her two hands on, thoroughly and with her whole heart and soul. In that lay the key to her character. There was no half-way with her. When she gave, it was open-handedly, with no reservation; where she loved or hated, it was unreservedly; if she gave a dance it would be a dance for the countryside to remember.

Yesterday Hampton had wondered, grinning, what he'd look like in a dress-suit again. Hadn't had a thing on here of late but his war togs. Whereby he called attention to his turned-up overalls, soft shirt, battered hat, and flapping vest with the tobacco-tag hanging out.

Bud Lee turned down the wick of his lamp, which had been smoking, and sat staring at it another five minutes.

"By thunder," he said softly to himself. "I'll do it."

He shoved the bunk away from its place in the corner, opened a trap-door in the floor and, lamp in hand, went down into the cabin's cellar. Here was a long pine box, hooped with tin bands for shipping, its lid securely nailed on. He set down his lamp and with shirt-sleeve wiped off some of the accumulation of dust and spider-web. A card with the words, "David Burrill Lee, Rocky Bend," tacked to it made its appearance. Lee shook his head and attacked the lid.

"It's like digging out a dead man," he muttered. "Well, we'll bury him again to-morrow."

It was a box of odds and ends. Clothing, a few books, a pack of photographs, an ornate bridle, a pair of gold-chased spurs, a couple of hats, gloves, no end of the varied articles which might have gone hastily into such a receptacle as this from the hurried packing in a bachelor's apartments.

Bud Lee, with a dress-suit and the articles it demands, even to tie and dancing-shoes, went back into the room above.

"Like Hampton," he mused, looking at the things in his hands, "I wonder what it'll feel like to get back into these! I'm a fool." He laughed shortly and set to work to improvise a flat-iron to take the worst wrinkles out of the cloth. "Once a fool, always a fool. You can't get away from it."

It was settled. He was going to Marcia's party. He insisted upon calling it in his mind, "Marcia's party." And he was wondering, as he shaved, how Judith was going to look.

XVIII
JUDITH TRIUMPHANT

As Bud Lee came through the lilacs into the courtyard, he heard the tinkle of a distant piano and the tremolo of a violin, so faint as hardly to be distinguished above the plash and gurgle of the fountains. The court, bathed in soft light, seemed a corner of fairyland, the music vanishing elfin strains of some mischievous troop putting sighs and love dreams into a sleeping maid's breast. The night was rich with stars, warm with summer, serene with the peace of the mountains. He was late. They were already dancing within.

He stood a moment, looking in at the outer edge of the flood of light which gushed through the wide doors. Behind him Japanese lanterns hanging from a vine-covered trellis; before him flowers, bright chandeliers, girls' dresses like fluttering, many-colored, diaphanous butterfly wings. He had been saying to himself: "I must hurry if I want to dance with Marcia." And something stirring restlessly within him shoved aside the thought of Marcia and put in its stead the old wonder: "What sort of a Judith would he see to-night?"

He found it difficult to form any picture of her here, among these gay, inconsequent merry-makers. Judith to him spelled a girl upon a horse, booted, spurred, with a scarf about her neck fluttering wildly behind her as she rode, the superb, splendid figure of a girl of the out-of-doors, alive with the hot pioneer blood which had been her rich inheritance, a sort of wonderful boy-girl. Remove her flapping hat, her boots, and spurs and riding-suit, and what was left of Judith?

Outside were half a dozen of the boys who had not mustered courage to set foot on the polished floors, Carson and Tommy Burkitt among them. Tommy stared at Bud Lee and his jaw dropped in amazement. Carson took swift stock of such clothes as he had never suspected a good horse foreman owned, and gasped faintly:

"The damn . . . lady-killer!"

But Lee had neither eyes nor thoughts for them, nor remembrance of his own change from working garb to that of polite society. The dance came to a lingering end, the couples throughout the big rooms strolled up and down, clapping their hands softly or vehemently as their natures or degree of enthusiasm dictated, and Lee forgot Marcia and sought eagerly for a glimpse of Judith.

Refused a second encore, the couples stood about chatting, the hum of lively voices bespeaking eager enjoyment. There was no early chill upon the assembly, to be dissipated as the dance wore on; the day of festivity outdoors had thawed the thin crust of icy strangeness which is so natural a part of such a function as this. Already it seemed that everybody was on the most cheerful terms with everybody else.

Suddenly Lee's eyes, still seeking Judith, found Marcia. Surrounded by a little knot of men, each of them plainly seeking to become her happy partner for the next dance, adorably helpless as usual, Miss Langworthy was allowing the men to fight it out among themselves. Lee moved a little nearer to see her better. In a pale-blue gown, fluffy as a summer cloud, her cheeks delicately flushed, a white rose like a snowdrop in the gold of her hair, she was flutteringly happy, reminding him of those little meadow blues that had flown palpitatingly about him that day in the fields. And she was obviously as much at her ease here, in an atmosphere of music and flattery, as the tiny butterflies in their own meadows.

Bud Lee came in, his tall form conspicuous, and went straight to Marcia. She saw him immediately; forget herself to stare almost as Carson had done; smiled at him brightly; waved her fan to him.

He took her hand and told her with his eyes how pretty she was. The delicate tint in Marcia's cheeks deepened and warmed, her eyes grew even brighter.

"Flatterer!" she chided him. "Are we to talk of the moth and the star again, Mr. Lee?"

The knot of men about her melted away. Lee stood looking down into her upturned eyes, measuring her gentle beauty. He had thought of her as a little blue butterfly--she was more like a wee white moth, fluttering, fluttering . .

The music, again from a hidden distance, set feet to tapping. Marcia plainly hesitated, flashed a quick look from Lee to the others about them, then whispered hurriedly:

"It's terrible of me, but----"

And she slipped her hand into his arm, cast another searching glance over her shoulder for a partner who had been too tardy in finding her, and yielded to the temptation to have this first dance with "the most terribly fascinating man there"! Lee slipped his arm about her, felt her sway with him, and lightly they caught the beat of the dance and lost themselves in it. And still, again and again turning away from Marcia, he sought Judith.

The dance over, their talk was interrupted by an excited and rather overdignified youth with a hurt look in his young worshipping eyes, who stiffly reminded Miss Langworthy that she had cut his dance. She was so contrite and helpless about it that the youth's heart was touched; she blamed herself for her terribly stupid way of always getting things tangled up, gave him the promise of the next dance, which she had already given to some one else, disposed of him with charming skill, and sighed as she turned again to Lee.

"I haven't paid my respects to our hostess," he said quietly. "Where is Miss Sanford?"

"She sent her excuses," Marcia told him. "Aren't we in a draft, Mr. Lee?"

He moved with her away from the soft current of air, a distinct disappointment moving him to the verge of sudden anger. What business had Judith to stay away?

"You mean she isn't coming at all?" he asked quickly.

"Oh, no," she told him, busy with the rose in her hair, her eyes bright on his. "Just as the dance was beginning she had to go to the telephone. Some ranch business, I don't know what. But she sent word she would be here immediately--I believe," and Marcia made her remark teasingly, though she did want to know, "that a certain mysterious gentleman who masquerades as a horse-breaker is very much interested in Judith."

"What makes you say a thing like that?" he asked, startled a little.

Marcia laughed.

"A woman's intuition, Sir Mystery!" she informed him gayly.

"What does the woman's intuition find to be the mysterious gentleman's interest in a certain Miss Langworthy?" he asked lightly.

"It tells her that he likes her; that it would be fun for him to come and play with her; that he would be kind and courteous; but that he considers her very much as he would a foolish little butterfly!"

Again she startled him. He looked at her wonderingly. But before he could frame a bantering reply, Marcia had involuntarily gripped at his arm with a look upon her face that first was sheer bewildered astonishment, and was crying for him to look yonder.

Judith had come.

Across the floor, now nearly deserted, Bud Lee and Marcia stared at her. She was coming toward them, her dainty little slippers seeming to kiss their own reflections in the gleaming floor. It was Judith and not Judith. It was some strange, unknown Judith. A wonderfully gowned, transcendently lovely Judith. A Judith who had long hidden herself, masquerading, and who now stepped forth smiling and bright and vividly beautiful; a Judith of bare white arms, round and soft and rich in their tender curves; a Judith whose filmy gown floated about her like a sun-shot mist; a Judith whose skin above the low-cut corsage was like a baby's, whose tender mouth was a red flower, whose hair was a shimmering mass of bronze-brown, whose eyes were Aphrodite's own, glorious, dawn-gray; a Judith of rare maidenly charm; a glorious, palpitant, triumphant Judith.

It might have been just because it was fitting that they should greet their hostess so; it might have been because the men and women who saw this new Judith were caught suddenly in a compelling current of admiration, that above the hum of voices rose from everywhere a quick clapping of hands as she came through the room. The color of her cheeks deepened, her eyes flashed a joyous acknowledgment of the greeting, and bright and cool and self-possessed she came on to Marcia.

"Marcia, dear," she said, taking Marcia's two hands--and Bud Lee found that even Judith's voice had taken on a new note, deeper, richer, gladder, fraught with the quality of low music--"forgive me for being late. I wanted to be here every little second to see you enjoy yourself." She put her lips closer to Marcia's ear, whispering: "You are the prettiest thing to-night I ever saw!"

Marcia shook her head, her eyes filled with frank wonder.

"Don't fib, Judith, dear," she answered. And, for Marcia, she was very grave. "I know you have a glass in your room. You wonderful, wonderful Judith!"

Their voices were indistinct to Bud Lee. Now at the moment when she was so rich in the splendor of her own sweet femininity he filled his heart with her. Judith had come in the only way Judith could come, surrendering herself utterly to the hour.

She turned to him, no surprise at his own costume in her happy eyes, and gave him her cool hand. A swift tremor ran through him at the contact, a tremor which was like that of the night in the cabin, which he could not conceal, which Judith must notice. She said something, but he let the words go, holding only the vibrant music of the voice.

She had stirred him, and now he did not seek a theory for a buckler; the sight of her, the brushing of her fingers against his, made riotous tumult in his blood.

The first strains of a waltz joined the lure of Judith's warm loveliness, whispering, counselling, commanding: "Take her." Marcia gasped and stepped back, startled by the look she saw in the eyes of this man who, having spoken no word since Judith came, put out his arms and took her into them. Judith flashed at him a look of quick wonder. His face was almost stern; no hint of a smile had come into his eyes. He merely caught her to him as though she were his, and swung her out into the whirl of dancers.

"You are rather--abrupt, aren't you?" said Judith coolly.

"Am I?" he asked gravely. "I don't know. It seems to me that I have been loitering, just loitering while----"

He didn't attempt to finish. He held Judith in his arms while for him the room was emptied of its gay throng, the music no longer pulsed; its beat was in the rhythm of their bodies, swaying as one.

The dance over, she was lost to him in the crowd of men who came eagerly to her. His eyes followed her wherever she went. A slow anger kindled in his heart that she should let other men talk with her, that she should suffer another man to take her in his arms.

A number of country dances followed. He stood by the door waiting a little before he went again to Judith. He saw Marcia across the room beckoning to him with her fan. There was nothing to do but to go to her. He frowned but went, still watching for Judith. Marcia wanted him to meet some of her friends. He shook hands with Hampton, was introduced to Rogers. Marcia explained that Mr. Lee was the gentleman who achieved perfect wonders in the education of his horses. She turned to introduce Farris, the artist. But Farris broke into Marcia's words with a sudden exclamation.

"Dave Lee!" he cried, as if he could not believe his eyes. "You! Here!"

"Hello, Dick," Lee answered quietly. "Yes, I'm here. I didn't know that you were the artist fellow Hampton had brought up with him."

Farris's hand went out swiftly to be gripped in Lee's. Marcia, mystified, looked from one to the other.

"You two know each other? Why, isn't that----"

She didn't know just what it was, so stopped, looking frankly as though she'd like to have one of them finish her sentence for her.

"But," muttered Farris, "I thought that you----"

"Never mind, Dick," said Lee quickly. And to Marcia's mystified expression: "You'll pardon us a moment, Miss Langworthy? I want to talk a little with Mr. Farris."

His hand on the artist's elbow, Bud Lee forced him gently away. The two disappeared into the little room off the library where Jose was placing a great bowl of punch on the table.

"Que hay, Bud," grinned Jose. "Your ol' nose smell the booze damn' queek, no?"

He set down his bowl and went out. Farris stared wonderingly at Lee.

"Bud, is it?" he grunted. "Breaker of horses; hired man at a dollar a day----?"

"Ninety dollars a month, Dick," Lee corrected g him, with a short laugh. "Give a fellow his true worth, old-timer."

Farris frowned.

"What devil's game is this!" he demanded sharply. "Isn't it enough that you should drop out of the world with never a word, but that you must show up now breaking horses and letting such chaps as Mrs. Simpson's Black Spanish chum with you? Not a cursed word in five years, and I've lain awake nights wondering. When you went to smash----"

"When a Lee goes to smash," said Bud briefly, "he goes to smash. That's all there is to it."

"But there was no sense, no use in your dropping out of sight that way----"

"There was," said Lee curtly, "or I shouldn't have done it. It wasn't just that I went broke; that was a result of my own incompetence in a bit of speculation and didn't worry me a great deal. But other things did. There were a couple of the fellows that I thought were friends of mine. I found out that they had knifed me; had helped pluck me to feather their own nests. It hurt, Dick; hurt like hell. Losing the big ranch in the South was a jolt, I'll admit; seeing those fellows take it over and split it two ways between them, sort of knocked the props out from under me. I believed in them, you see. After that I just wanted to get away and sort of think things over."

"You went to Europe?"

"I did not. I don't know how that report got out, but if people chose to think I had gone to take a hand in the fighting over there, I saw no need to contradict a harmless rumor. I took a horse and beat it up into the coast mountains. I tell you, Dick, I wanted to think! And I found out before I was through thinking that I was sick of the old life, that I was sick of people, the sort of people you and I knew, that there was nothing in the world but horses that I cared the snap of my finger about, that the only life worth living--for me--was a life in the open. I drifted up this way. I've been living my own life in my own way for five years. I am happier at it than I used to be. That's all of the flat little story, Dick."

"You might have let me know, it seems to me," said Farris a bit stiffly.

"So I might," answered Lee thoughtfully. "I was going to in the first place. But you'll remember that you were off somewhere travelling when the bubble broke. When Dick Farris travels," and his grave smile came back to him, "let no mad letter think that it can track him down. Then I hit my stride in this sort of life; I grew away from the old news; the years passed as years do after a man is twenty-five; and I just didn't write. But I didn't forget, Dickie, old man," he said warmly, and his hand rested on Farris's shoulder. "You can put it in that old black pipe of yours and smoke it, that I didn't forget. Some day I planned to hit town again, heeled you know, and remind you of auld lang syne."

"You are a fool, David Burrill Lee," said Farris with conviction. "Look here: you can take a new start, pull yourself together, come back--where you belong."

But Lee shook his head.

"That's like the old Dick Farris I used to know," he said gently. "But this is where I belong, Dick. I don't want to start over, I don't want to come back to the sort of thing we knew. The only thing in the world I do want is right here. And I don't see that it would do any good for you to go stirring up any memories about the old Lee that was shot 'somewhere in France.'"

When Farris had to go and claim a dance, Lee watched him with eyes soft with affection. Then he, too, left the room and went back to the outer door, to his old spot, looking for Judith.

"The only thing I want is right here," he repeated softly.

He watched Farris join Marcia and Judith. He noted the eager excitement in Marcia's eyes, saw her turn impulsively to Farris. The artist shook his head and left them, ostensibly going in search of his partner. Marcia was speaking excitedly to Judith. Lee frowned.

Once more that night he held Judith in his arms. He meant to make amends for his brusque way with her before. But again the magic of her presence was like a glorious mist, shutting them in together, shutting all of the world out. They spoke little and the music had its will with them. Judith did not know that she sighed as the dance ended. She seemed moving in a dream as Lee led her through the door. They were out in the courtyard, the stars shining softly down on them. In the sub-dued light here he stood still, looking down into her pleasure-flushed face. Again the insistent tremor shot down his blood.

Here in this tender light she looked to him the masterpiece of God striving for the perfect in a woman's form. Her gown, gently stirred by the warm breeze, seemed a part of her, elusive, alive, feminine. The milk-white of bare throat and shoulder and rounded arm, the rise and fall of her breast, the soft lure of her eyes, the tender smile upon her lips, drew him slowly closer, closer to her. She lifted her face a little, raising her eyes until they shone straight into his.

"Judith," he said very quietly, very gravely, making her wonder at the tone and the words to follow: "You have had your way with me to-night. Do you understand all that means? And now--I am going to have my way with you!"

He caught her in his arms, crushed her to him, kissed her. Then he let her go and stood, stern-faced, watching her.

For a moment he thought that the hand at her side was rising to strike him full in the face. But he did not move.

Had such been Judith's intention, suddenly it changed.

"So," she cried softly, "this is the sort of fine gentleman into which a dress-suit has made Bud Lee, horse foreman! For so great an honor surely any woman would thank him!"

She made him a slow, graceful courtesy, and laughed at him. And so she left him, her laughter floating back, taunting him.

Lee watched her until she had gone from his sight. Then he turned and went down the knoll, into the night.

XIX
BUD LEE SEEKS CROOKED CHRIS QUINNION

Going down the knoll to the bunk-house, Bud Lee cursed himself at every stride. He cursed Carson when the cattle foreman, turning to follow him, addressed a merry remark to him concerning his "lady-killing clothes." The words reminded him of Judith's and he didn't cherish the remembrance. In the bunk-house Carson watched him curiously over his old pipe as Lee began ripping off his dress-suit.

"A feller called you up a while ago," said Carson, still bright-eyed with interest but pretending that that interest had to do with the new wall telephone recently installed. "Sandy Weaver, it was. Said----"

"What did he want?" demanded Lee, swinging suddenly on Carson, his coat balled up in his hand and hurled viciously under a bunk.

"Wasn't I telling you?" Carson grunted. "What's eating you, Bud? You ac' mighty suspicious, like a man that had swallered poison or else was coming down with the yeller jaundice or else was took sudden an' powerful bad with love. They all treats a man similar----"

"Damn it," growled Lee irritably, "can't you tell me what Weaver said?"

"Said, call him up, real pronto," replied Carson cheerfully. "Say, Bud, where in heck *did* you get that outfit? By cripes, if I had a regalia like that I'd be riding herd in 'em ev'ry Sunday! On the square now----"

But Lee wasn't listening to him and Carson knew it. He had gone quickly to the telephone, had rung the one bell for "Central," and a moment later was speaking with Sandy Weaver of the Golden Spur saloon. Carson sucked at his pipe and kept his eyes on Lee's face.

The ensuing conversation, only one side of which came to Carson, was brief.

Most of the talking was done by Sandy Weaver. Lee asked three questions; the third a simple,

"Sure of it, Sandy?"

Then he jammed the receiver back upon its hook, and with no remark continued his hurried dressing. When he had come in, his face had been flushed; now it was suddenly red, the hot red of rage. His eyes, when they met Carson's once, were stern, bright with the same quick anger. When he had drawn on his working garb and stuffed his trousers into his boots, he went to his bunk and tossed back the blanket. From the straw mattress he took a heavy, old style Colt revolver. Carson, still watching him, saw him spin the cylinder, slip a box of fresh cartridges into his pocket and turn to the door.

"Riding, Bud?" He got to his feet, stuffed his pipe into his pocket and reached for his hat. "Care if I mosey along?"

"What for?" asked Lee curtly.

"Oh, hell, what's the use being a hawg," Carson grumbled deep down in his brown throat. "If you're on your way to little ol' Rocky hunting trouble, if they's going to be shooting-fun, why can't you let me in on it?"

Lee stood a moment framed in the doorway, frowning down at Carson. Then he turned on his heel and went out, saying coolly over his shoulder:

"Come on if you want to. Quinnion's in town."

As their horses' hoofs hammered the winding road for the forty miles into Rocky Bend the two riders were for the most part silent. All of the explanation which Lee had to give, or cared to give, was summed up in the brief words:

"Quinnion's in town."

To Judith, Lee had said that night they fought together at the Upper End that he had recognized Quinnion's voice; "I played poker with that voice not four months ago." That he had had ample reason to remember the man as well, he had not gone on to mention. But Carson knew.

Carson had sat at Lee's left hand that night, across the table from Chris Quinnion, and had seen the look of naked hatred in two pairs of eyes when Lee had risen to his feet and coolly branded Quinnion as a crook and a card sharp. For a little the two men had glared at each other, their muscles corded and ready, their eyes alert and suspicious, their hands close to their pockets. Then Quinnion had sneered in that evil voice of his: "You got the drop on me this time. Look out for the next." He too had risen and with Lee's eyes hard upon him had gone out of the room. And Carson had been disappointed in a fight. But now--now that Bud Lee in this mood was going straight to Rocky Bend and Quinnion, Carson filled his deep lungs with a sigh of satisfaction. Life had grown dull here of late; there wasn't a fresh scar on his battered body.

Though the railroad had at last slipped through it, Rocky Bend was still a bad little town and proud of its badness. To the northeast lay the big timber tracts into which the Western Lumber Company was tearing its destructive way; only nine miles due west were the Rock Creek mines, running full blast; on the other sides it was surrounded by cattle ranges where a lusty brood of young untamed devils were constrained to give themselves soberly to their work during the long, dusty days. But at night, always on a Saturday evening, there came into Rocky Bend from lumber-camps, mines, and cow outfits a crowd of men whose blood ran red and turbulent, seeking a game of cards, a "whirl at the wheel," a night of drinking or any other amusement which fate might vouchsafe them. Good men and bad, they were all hard men and quick. Otherwise they would not have come into Rocky Bend at all.

Lee and Carson riding out of the darkness into the dim light of the first of the straggling street-lamps, passed swiftly between the rows of weather-boarded shacks and headed toward the Golden Spur saloon.

Though the hour was late there were many saddle-ponies standing with drooping heads here and there along the board sidewalks; from more than one barroom came the gay ragtime of an automatic piano or the scrape and scream of a fiddle. Men lounged up and down the street, smoking, calling to one another, turning in here or there to have a drink or watch a game.

The two newcomers, watching each man or group of men, rode on slowly until they came to the building on whose false front was a gigantic spur in yellow paint. Here they dismounted, tied their horses, and went in. Carson, with a quick eye toward preparedness for what might lie on the cards, looked for Lee's gun. It wasn't in his pocket; it wasn't in his waistband, ready to hand. It wasn't anywhere that Carson could see. At the door he whispered warningly:

"Better be ready, Bud. Ain't lost your gun, have you?"

Lee shook his head and stepped into the room. At the long bar were three or four men, drinking. Quinnion was not among them. There were other men at the round tables, playing draw, solo, stud horse. One glance showed that Quinnion was not in the room. But there were other rooms at the rear for those desiring privacy. Lee, nodding this way and that to friends who accosted him, made his way straight to the bar.

"Hello, Sandy," he said quietly.

Sandy Weaver, the bartender, looked at him curiously. A short, heavy, blond man was Sandy Weaver, who ran a fair house and gave his attention strictly to his own business. Save when asked by a friend to do him a favor, such a favor as to keep an eye on another man.

"Hello, Bud," returned Sandy, putting out a red hand. All expression of interest had fled from his placid face. "Come in right away, eh? Hello, Carson. Have somethin'; on me, you know."

Lee shook his head.

"Not to-night, Sandy," he said. "Thanks just the same."

"Me," grinned Carson, "I'll go you, Sandy. Same thing--you know."

Sandy shoved out whiskey-bottle and glass. Then he turned grave eyes to Lee.

"One of these fellers can tend bar while we talk if you want, Bud," he offered.

"You say Quinnion has been talking?" asked Lee.

"Yes. Considerable. All afternoon an' evening, I guess. I didn't hear him until I called you up."

"Then," continued the man from Blue Lake ranch, "I don't see any call for you and me to whisper, Sandy. What did he say?"

"Said you was a liar, Bud. An' a skeerd-o-your-life damn bluff."

A faint, shadowy smile touched Lee's eyes.

"Just joshing, Sandy. But that wasn't all, was it?"

"No," said Sandy, wiping his bar carefully. "There was the other word, Bud. An'--say, Billy, tell him what Quinnion had to say down to the Jailbird."

Lee turned his eyes to Billy Young. Young, a cattleman from the Up and Down range, shifted his belt and looked uncomfortable.

"Damn if I do!" he blurted out. "It ain't none of my funeral. An' if you ask me,

I don't like the sound of that kind of talk in my mouth. Maybe I can't find my way to church of a Sunday for staggerin' with red-eye, but I ain't ever drug a nice girl's name into a barroom."

"So," said Lee very quietly, "that's it, is it?"

"Yes," said Sandy Weaver slowly, "that's it, Bud. Us boys knowed ol' Luke Sanford an' liked him. Some of us even knowed his girl. All of us know the sort she is. When Quinnion started his talk--oh, it's a song an' dance about you an' her all alone in some damn cabin, trying to crawl out'n the looks of things by accusin' Quinnion of tryin' to shoot you up!--well, folks jus' laughed at him. More recent, somebody must have took him serious an' smashed him in the mouth. He looks like it. But," and Sandy shrugged his thick shoulders elaborately, "if it's up to anybody it's up to you."

For a moment Bud Lee, standing very straight, his hat far back, his eyes hard and cold, looked from one to another of the men about him. In every face he saw the same thing; their contempt for a man like Quinnion, their wordless agreement with Sandy that it "was up to Bud Lee." Lee's face told them nothing.

"Where is he?" he asked presently.

"Mos' likely down to the Jailbird," said Billy, Young. "That's where he hangs out lately."

Lee turned and went out, Carson at his heels, all eyes following him. In his heart was a blazing, searing rage. And that rage was not for Quinnion alone. He thought of Judith as he had seen her that very night, a graceful, gray-eyed slip of a girl, the sweetest little maid in all of the world known to him--and of how he, brutal in the surge of love for her, had swept her into his arms, crushed her to him, forced upon her laughing lips the kiss of his own.

"My God," he said within himself, "I was mad. It would be a good thing if I got Quinnion to-night--and he got me. Two of a kind," he told himself sneeringly.

As he made his way down the ill-lighted street, his hat drawn over his eyes now. Bud Lee for a moment lost sight of the rows of rude shanties, the drowsing saddle-ponies, the street-lamps, and saw only the vision of a girl. A girl clean and pure, a girl for a man to kneel down to in worship, a girl who, as he had seen her last, was a fairylike creature born of music and soft laughter and starlight, a maid indescribably sweet. In the harshness of the mood which gripped him, she seemed to him superlatively adorable; the softness of her eyes at the moment before he had kissed her haunted him. As he strode on seeking Quinnion, who had spoken evil of her, he carried her with him in his heart.

The horrible thing was that her name had already been bandied about from a ruffian's lips. Lee winced at that even as he had winced at the remembrance of having been brutally rough with her himself. But what was past was past; Quinnion had talked and must talk no more.

"He'll start something the minute he sees you," cautioned Carson, his own revolver loose in the belt under his coat, his hard fingers like talons gripped about the butt. "Keep your eye peeled, Bud. Better cool off a speck before you tie into him. You're too mad, I tell you, for straight, quick shooting."

Lee made no answer. Side by side the two men went on. They had left the sidewalk and walked down the middle of the rusty, rut-gouged street. Every man they met, every figure standing in the shadows, received their quick, measuring looks.

"Most likely," suggested the cattle foreman, "by now he's got drunk an' gone to sleep it off."

But Lee knew better than that. Quinnion wasn't the sort that got drunk. He'd drink until the alcohol stirred up all of the evil in his ugly heart; then he'd stop, always sure of his eye and his hand. It was far more likely that with a crowd of his own sort he was gambling in the card-room of the Last Chance saloon, the Jailbird saloon as "white" men called it. For there was an ill-famed hang-out at the far end of the straggling town, just at the edge of the Italian settlement, that of late had come to be frequented by such as Quinnion; men who were none too well loved by the greater part of the community, men who, like Quinnion, had served time in jail or penitentiary. Black Steve, who was both proprietor and bartender, and who looked like a low-class Italian, though he spoke the vernacular of the country, was the god of the "dago" quarter, the friend of those who had gotten entangled with the law. Only last year he had killed his man in his own saloon, then gone clear, through the combined perjury of his crowd.

The street grew steadily gloomier, filled with shadows. In front of the Jailbird the only light came from within and made scant war on the lurking darkness without. Lee's ears were greeted with the crazy whine of an old accordion, and with men's voices lifted in laughter. He shoved the swing door open with his shoulder, Carson pushed the other half back, and the two stood on the threshold, their eyes swiftly seeking Quinnion.

As though their presence had been a command for silence, a sudden hush fell over the Jailbird. The accordion man drew out a last gasping note and turned black round eyes upon them. Black Steve, oily and perspiring behind his bar, caressed a heavy black mustache and looked at them out of cold, expressionless eyes.

The first glance had shown Lee that Quinnion was not there. At least not in the main room, but there were the card-rooms at the rear. He gave no sign of having felt the hostility of the many eyes turned upon him, but went quickly down through the room, turning neither to right nor left.

"Hol' on there," came the big booming voice of Steve. "What you fellers want, huh?"

Lee gave him no answer but strode on. Carson, at Lee's heels like a grim old dog, showed his teeth a little. Steve, striking the bar with a heavy hand, shouted in menacing tones:

"Hol' on, I say! Nobody goin' to break in on a play that's running in my card-rooms. If you fellers want anything, you ask me."

"Go ahead, Bud," said Carson jocosely. "It's only the ol' black calf bawling same as usual."

But Lee needed no urging. He had heard voices beyond the closed door in front of him, among them a certain high-pitched, snarling, indescribably evil voice which he knew. He put his hand on the knob and found that the door was locked. With no waste of time, he drew back a step, lifted his foot and drove his heel smashing into the lock. Then, throwing himself forward, driving his shoulder into the door, he burst it off its hinges.

At last he had found Quinnion.

Here were half a dozen men, not playing cards, but interrupted in a quiet talk. Standing on the far side of the table was a man who was as evil a thing to see as was his voice to hear; his face twisted, drawn to the left side, the left eye a mere slit of malevolence, the uneven teeth showing in an eternal, mirthless grin, a man whose hands, when his arms were lax as now, hung almost to his knees, a man twisted morally, mentally, and physically.

Bud Lee had eyes only for this man. But suddenly Carson had seen another man, seeking to screen himself behind the great, misshapen bulk of Quinnion, and with new eagerness was crying:

"It's Shorty, Bud! He's mine!"

But Shorty was no man's yet. At his back was a window; it was closed and the shade was drawn, but to Shorty it spelled safety. Head first he went through it, tearing the green shade down, crashing through the glass, leaving discussion behind him. With a bellow of rage Carson went after him, forgetful in the instant that there was another matter on hand to-night. Shorty, consigned to Carson's care and the grain-house, had slipped away and had laughed at him. Ever since, Carson had been yearning for the chance to get his two hands on Shorty's fat throat. Before the smash and tinkle of falling glass had died away Carson, plunging as Shorty had plunged, was lost to the bulging eyes which sought to follow him, gone head first into the darkness without.

Lee kept his eyes hard on Quinnion's. He moved a little, so that the wall was at his back. His coat was unbuttoned; his left hand was in his pocket, his arm holding back his coat a little on that side. The right hand was lax at his side, like Quinnion's.

He had seen the other men, though his eyes had seemed to see only one man. One of them he knew; the others he had seen. They were the sort to be found in Quinnion's company. They were the nucleus of what was spoken of as Quinnion's crowd.

"Quinnion," said Lee quietly, "you are a damned dirty-mouthed liar."

The words came like little slaps in the face. Of the four men still in the room with Quinnion three of them moved swiftly to one side, their eyes on their leader's face, which showed nothing of what might lie in his mind.

"I have taken the trouble," went on Lee coolly, when Quinnion, leering back at him, made no reply, "to ride forty miles to-night for a little talk with you. You are a crook and a card-cheat. I told you that once before. You have been telling men that I am a coward and a four-flusher. For that I am going to run you out of town to-night. Or kill you."

Then Quinnion laughed at him.

"Just for that?" he jeered. "Or because I've been tellin' a true story about you an'----"

He didn't get her name out. Perhaps he hadn't expected to. His eyes had been watchful. Now, as he threw himself to one side, he whipped out his gun, dropping to one knee, his body partly concealed by the table. At the same second Bud Lee's right hand, no longer lax, sped to the revolver gripped under the coat at his left arm-pit.

It was a situation by no means new to the four walls of the Jailbird nor to the men concerned. It was a two-man fight, with as yet no call for the four friends of Quinnion to interfere. It would take the spit and snarl of a revolver, the flash of flame, the acrid smell of burning-powder to switch their sympathetic watching into actual participation. No new situation certainly for Chris Quinnion who took quick stock of the table with its heavy top and screened his body with it; no new situation for Steve, the big bartender who was at the shattered door almost as Bud Lee sent it rocking drunkenly.

Since a fight like this in a small room may end in three seconds and yet remain a fight for men to talk of at street corners for many a day thereafter, it is surely a struggle baffling adequate description. For while you speak of it, it is done; while a dock ticks, two guns may carry hot lead, and cut in two two threads of life.

Quinnion was down and shooting, with but ten steps or less between him and the man whom he sought to kill; Bud Lee was standing, tall and straight, back to wall, his first bullet ripping into the boards of the table, sending a flying splinter to stick in Quinnion's face, close to a squinting, slitted eye; and as the two guns spoke like one, a third from the open barroom shattered the lamp swinging from the ceiling between Lee and Quinnion. Steve, the bartender, had taken a hand.

The card-room was plunged in darkness so thick that Lee's frowning eyes could no longer make out Quinnion's head above the table, so black that to Quinnion's eyes the tall form of Lee against the wall was lost in shadow.

XX
THE FIGHT AT THE JAILBIRD

As Steve fired his shot into the lamp, Bud Lee understood just what would be Steve's next play; the bartender had given his friends brief respite from the deadly fire of the Blue Lake man, and now would turn his second shot through the flimsy wall itself on the man standing there. Lee did not hesitate now, but with one leap was across the room, avoiding the table, seeking to come to close quarters with Quinnion and have the thing over and done with. In the bitterness still gnawing at his heart, he told himself again that it would be no calamity to the world if the two men who had insulted Judith Sanford went down together.

Again Steve fired. His bullet ripped into the wall, tearing a hole through the partition where a brief instant ago Lee had stood. The light out in the barroom was extinguished. In the cardroom it was utterly, impenetrably dark now, only a vague square of lesser darkness telling where was the window through which Shorty had fled.

A red flare of flame from where Quinnion crouched, and Lee stood very still, refusing the temptation to fire back. For Quinnion's bullet had sped wide of the mark, striking the wall a full yard to Lee's left. Quinnion's eyes had not found him, would not find him soon if he stood quite motionless. The fight was still to be made, Quinnion's friends would be taking a hand now, Steve had already joined issue. There were six of them against him and with one shot fired from his heavy Colt there were but five left. No shot to be wasted.

A little creaking of a floorboard, a vague, misty blur almost at his side, and still Lee saved his fire. Quickly he lifted the big revolver, held welded to a grip of steel, throwing it high above his head and striking downward. There was almost no sound; just the thudding blow as the thick barrel struck a heavy mat of hair, and with no outcry a man went down to lie still. At the same moment the dim square of the window showed a form slipping through; one man was seeking safety from a quarrel not his own. And as he went, there came again a soft thudding blow and Carson's dry voice outside, saying calmly:

"Shorty got away, but you don't, pardner. Give 'em hell, Bud. I'm in the play again."

"Two men down," grunted Lee to himself with grim satisfaction. "And old Carson back on the job. Only two to our one now."

The form in the window crumpled and under Carson's quick hands was jerked out. Suddenly it was very still in the little room. Steve did not fire a third time; Quinnion held his fire. For Lee had made no answer and they were taking heavy chances with every shot now, chances of shooting the wrong man. Each of the four watchful men in the narrow apartment breathed softly.

Once more Lee lifted his gun above his head. As he held it thus, he put out his left hand gently, inch by inch, gropingly. Extended full length, it touched nothing. Slowly he moved it in a semi-circle, the gun in his right hand always ready to come crashing down. His fingers touched the wall, then moving back assured him that no one was within reach. Lifting a foot slowly, he took one cautious step forward, toward the spot where he had last seen Quinnion. Again his arm, circling through the darkness, sought to locate for him one of the men who must be very near him now. Suddenly it brushed a man's shoulder.

There was a sharp, muttered exclamation, and again a flare of red flame as this man fired. But he had misjudged Bud Lee's position by a few inches, the bullet cut through Lee's coat, and Lee's clubbed revolver fell unerringly, smashing into the man's forehead. There was a low moan, a revolver clattered to the floor, a body fell heavily.

"A new situation," thought Lee. Three men down before a clock could tick off as many minutes and not a single man shot. It was a place for a man like Charlie Miller with his old pick-handle.

"Bud," called Carson's voice sharply, "are you all right?"

"Yes," answered Lee briefly, and as he answered moved sharply to one side so that his voice might not draw a shot from Quinnion or the other men. There came two spurts of flame, one from each of the corners of the room opposite him, the reports of the two shots reverberating loudly. But this was mere guesswork--shooting at no more definite thing than a man's voice, and Lee having moved swiftly had little fear. And he knew pretty well where those two men were now.

So did Carson, who from without fired in twice through the window. Then again it grew so silent that a clock ticking somewhere out in the barroom was to be heard distinctly, so that again the men guarded their breathing.

Lee thought that he knew where Quinnion was, in the corner at his right close to the rear wall. Not square in the corner, of course, for having fired he was fox enough to shift his position a little. True, no sound had told of such a movement. But Quinnion could be trusted to make no sound at a time like this. Lee, equally silent, again set a slow foot out, moving cautiously toward the spot where his eyes sought Quinnion in the dark.

He was calculating swiftly now: Quinnion had fired twice from the screen of the table just as Steve shot out the light; he had fired again just now, it was a fair bet that at least one of the other shots had been his. That meant that he had fired four times. If Quinnion still carried his old six-shooter he had but two shots at most left to him, for there had been no time which he would risk in reloading.

Lee swept off his hat and tossed it out before him to the spot where he believed Quinnion was and dropped swiftly to his knee as he did so. There was a snarl, Quinnion's evil snarl, and a shot that sped high above his head. His hat had struck Quinnion full in the face. Then Lee again sprang onward, again struck out with his clubbed revolver. The blow missed Quinnion's head but caught him heavily on the shoulder and sent him staggering back against the wall. Lee could hear the bulk of his body crashing against the boards. And again leaping, he struck the second time at Quinnion. This time there was no snarl, but a falling weight and stillness.

There was a sound of a chair violently thrown down, the scuffle of hasty feet and in the door the faint blur of a flying figure seeking refuge in the bar. Lee flung the crippled door shut after the fugitive and then with his left hand struck a match, his revolver ready in his right.

Holding the tiny flame down toward the floor, he made out two prone bodies. One, that of the first man he had struck down, a man whom he knew by name as Lefty Devine, a brawler and boon companion of Quinnion. The other Quinnion himself. Devine lay very still, clearly completely stunned. Quinnion moved a little.

Carson's weather-beaten face peered in at the window.

"Better do the hot foot, Bud," he grunted softly, "while the trail's open. Steve will be mixing in again."

But Lee seemed in no haste now. When the match had burned out, he dropped it and slipped fresh cartridges into his gun. That done, he stooped, gathered up Quinnion's feebly struggling body in his arms and carried it to the window.

"Here," he said coolly to Carson. "Take him through."

"What the hell do you want of him?" Carson wanted to be told. "Ain't going to scalp him, are you, Bud?"

"Take him out," commanded Lee with no explanation. Carson obeyed, jerking the now complaining Quinnion out hastily and unceremoniously. Lee followed as Steve threw open the barroom door.

"It's a new one on me, just the same," said Carson dryly as he watched Lee stoop and gather Quinnion up in his arms. "After a little party like this one, I'm generally travelling on an' not stopping to pick flowers an' gather sooveneers! You ain't got cannibal blood in you, have you, Bud?"

While Carson was cudgelling his brains for the answer and Steve was making cautious examination of the card-room, Lee with his burden in his arms passed through the darkness lying at the rear of the saloon and out into the street. Carson followed to take care of a sortie should Steve and the rest not have had all they wanted for one night. He chuckled, remarking to himself that Bud Lee and Quinnion were the very picture of a young mother and her babe in arms.

Not until they again reached the Golden Spur did Lee's burden completely recover consciousness. Many a man on the street looked wonderingly after them, demanded to know "what was up," and, receiving no answer, swung in behind Carson.

In the Golden Spur the arrivals were greeted by a heavy silence. Sandy Weaver forgot to set out the drinks which had just been ordered by three men who, in their turn, forgot that they had ordered. Men at the tables playing cards put down their hands and rose or turned expectantly in their seats.

Lee put Quinnion down on the floor. The man lay there a moment blinking at the lights above him and at the faces around him. At length his eyes came to Lee.

"Damn you," he muttered, trying to rise, and slowly getting to his feet with the aid of a chair, "I'll get you----"

Then Bud Lee gave his brief explanation, cutting Quinnion's ugly snarl in two.

"This is Quinnion's farewell party," he said bluntly. "He is a liar and a crook and an undesirable citizen. I have told him all that before. He took it upon himself to say about town that I am all of those things which he is himself. I have damn near killed him for it; I am going to give him ten minutes to get out of town. If he doesn't do it, I am going to kill him. And in that ten minutes he is going to find time to eat his words."

"I'll see you in--" began Quinnion, as something of the old bluster came back to him.

"Shut up!" snapped Lee. "Carson, let me have your gun."

Carson, wondering, gave it. Lee dropped it on the floor at Quinnion's foot.

"Pick that gun up and we'll finish what we've begun," he said coolly to Quinnion. "I won't shoot until you've got it in your hand and have straightened up. Then I'll kill you. Unless first you admit that you are the contemptible liar every one knows you are, and second, get out of town and stay out. It's up to you, Quinnion."

Knowing Quinnion, the men moved swiftly so that they did not stand behind either him or Lee. Sandy Weaver, shifting a few feet along his bar, shook his head and sighed.

"It'll be both of them," he muttered.

Quinnion turned his head a little, his red-rimmed eyes going from face to face, his tongue moving back and forth between his lips. For an instant his eyes dropped to the gun at his feet, and a little spasmodic contraction of his body showed that he was tempted to take up the weapon. But he hesitated, and again turned to Lee.

"It's up to you," repeated Lee. "If you're not a coward after all, pick it up." Lee's hands were at his sides, his own revolver in his pocket. Quinnion was tempted. The evil lights in his eyes danced like witch-fires. Again he hesitated; but his hesitation was brief. With his whining, ugly laugh he lurched to the bar.

"Gimme a drink, Sandy," he commanded.

"Neither now nor after a while," Sandy told him briefly. "I ain't dirtyin' my glasses that-a-way."

"There you are," jeered Quinnion, with a sullen sort of defiance. "You swat me over the head while I ain't lookin' an' then bring me in here where they're all your friends. If I drop you I get all mussed up with their bullets. No, thanks."

"For the last time," said Lee, and his low voice was ominous, "I tell you what to do. If you don't do it, I'll kill you just the same. You've got your chance. Count ten seconds, Sandy."

"One," said Sandy, watching the clock on the wall, "two, three, four, five, six, seven----"

"Curse you!" cried Quinnion then, a look of fear at last in his eyes. "I'll get you for this some day, Bud Lee. Now you've got me----"

"Keep on counting, Sandy," commanded Lee.

"Eight," said Sandy, "nine----"

"I lied!" snapped Quinnion. "An' I'm leavin' town for a while."

And lurching as he walked, he made his way out of the room, his eyes on the floor, his face a burning red.

"Carson and I are riding back to the ranch as soon as our horses rest up and get some grain," said Lee, his fingers slowly rolling a brown cigarette. "We'll mosey out now, see Quinnion on his way and drop back to make up a little game of draw for a couple of hours. Strike you about right, Billy? And you, Watson? And you, Parker?"

They listened to him, took the cue from him, and allowed what lay between him and Chris Quinnion to lie in silence. But there was not a man there but in his own fashion was saying to himself:

"It's a good beginning. But where's the end going to be?"

XXI
BURNING MEMORY

As June had slipped by, so did July and August. On Blue Lake ranch life flowed smoothly. Men were too busy with each day's work to sit into the nights prophesying trouble ahead. And in truth it seemed that if Bayne Trevors had ever actively opposed the success of the Sanford venture he had by now accepted the role of inactivity forced upon him by circumstance. He was with the Western Lumber Company, as director and district superintendent, seemingly giving all his dynamic force to the legitimate affairs of the company.

But there were those who placed no faith in the obvious. Bud Lee kept in touch with Rocky Bend and learned that Quinnion had not come back; that no one knew where he had gone. Carson's man, Shorty, was sought by Emmet Sawyer and his disappearance was like that of a pricked bubble; it seemed that Shorty had no actual physical existence or that, if he had, he had taken it into some other corner of the world. Quinnion's friends had also gone from Rocky Bend, like Quinnion leaving behind them no sign to show where they had gone.

Knowing Quinnion as he did, and having his own conception of the character of Bayne Trevors, Bud Lee said to himself that too great a quiet portended strife to come. If Quinnion was the man to carry in his breast the hate that drove him to the murder of Judith's father, then he was the man to remember the humiliation he had suffered at Lee's hands, to remember and to strike back when the time was ripe.

Judith had heard of the night in Rocky Bend, a lurid and wonderfully distorted account from Mrs. Simpson, who had received it in a letter from her daughter.

"So that was what Bud Lee did after he kissed me!" mused Judith.

She sent immediately for Carson and forced from him the full story. Dismissing Carson, she remained for a long while alone. Only one remark had she made to the cattle foreman, and that a little aside from the issue occupying his mind:

"Keep your weather eye open for what's in the wind," she told him briefly. "Behind Quinnion is Trevors, and the year isn't over yet."

The ranch was stocked to its utmost capacity. Carson had bought another herd of cattle; Lee had added to his string of horses. The dry season was on them, herds were moved higher up the slopes into the fresh pastures. Carson, converted now to the silos, was a man with one idea and that idea ensilage. Again the alfalfa acreage was extended, so that each head of cattle might have its daily auxiliary fodder. Carson now agreed with Judith in the matter of holding back sales for the high prices which would come at the heels of the lean months.

The man Donley, who had brought to the ranch the pigeons carrying cholera, was tried in Rocky Bend. The evidence, though circumstantial, was strong against him, and the prosecution was pushed hard. But it was little surprise to any one at the ranch when the trial resulted in a hung jury. The ablest lawyer in the county had defended Donley, and finally, late in August, secured his acquittal The man himself did not have ten dollars in the world; the attorney taking his case was a high-priced lawyer. Obviously, to Judith Sanford at least, Bayne Trevors was standing back of every play his hirelings made.

Doc Tripp had the hog-cholera in hand. And every day, out with the live stock whose well-being was his responsibility, he worked as he had never worked before, watchful, eager, suspicious. "If they'll drop cholera down on us out of the blue sky," he snapped, "I'd like to know what they won't try."

For the first few days following the dance Bud Lee had within his soul room but for one emotion: he had held Judith in his arms. He had set his lips on hers. He went hot and cold with the remembrance. Being a man, he made his man-suppositions of the emotions that rankled in her breast. He imagined her contempt of a man who by his strength had forced her lips to wed his; he pictured her scorn, her growing hatred. He told himself that he should go, rid the ranch of his presence, take his departure without a word with her. For, already, he had fitted her into his theory of the perfect woman, lifting her high above himself and above the human world. It was a continued insult for him to remain here.

But, after careful thought, he remembered what Judith had already told him; he was one of the men whom she could trust to do her work for her, one of the men she most needed, a man whom she would need sorely if Bayne Trevors were lying quiet now but to strike harder, expectedly, later.

Judith did not dismiss him, as at first he had been sure she would. So he stayed on, remaining away from the ranch headquarters, sleeping when he could in the cabin above the lake, spending his days with his horses, avoiding her but keeping her personality in his soul, her interests in his heart. When the winter had passed, when she had made her sales and had the money in hand for the payments upon the mortgages, then he would go. Whereat, no doubt, the high gods smiled.

As time passed, there came about a subtle change in the attitude of the outfit toward Pollock Hampton, whom they had been at the beginning prone to accept as a "city guy." It began to appear that under his lightness there was often a steady purpose; that if he didn't know everything about a ranch, he was learning fast; that in his outspoken admiration of things rough and manly and primal there were certain lasting qualities. Whereas formerly his being thrown from a spirited mount was almost a daily occurrence, now he rode rather well. With tanned face and hard hands, he was, as Carson put it, "growing up."

He came to Judith one day serious-faced, thoughtful-eyed.

"Look here, Judith," he began abruptly, "I'm no outsider just looking on at this game. You're the chief owner and the boss and I'm not kicking at that any longer. Your dad raised you to this sort of thing and you have a way of getting by with it. But, on the other hand, I'm part owner and you've got to consider me."

Judith smiled at him.

"What now, Pollock?" she asked.

"You're the boss," he repeated stoutly. "But I've got a right to be next in authority. Under you, you know. Why, by cripes, I go around feeling as if I had to take orders from Carson or Tripp or any other of the foremen!"

"'By cripes' is good!" laughed Judith. "Go ahead."

"That's all," he insisted. "You can tell them, when you get a chance, that I am your little old right-hand man. Suppose," he suggested vaguely, "that you left the ranch a day or so. Or even longer, some time. There's got to be some one here who is the head when there is need for it."

Judith mirthfully acquiesced. Hampton's interest was sufficiently heavy for him to be entitled to some consideration. Besides, she had come to experience a liking for the boy and had seen in him the change for the better which his new life was working in him. Further, she meant to make it her business that she did not leave the ranch for a day or so, or an hour or so, when she should be there. Consequently, within a week Pollock Hampton was known humorously from one end to the other of the big ranch as the Foreman-at-Large.

Marcia Langworthy, visiting in southern California, wrote brief, sunny notes to Hampton, intricate letters to Judith. The mystery of Bud Lee of which she had had a glimpse when the artist, Dick Farris, and Lee recognized each other as old friends had piqued her curiosity in a way which allowed that young daughter of Eve no rest until she had made her own investigations. She wrote at length, telling Judith all that she had learned of Lee. How he had been quite the rage, my dear. Oh, tremendously rich, with great ranch in the South, a wonderful adobe hacienda of the old Spanish days, where, like a young king, he had entertained lavishly. How, believing in his friends, he had lost everything, then had dropped out of the world, content equally to allow that world to believe him soldiering in France or dead in the trenches and to take his wage as a common laborer. Wasn't it too romantic for anything?

In due course, following up her letters, Marcia herself came back to the Blue Lake ranch, Judith's guest now. The major and Mrs. Langworthy were visiting in the East--it seemed that they always visited somewhere--and Marcia would stay at the ranch indefinitely. Hampton drove into Rocky Bend for her and held the girl's breathless admiration all the way home, handling the reins of his young team in a thoroughly reckless, shivery manner.

"Isn't he splendid?" cried Marcia when she slipped away with Judith to her room.

Under the bright approval of Marcia's eyes Hampton flushed with pleasure Could Mrs. Langworthy have seen them together she would have nudged the major and whispered in his ear.

During the two months after the dance, Bud Lee and Judith had seen virtually nothing of each other. When routine duties or a necessary report brought them for a few minutes into each other's society there was a marked constraint upon them. Never had the man lost the stinging sense of his offense against her; never had Judith condescended to be anything but cool and brief with him. While no open reference was made to what was past, still the memory of it must lie in each heart, and though Lee held his eyes level with hers and drank deep of the warm loveliness of her, he told himself angrily that he was beneath her contempt. The chivalry within him, so great and essential a part of the man's nature, was a wounded thing, hurt by his own act. The old feeling of camaraderie which had sprung up between them at times was gone now; they could no longer be "pardners" as they had been that night in the old cabin.

He told himself curtly that he did not regret that; that now it was inevitable that they should be less than strangers since they could not be more than friends. That the girl was ready to forgive him, that she had never been as harsh with him as he was himself, that there was a golden, delicious possibility that she should feel as he did--so mad an idea had not come to Bud Lee, horse foreman.

A few days after Marcia's arrival there came to the ranch a letter which was addressed:

> Pollock Hampton, Esq.,
> General Manager,
> Blue Lake Ranch.

It was from Doan, Rockwell & Haight, big stock-buyers of Sacramento, submitting an unsolicited order for a surprisingly large shipment of cattle and horses. The price offered was ridiculously low, even for this season of low figures due to the fact that many overstocked ranches were throwing their beef-cattle and range horses on the market. So low, in fact, that Judith's first surmise when Hampton brought it to her was that the typist taking the company's dictation had made an error.

Judith tossed the note into the waste-basket. Then she retrieved it to frown at it wonderingly, and, finally, to file it. It began by having for her no significance worthy of speculation. It soon began to puzzle her. Finally, it faintly disturbed her.

Here were two points of interest. First: Doan, Rockwell & Haight was the company to which Bayne Trevors, when general manager, had made many a sacrifice sale. Because the Blue Lake had knocked down to them before, did they still count confidently upon continued mismanagement? Surely they must know that the management of the ranch had changed. And this brought her to the second point: How did it come about that they had addressed, not her, but Pollock Hampton? Was this just a trifle?

Long ago Judith had told herself that she must keep her two eyes wide open for seeming trifles. In spite of her, though she scoffed at her "nerves," the girl had the uneasy conviction that this offer had been prompted by Trevors; that Trevors, for purposes of his own, had given instructions that the letter be addressed to Hampton; that this was the first sign of a fresh campaign directed against her from the dark; that trouble was again beginning.

Thoughtfully she smoothed out the letter, impaling it on her file.

XXII
PLAYING THE GAME

Pollock Hampton, Foreman-at-Large, came and went on the ranch, carrying orders, taking always a keen interest in whatever work fell to hand, an interest of a fresh kind, in that it was born of a growing understanding. The men grew to like him; Bud Lee tactfully sought to acquaint him with many ranch matters which would prove of value to him. Carson, however, grown nervous over the new method in stock-raising still in its experimental stage, was given to take any suggestion from Hampton in the light of a personal affront.

"Damn him," he growled deep in his throat when Hampton had ridden out with word to shift one of the herds into a fresh pasture, an act on which Carson had already decided, "some day I'll just take him between my thum' an' finger an' anni-hilate him."

The greater bulk of the stock had been steadily shifted higher in the hills. The hogs grazed on the slopes at the north of the Lower End; cattle and horses had been pushed eastward to the little valleys in the mountains about the lake. Even the plateau, where the old cabin stood, was now stocked with Lee's prize string of horses. Then, one day Hampton came galloping through the herds of shorthorns, seeking Carson.

"Crowd them down to the Lower End again," he shouted above the din. "Cut out the scrawny ones and haze the rest into the pens."

Carson's steel-blue eyes snapped, his teeth showed like a dog's.

"Drunk?" he sneered. "What's eating you?"

"Do as you're told," retorted Hampton hotly. "Those are orders from headquarters and it's up to you to obey them. Get me?"

"If ever I do get you, sonny," grunted Carson, "there won't be enough of you left for the dawgs to quarrel over. Orders or no orders, I ain't going to do no such fool thing."

Hampton reined his horse in closer, staring frowningly at the old cattleman. The purplish color of rage mounted in Carson's tanned cheeks.

"You'll do what you're told or go get your time," he announced tersely. "We've got an order for five hundred beef cows and we're selling immediately.'

Carson's jaw dropped.

"What?" he demanded, not quite believing his ears. "Say that again, will you?"

"I said it once," retorted Hampton. "Now get busy."

"Who are we selling to? I ain't heard about it."

"An oversight, my dear Mr. Carson," laughed Hampton, his own anger risen. "Quite an oversight that you were not consulted. We are selling to Doan, Rockwell & Haight. Ever heard of them?"

"Who says we're selling?"

"I say so. And, if you've got to have all the news, Miss Sanford says so."

"She does, does she? Hm-m. First I knew of it. What figger?"

"Really, does that concern you? If the price suits me and Miss Sanford, who own the stock, does it in any way affect you? I don't want to quarrel with you, Carson, and I do appreciate that you are a good man in your way. But just because you have worked here a long time, don't make the mistake of thinking that you own the ranch."

With that he whirled his horse, and was gone. Carson, with puckered brows, stared after him.

But orders were orders, and Carson though the heart was sore, barked out his commands to his herders to turn the cattle back toward the lower fields. He had been converted to the new way, he had grown to dream of the fat prices his cow brutes would fetch in the winter market, he knew that prices now were rock-bottom low, that Doan, Rockwell & Haight were close buyers who before now had cut the throat of the Blue Lake ranch in sacrifice sales when Bayne Trevors ran the outfit.

"We're standing to lose thousan's an' thousan's of dollars," he told himself in disgust. "All we've spent on irrigation an' fences an' silos an' ditches, all gone to heck in a han'-basket. Not counting thousan's of more dollars lost in selling at what we can get this time of year. It makes me sick, damn throwin'-up sick."

Riding down a long, winding trail, out through a patch of chaparral into a rocky gorge, Hampton turned east again toward the higher plateau. Taking the roundabout way which led from the far side of the lake and along the flank of the mountain to the table-land, he came to a scattering band of horses and Tommy Burkitt.

"Where's Lee?" called Hampton.

Burkitt grinned at him by way of greeting, and then pointed across the plateau to a ravine leading to a still higher, smaller, shut-in valley. Hampton galloped on and a quarter of an hour later came up with Lee. The horse foreman was sitting still in his saddle, his eyes taking stock of a fresh bit of pasture into which he planned turning his horses a little later. It was one of a dozen small meadows on the mountain creeks where the canon walls widened out into an oval-shaped valley, less than a half-mile long, where there was much rich grass.

"Hello, Hampton," called Lee pleasantly. "What's the word?"

The perspiration streaming down Hampton's face had in no way dampened his ardor.

"Big doings," he cried warmly. "We're cutting loose, Bud, at last and piling up the shining ducats! You're to gather up a hundred of the most likely cayuses you've got and shove them down to the Lower End. We're selling pretty heavily to Doan, Rockwell & Haight."

A new flicker came into Lee's eyes. Then they went hard as polished agate.

"I didn't quite get you, Hampton," he said softly. "You say we're selling a hundred horses? Now?"

Hampton nodded, understanding nothing of what lay in Lee's heart.

"On the jump, just as fast as we can get them on the run," he said triumphantly. "Judith wanted me to tell you."

"I see," answered Lee slowly.

His eyes left Hampton's flushed face and went to the distant cliffs. It was no way of Bud's to hide his eyes from a man, and yet now he did hide them. He did not want Hampton to see what they showed so plainly, in spite of his attempt to master his emotion. He was hurt. Long ago he had offended Judith, and she had waited until now to repay his rude insult with this cool little slap in the face. She had not consulted him, she had not mentioned a sale to him, and now she sent Hampton and did not even come to him with a word of explanation. It was quite as if she had said:

"You are just a servant of mine, like the rest, Bud Lee, and I treat you accordingly."

Until Judith had come, there had been nothing that this man loved as he did his work among his horses. He watched them as day after day they grew into clean-blooded perfection; he appraised their values; he saw personally to their education, helping each one of them individually to become the true representative of the proudest species of animal life. Had he turned his eye now to the herd down yonder he could have seen the animal he had selected for a brood-mare next year, the three-year-old destined to draw all eyes as he stepped daintily among the best of the single-footers in Golden Gate Park, the rich red bay gelding that he would mate for a splendid carriage team. . . . Oh, he knew them all like human friends, planned the future for each, the sale of each would be no sorrow but rather a triumph of success. And now, to see them lumped and sold to Doan, Rockwell & Haight--even that hurt. But most of all did Judith's treatment of him cut, cut deep.

"You're a fool, Bud Lee," he told himself softly. "Oh, God, what a fool!"

"The buyers will be here the first thing to-morrow," said Hampton. "Judith says we're to have everything ready for them."

"I'll not keep her waiting," answered Lee quietly. And with a quick touch of the spur he whirled his horse and left Hampton abruptly, going straight to the plateau.

"Round 'em up, Tommy," he said sharply. "Every damned hoof of them: They go back to the corrals."

Though quick questions surged up in Tommy's brain, none of them was asked just yet, for he had seen the look on Lee's face.

It was early in the afternoon when Hampton carried his messages to Carson and Lee. It was after dark when Lee, his work done, his heart still sore and heavy, came into the men's bunk-house. It was very still, though close to a dozen men were in the room. Lee's eyes found Carson and he guessed the reason for the silence. Carson was in a towering rage that flamed red-hot in his eyes; under the spell of his dominating emotion, the men sat and stared at him.

"Well, what's wrong?" asked Lee coolly from the door.

"Good goddlemighty!" growled Carson snappishly. "You stan' there an' ask what's the matter. If they's anything that ain't the matter an' you'll spell its name to me I'll put in with you. The whole outfit's going to pot, an' I, for one, don't care how soon it goes."

"Rather a nice way for a cattle foreman to talk about his ranch, isn't it?" asked Lee colorlessly.

"Cattle foreman?" sniffed Carson with further expletives. "Now will you stan' on your two feet an' explain to me how in blue blazes a man can be a cattle foreman when there ain't no cattle!"

"So that's it, is it? I didn't know how close you were selling off----"

"Don't say *me* selling! Why, I got silage to run my cow brutes all winter, what with the dry feed in them canons----"

Lee didn't hear the rest. It had been his intention to come in and smoke with the boys, and perhaps play a game of whist. Anything to keep from thinking. But now, moving on impulse, he turned and left the shack, going swiftly up the knoll to the ranch-house.

Just stepping into the courtyard soft under the moon, tinkling with the play of the fountains, stirred his heart to quicker beating. He had not set foot here for over two months, not since that night which he knew he should forget and yet to whose memory he clung desperately. This was the first time in many a long week that he had gone out of his way to seek Judith. And now words which Judith herself had spoken to him one day were now at least a part of the cause sending him to speak with her. She had said that he was loyal, that she needed loyal men. He still took her wage, he was still a Blue Lake ranch-hand, he still owed her his loyalty, though it came from a sore heart.

If she were hard driven in some way which she had not seen fit to confide to him, if she were forced to make this tremendous sale, if she were mad or had at last lost her nerve, frightened at the thought of the heavy sums of money to be raised at the end of the winter, well, then it still could do no harm for him to speak his mind to her. Hampton had told him the price which the horses were to bring; it was pitifully small and Lee meant to tell her so, to tell her further that he would guarantee an enormous gain over it if she gave him time. He would be doing his part though she called him meddler for his pains. Marcia Langworthy, hidden in a big chair on the veranda, watched him approach with interest, though Lee was unconscious of her presence. He had lifted a hand to rap at the door when she called to him, saying:

"Good evening, Mr. Mysterious Lee. Have you forgotten me?"

Though he had pretty well forgotten her, it was not necessary to tell her that he had. He came toward her, putting out his hand.

"Good evening, Miss Langworthy," he said cordially. "I haven't seen much of you this time, have I? Two reasons, you know: busy all day and half the night, for one thing, and for another, Hampton has monopolized you, hasn't he?"

Marcia laughed softly.

"To a man your size the second reason is absurd. . . . Will you sit down? You see, I am taking it for granted that you come here to see me. Unless," and her eyes twinkled brightly up at him, "you were surreptitiously calling on Mrs. Simpson?"

"I'd love to talk with you," he assured her. "But, as I've just hinted, my work here has got into the habit of running away with me into the night. I really came up for a word with Miss Sanford."

"Oh, didn't you know?" asked Marcia. "Judith isn't here."

"Isn't here?" He frowned. "No, I didn't know. I haven't seen much of her lately and didn't know her plans. Where is she?"

"In San Francisco. Her lawyers sent for her, you know. Something about a tangle in her father's business. Funny you hadn't heard; she left Saturday night."

Saturday? This was Tuesday evening. Judith had been away three full days. Lee, thinking hurriedly, thought that he saw now the explanation of Judith's ordering a sale like this. Her lawyers had found what Marcia called a "tangle" in Luke Sanford's affairs; there had been an insistent call for a large sum of money to straighten it out, and Judith had accepted the only solution.

Still, it didn't seem like Judith to sell like this at a figure so ridiculously low. Doan, Rockwell & Haight were not the only buyers on the coast. Lee himself could get more for the horses if he had two days' time to look around; the cattle were worth a great deal more than they were being sold for, even with the market down.

"Did she have an idea what the trouble was before she left?" he asked finally.

"Why," said Marcia, "I don't know. You see, she slipped out late Saturday night after we'd all gone to bed. There was a message for her over the telephone; she got up, dressed, saddled her own horse and rode into Rocky Bend alone, just leaving a note for me that she might be gone a week or two."

Just why he experienced a sense of uneasiness even then, Lee did not know. It was like Judith to act swiftly when need be; to go alone and on the spur of the minute to catch her train; to slip out quietly without disturbing her guest.

"You have heard from her since?" he demanded abruptly.

"Not a word," said Marcia. "She doesn't like letter-writing and so I haven't expected to hear from her."

Lee chatted with her for a moment, then claiming work still to be done, turned to go back down the knoll. A new thought upon him, he once more came to Marcia's side.

"I expect I'd better see Hampton," he said. "Do you know where he is?"

"Where he has been every night since Judith left," laughed Marcia. "He's old Mr. Business Man these days. In the office."

There Lee found him. Hampton, his hair ruffled, Judith's table littered with market reports, and many sheets of paper covered with untidy figures, looked up at Lee's entrance.

"Hello, Bud," he said, reaching for cigarette and match. "Got everything ready for to-morrow?"

"Why didn't you tell me Miss Sanford had gone away?" was Lee's sharp rejoinder. Hampton flushed.

"Devil take those two eyes of yours, Bud," he said testily. "They've got a way of boring through a man until he feels like they were scorching the furniture behind him. Well, I'll tell you. While Judith is away I am running this outfit. And if the men think I'm coming straight from her with an order they obey it. If they get the notion she isn't here, they're apt to ask questions. That's why."

"This sale to Doan, Rockwell & Haight," said Lee quickly. "You didn't cook that up, did you, Hampton?"

"Lord, no!" cried Hampton. From its place on a file he took a yellow slip of paper, tossing it to Lee. "She sent me that this morning."

It was a Western Union telegram, saying briefly:

POLLOCK HAMPTON,   Blue Lake Ranch.

Am forced to sell heavily. Sending Doan, Rockwell & Haight Wednesday morning, one hundred horses; as many beef cattle as Carson can round up. Accept terms made in their letter to you last week.

JUDITH SANFORD.

The date-line upon the message gave the sending point as San Francisco.

"They wrote *you* a letter offering to buy?" said Lee thoughtfully, his eyes rising slowly from the paper in his fingers. "How'd it happen they didn't write to *her*?"

"Well, it's a natural enough mistake, isn't it? Knowing that she and I were both part-owners, knowing that we were both here, isn't it quite to be expected that they would write to the man instead of to the woman? Of course I gave her the letter as soon as I had opened it."

"Of course," answered Lee.

But his thoughts were not with his answer. They were with Bayne Trevors. He knew that Trevors had long ago sold to these people; he knew, too, that at least two of the heavy shareholders in the Western Lumber Company were interested in Doan, Rockwell & Haight. Tom Rockwell himself was second vice-president of the lumber company.

"Have you had any other word from Miss Sanford?" he asked.

"No."

"Know who her lawyers are?"

"No. I don't."

"Anything in her papers here that would tell us?"

"No. Her papers are in the safe yonder and it's locked and I don't know the combination."

"Know what hotel she is stopping at in the city?"

"No. Look here, Bud; what are you driving at? I don't get you."

"No?" answered Lee absently.

What Bud Lee was thinking was: "Here are too many coincidences!" Little things, each one in itself safe from suspicion. But when he meditated that the offer had come from this particular firm, that it had come just a few days before Judith's first departure from the ranch, that it had been addressed not to her but to Hampton, so that he must have the opportunity to read it, that she had been called sucdenly to the city, that that call had come after the house was quiet, its occupants in bed, that no letter had come since she had left, that no one knew where to reach her--when he passed all of these things in review the bitterness in his heart died under them and the first anxiety sprang up anew, grown almost into fear for her.

"There's just one thing, Hampton," he said, his eyes hard on the boy's face. "We don't sell a single hoof in the morning. Not a cow nor a horse until Judith is here herself."

Hampton, new in his role of general manager, flushed hotly, his own eyes showing fight.

"I like you, Lee," he said sharply, his tone that of master to man. "And I don't want us to quarrel. But Judith wired me to sell, I've wired the buyers an acceptance and we do sell in the morning!"

For a full minute Bud Lee stood stone still, staring into Hampton's face. Then, tossing the telegram to the table, he turned and went out. His face had gone suddenly white.

"They've got you somehow, Judith girl," he whispered through tense lips. "But the fight is still to be made. And, by God, there's a day of squaring accounts coming for a man named Bayne Trevors!"

He went to the bunk-house, neither seeing Marcia nor hearing her when she called after him, and with a word to Carson brought the irate cattle foreman hurriedly outside.

XXIII
THE WRATH OF POLLOCK HAMPTON

Bayne Trevors's way had ever been to play safe, the way of a coward or a wise man. Even now, no doubt he was giving an account of himself in legitimate endeavor at the lumber camp, putting in his appearance at his regular hour, safe miles lying between him and that which might occur upon the Blue Lake ranch, establishing alibis, conducting himself like the man he wished the world to think him. But in the mind of Bud Lee there was no question, no doubt. Bayne Trevors, or one of Bayne Trevors's gang, was even at this instant holding Judith somewhere until this colossal deal could be put over. Trevors or one of his gang--and Lee's face went whiter, his hands shut tighter into hard fists, as there came to his mind the picture of Quinnion's twisted face and evil, red-rimmed eyes.

"Well?" snapped Carson. "What now?"

"There's going to be no sale in the morning," said Lee, and at the new strange tone in Lee's voice Carson jerked up his head, thrusting it forward, peering at the other through the moon-lit night.

"Say it again," muttered Carson. "Who said so? Miss Judith?"

"She isn't here," replied Lee briefly. "Hasn't been here since Saturday night."

Now, with more cause than ever, did Carson stare at him.

"Then what did Pollock Hampton say sell for? By cripes, if this is one of that young hop-o'-my-thumb's jokes, I'm going up to the house an' murder him. That's all. An' right now."

Lee laid a hand on Carson's arm.

"Hold on, old-timer," he said shortly. "We'll have a talk with him after a while. Now I want to talk with you."

Contenting himself with the coldest of brief outlines, Bud Lee told Carson of Judith's absence and of his own suspicions. Carson, who had listened to him gravely, at the end shook his head.

"That's a pretty bald play, Bud," he said slowly. "I don't believe Trevors would get that coarse in his work. It doesn't look like him a little bit."

"Does this sale look the least little bit like Judith?" demanded Lee sharply. "Is it her style to go over our heads this way, Carson? If she's got to sell heavily, why pick out this particular set of buyers? Why is the deal rushed through while she's away? I tell you there's a nigger in the wood-pile and it's up to you and me to smoke him out. Come up to the house with me."

Marcia did not see them as they drew near in the moonlight. For, with a plan shaping in his brain, Lee judged best that they should not be seen. He and Carson passed in a wide arc about the left end of the courtyard, around the end of the house and so to a door opening front the office to the back of the house. This door he found unlocked and pushed quietly open.

Hampton lifted swift eyes, sensing something stern and ominous in this silent approach.

"We want to talk things over with you," began Lee.

"If you've come to bulldoze me out of that deal in the morning," retorted Hampton, "you might as well keep still. I'm going to sell."

"I don't know that you'd exactly call it bull-dozing," smiled Lee, determined to be pleasant with the young fellow as long as possible. "But you've got sense enough to listen to reason, Hampton."

"Have I?" jeered Pollock. "Thanks."

"If Miss Sanford wants the deal to go through," continued Lee, "why, then, of course, through it goes. If she doesn't, there's going to be no sale."

"I tell you she wired me to sell; I showed you the telegram----"

"But you didn't prove to me that she sent it. You didn't know yourself whether it had been sent by her or Doan, Rockwell & Haight, or by Bayne Trevors or the devil himself." He took up the telephone and said into it, "Western Union, Rocky Bend. . . . That you, Benton? This is Lee of the Blue Lake. We want to get in communication with Miss Judith Sanford, somewhere in San Francisco. Send this message to every hotel there, will you? And rush it: 'Must have word with you immediately. Important. Telephone.' Got it? Oh, sign it, Carson and--and Tripp. Rush it, I tell you, Benton. And if you get in touch with Miss Sanford in any way, tip us off here, will you? Thanks."

"She might be visiting with friends," muttered Hampton, little pleased at the thought that Lee and Carson were seeking to rob him of his newly acquired importance.

"Where's Mrs. Simpson?" asked Lee.

"Gone to bed," answered Hampton.

"And Miss Langworthy is still on the veranda. Now Hampton, Carson and I want a look at Miss Sanford's room. Come with us, will you?"

"I'm damned if I will!" cried the boy hotly. "I don't know what you are up to, but I'm boss here and I'm giving orders, not taking them. If there's any reason in all this, I've got the right to know what it is."

"Yes," answered Lee thoughtfully. "You've got the right. I just don't like the looks of affairs, Hampton. I don't believe all that I hear. I don't believe Miss Sanford sent that wire. I don't believe she is in San Francisco. I do believe that your friend Trevors has got hold of her somehow, and that he is playing you for a sucker. That's our reason in this. Now will you come with us to her room?"

"Trevors?" said Hampton. Then he laughed. "You are like the rest, Bud. Trevors is a gentleman, and you try to make him a crook. Such a scheme as you imagine is absurd and ridiculous. And I won't go prying with you into Judith's room."

"Come on, Carson," said Lee. "If Hampton wants to stay here, let him."

But the young fellow was on his feet, his face flushed, his eyes excited.

"You'll get out of this house and do it quick!" he cried sharply. "If you think for one little minute that I'll stand for your high-handed actions, you're mistaken."

At a look from Lee, Carson stepped quickly forward, so that Hampton stood between them.

"You come with us," and now Lee no longer sought to be pleasant. "And keep still or we'll stop your mouth with a yard of cloth. This way, Carson."

With right and left arms gripped, with lagging feet and furious eyes, Hampton went between them to the door. For an instant only did he struggle; then, with a snort of disgust, seeing the futility of making a fool of himself, he went quietly.

Just what he expected as a result of a visit to the girl's room, Lee did not know.

He hoped for some sign to tell him something, anything.

Quietly the three went through the house until they came to Judith's dainty blue-and-white bedroom. Here all had been set in order by Mrs. Simpson. A great vase of rosebuds, brought by Jose this morning, accepted by Mrs. Simpson with suspicion and searched carefully for a lurking scorpion or a coiled rattlesnake, stood on a table by the window. On entering the room a sort of awkward shyness fell over both Lee and Carson. Hampton, freed now and standing alone, though under Carson's hard eye, stared at them angrily.

"When you get through with this foolishness," he told them stiffly, "you can either apologize or call for your time."

Neither answered. Carson little by little had come to share Lee's uncertainty and anxiety; and now, like Lee, sought eagerly to find a sign--something to tell that Judith had been lured away by Trevors or Quinnion; or that she had been overpowered here and taken out, perhaps through a window.

But Judith had gone Saturday night, and Mrs. Simpson had done her work thoroughly. It might be well to call the housekeeper and question her. Had she found a chair overturned, a rug rumpled, a table shoved a little from its accustomed place? But, again, it would be as well not to start suspicion and surmise in other minds; if, after all, there were no true cause for it. Judith *might* be in San Francisco; she *might* have sent the order to sell.

"Chances is we're smelling powder where there wasn't no shot," said Carson hesitatingly.

"Bright boy!" mocked Hampton. "You'll make a great little gumshoe artist one of these days."

Had Bud Lee not loved Judith as he did, with his whole heart and soul, it well might have been that he and Carson and Hampton would have gone out of the room knowing no more than when they had come in. But it seemed to Lee that the room which knew Judith so intimately, was seeking to open its dumb lips to whisper to him of danger to her. He had come here troubled for her; he stood, looking about him frowningly, his heart heavy, fear mounting within him. And at length he found a sign.

At the far end of the room, in a corner, was Judith's writing-table, on which were several opened letters, pen and ink, a pad of paper. Lee stepped to it. If she had been lured away after nightfall, then some message had come to her. If that message had come by word of mouth, there was no need seeking it; if it had been a note, fate might have kept it here.

Impaled on a sharp file was a sheet of note-paper. The note was brief, typewritten, even to the signature--that of Doc Tripp. It ran:

DEAR JUDITH:

I am afraid of a new trouble. Have spotted another one of T's gang working for us. Also have got a bullet-hole in my right hand. Nothing serious so far. Come down right away. Don't let any one see you as I want to spring a surprise on them. Am not even using the telephone, as I've a notion they are watching me. Hurry.

TRIPP.

"Come back to the office," said Lee bluntly. And well in front of Carson and Hampton, who stared wonderingly at the paper in his hand, he went to the office telephone and called for Tripp.

"How's your hand?" he asked when Tripp answered.

"All right," replied Tripp. "Why?"

"Get it hurt?"

"No."

"Did you write Miss Sanford a hurry-up note within the last few days?"

"No."

"Sure of that, Doc? Typewritten note?"

"Of course I'm sure," snapped Tripp. "What's wrong?"

"God knows," answered Lee shortly. "But you'd better come up here and come on the jump. Also, keep your mouth shut until you can get a chance to talk with me or Carson."

He clicked up the receiver and turned terrible eyes on the two men watching him.

"They've got her," he said slowly. "They've got her, Carson. They've had her since Saturday night!"

Carson read the note. Only then did it pass into Hampton's hands. The boy, angered at the way in which he had been ignored, insulted in his sense of dignity by those words of Lee's to Tripp, "Talk with me or Carson," seeing the reins of power being snatched from his hands, was speechless with wrath.

"You fellows have butted in all I'll stand for!" he cried at them, his shut fists shaking. "I tell you I'm running this outfit and what I say goes. I don't believe that Trevors or any man living would do a trick like that. I tell you it's ridiculous. And, no matter where Judith is, when she is not here I run the ranch. I need money; she needs money; we've got a fair chance to sell; I've passed my word we are going to sell; and by God, we are going to sell."

In another mood, Hampton would not have spoken this way. In another mood and with time for argument, Bud Lee would have expostulated with him. Now, however, Lee said tersely:

"Carson, it's up to you and me. Get the boys out, to the last man of them. Turn every hoof of cattle and horses back into the Upper End. We've got to do it to-night. Get them into the little valley above the plateau. We can hold them there, even if they try to force our hands, which will be like them. I take this to be Trevors's last big play. And, by thunder, he has mighty near gotten away with it!"

"Don't you dare do it!" blazed out young Hampton. "Carson, you take orders from me. Get out of this house and leave the stock where they are. In the morn-ing----"

"Go ahead, Carson," cut in Lee's hard voice. "I'll take care of Hampton here."

"You will, will you?" cried Hampton.

With one bound he was at the table, jerking open a drawer. As his hand sought the weapon lying there, Bud Lee was on him, throwing him back. Carson looked at them a moment, then went to the door.

"You're right, Bud," he said calmly as he went out.

Lee, forcing himself to show a calmness like Carson's, said gently to Hampton:

"Can't you see the play? It's up to you to kick in and stop it. There's a tele-phone; call up the buyers in Rocky Bend. They're there now, or at least their driv-ers are, if they're coming out here in the morning. Tell them the deal is off."

"Can't I see?" said Hampton, writhing out of Lee's hands, on his way to the door. "You bet I can see! If you and Carson think that you can run me----"

Then, for good and all, Lee gave over trying to reason with Hampton. There was too much to be done to waste time. He drew Hampton back, forcing him against the wall. As he tried to call out, Lee's hand over his mouth smothered his words.

"You're coming with me," he said sharply. "Right now."

Though he struggled, Hampton was little more than a baby in the horse fore-man's muscular grip. Tripped, with a heel behind his calf, he fell heavily, Lee upon him. Both arms were pinioned behind him, and Lee's neckerchief thrust into his mouth. He writhed in impotent rage. His outcries died in his throat, the loudest of them not reaching Marcia's ears above the creaking of her rocking-chair. Lee still held Hampton's tied hands gripped in his own. So the two men went out the back door, down toward the corrals.

Seeing men hurrying from the bunk-house to the stables under Carson's snap-ping orders. Lee called out for Tommy Burkitt. And in a moment, with bulging eyes, Burkitt came running.

"Bring out three horses, Tommy," Lee commanded, giving no explanation. "Hurry, and keep your mouth shut."

Burkitt obeyed Lee as he always did, silently and unquestioningly. Very soon he returned, riding, leading two saddled horses.

"Get into the saddle, Hampton," said Lee sternly. "There's no time for non-sense. Get up or I'll put you up."

"Curse you," Hampton said in smothered anger, his tone making clear the meaning of the indistinct mutter. But he climbed into the saddle.

"Come on, Tommy." Lee, too, was up, his hand on Hampton's reins. "We're going up to the old cabin. You're going to ride herd on Hampton while I do some-thing else. I'll tell you everything when we get there."

So they rode into the night, headed toward the narrow passes of the Upper End, Hampton and Lee side by side, Tommy Burkitt staring after them as he fol-lowed. No longer were Bud Lee's thoughts with his captive, nor with the herds Carson's men were driving back to the higher pastures. They were entirely for Ju-dith, and they were filled with fear. She had been gone for three full days; she was somewhere in the clutch of Trevors or of one of his cutthroats. He thought of her, of Quinnion's red-rimmed, evil eyes, and as he had not prayed in all the years of his life Bud Lee prayed that night.

XXIV
A SIGNAL-FIRE?

L
ee left Hampton securely bound and under Tommy Burkitt's watchful eyes in the old cabin, and rode straight back to the ranch-house. Marcia was not yet in bed and he made his first call upon her. Marcia was delighted, then vaguely perturbed, as he made known his errand without giving any reason. He wanted to see the note from Judith. Marcia brought it, wondering. He carried it with him to Judith's office and compared it carefully with scraps of her handwriting which he found there. The result of his study was what he had expected: the writing of the note to Marcia was sufficiently like Judith's to pass muster to an uncritical eye, looking, in fact, what it purported to be, a very hasty scrawl. But Lee decided that Judith had not written it. He slipped it into his pocket.

Tripp was waiting for him, impatient and worried, when he came back from the Upper End. From Tripp he learned that one of the men, a fellow the boys called Yellow-jacket, had unexpectedly asked for his time Saturday afternoon and had left the ranch, saying that he was sick.

"He's the chap who brought the fake note from you," said Lee. "It's open and shut, Doc. Another one of Trevors's men that we ought to have fired long ago. The one thing I can't get, is why he didn't do a finished job of it and hang around until Miss Sanford left, then get away with the note. It would have left no evidence behind him."

"She must have locked her door and windows when she went out," was Tripp's solution. "And probably he didn't hang around wasting time and taking chances."

Tripp's boyish face had lost its youthful look. His eyes, meeting Lee's steadily, had in them an expression like Lee's.

"If it's Quinnion--" Tripp began. Then he stopped abruptly.

Lee and Tripp were together in the office not above fifteen minutes. Then Tripp left to return to the Lower End, to get the rest of the men out, to help in the big drive of cattle and horses which must be returned to the shut-in valleys of the Upper End. Lee went to the bunk-house, slipped revolver and cartridges into his pockets, took a rifle and rode again to the old cabin.

"It's Trevors's big, last play," he told himself gravely, over and over. "He'll be backing it up strong, playing his hand for all that there's in it, and he'll have taken time and care to fill in his hand so that we're bucking a royal flush. And there's only one way to beat a royal flush, and that's with a gun. But I can't quite see the whole play, Trevors; I can't quite see it."

There were enough men to do the night's work without him and Tommy Burkitt, and Lee gave no thought now to Carson, swearing in the darkness of some shadow-filled gorge. He did not know what the morrow's work would be for him, but he made his preparations none the less, eager for the coming dawn. He fried many slices of bacon while Hampton glared at him and Tommy watched him interestedly; he made a light, compact lunch, such as best "sticks to a man's ribs," wrapped it in heavy paper and slipped the package into the bosom of his shirt. He completed his equipment with a fresh bag of tobacco and many matches. He loaded his rifle, added a plentiful supply of ammunition to his outfit from the box on the shelf. Then he went outside to be alone, to frown at the black wall of the night, to think, to await the dawn.

"I'm coming to you, Judith girl," he whispered over and over to himself. "Somehow."

Dawn trembled over the mountain-tops, grew pale rose and warm pink and glorious red in the eastern sky, and Bud Lee, throwing down his coiled rope which had been put into service a dozen times during the night, said shortly:

"Here we camp, boys. I'll leave you my fried bacon, Tommy, and take the raw with me. You're not even to light a fire. And you're to stick here until I come for you."

They had travelled deeper and deeper into the fastnesses of the mountains, mounting higher and higher until now, in a nest of crags and cliffs, on a flank of Devil's Mountain, they could look far to the westward and catch brief glimpses of the river from Blue Lake slipping out of the shadows. They had gone a way which

Lee knew intimately, travelling a trail which brought them again and again under broken cliffs, where they must use hands and feet manfully, and now and then make service of a loop of rope cast up over an outjutting crag.

"They'll never follow us here, Tommy," he said confidently. "If they do, you've got the drop on them and you've got a rifle. You know what to do, Tommy, old man."

"I know, Bud," said Tommy, his eyes shining. For never before had Bud Lee called him that--"old man."

Long ago the gag had been removed from Hampton's mouth. Long ago, consequently, Hampton had said his say, had made his promises. When he got out of this--glory to be! wouldn't he square the deal, though! Did Lee know what kidnapping was? That there were such things as laws, such places as prisons?

"Here," said Lee not unkindly, "I'll loosen the rope about your wrists. That's all the chances we're going to take with you. Come, be a sport, my boy. You're the right sort inside; just as soon as this fracas is over, when you know that we were right and that all this is a put-up job on you, your friend Trevors playing you for a sucker and getting Miss Sanford out of the way, you'll say we were right and I know it."

"That so?" snapped Hampton. "You just start now and keep going, Bud Lee, if you don't want to do time in the jug."

Tommy Burkitt, staring back across the broken miles of mountain, canon, and forest, his eyes frowning, was muttering:

"Look at that, Bud. What do you make of it?"

For a little Lee did not answer. He and Tommy and Hampton, standing among the rocks, turned their eyes together toward the hills rimming in the northern side of Blue Lake ranch.

"I make out," said Lee slowly, "that Trevors means business and that Carson has got his work cut out for him this morning, Tommy."

For the thing which had caught the boy's eyes was a blaze on the ridge, its flames leaping and ricking at the thinning darkness, its smoke a black smudge on the horizon, staining the glow of the dawn. And farther along the same ridge was a second blaze, smaller with distance, but growing as it licked at the dry brush. Still farther a third.

"If that fire ever gets a good start," muttered Lee heavily, "it's going to sweep the ranch. God knows where it will stop. And just how Carson is going to fight fire with one hand and hold his stock with the other, I don't know."

But even then he turned his eyes away from the ranch, sweeping the ragged jumble of mountains about him. Judith was gone. Judith needed him and he did not dare try to estimate the soreness of her need. What did it matter that Carson and Tripp and the rest had their problems to face back there? There was only one thing all of the wide world that mattered. And did not even know where she was, north, south, east, or west! Somewhere in these mountains, no doubt. But where, when a man might ride a hundred miles this way or that and have no sign if he passed within calling distance of her?

In his heart Bud Lee prayed, as he had prayed last night, asking God that he might come to Judith. And it seemed to him, standing close to God on the rocky heights, that his prayer had been heard and answered. For, far off to the east, still farther in the solitude of the mountains, rising from a rugged peak, a thin line of smoke rose into the paling sky.

It might be that Judith was there. It might be that she was scores of miles from the beckoning smoke. But Lee had asked a sign and there, like a slender finger pointing to the brightening sky, was a sign.

He stooped swiftly for rifle and rope and packet of bacon.

"Where you goin', Bud?" asked Tommy.

"To Judith," answered Bud Lee gently.

For in his heart was that faith which is born of love.

XXV
THE TOOLS WHICH TREVORS USED

To Judith life had changed from a pleasant game in the sunshine to a hideous nightmare. In a few dragging hours she had come to know incredulity, anxiety, misery, dejection, black hopelessness, and icy terror. She had come to look through a man's eyes at that which lay in his heart, to feel for the first time in her fearless life that the fortitude was slipping out of her bosom, that the strength was melting in her.

She lay on a rude bed of fir-boughs, an utter, impenetrable blackness like a palpable weight on her eyeballs. When it was silent about her, and for the most part silence reigned with the oppressive gloom, she yearned so for a little sound that she moved her foot along the rock floor under her or snapped a dry twig between her fingers or even listened eagerly for the coming of the terrible woman who was her jailer.

Gropingly, again and again she went over in her thoughts the long journey here, seeking fruitlessly to know whether she had come north, south, or east from the ranch-house. It was one of these three directions, for there were no such mountains as these to the west, no such monster cliffs, no deep cavern reaching into the bowels of the earth The sense that, even were she freed, she had no slightest idea where she was, which way she must go, stunned her.

"Will I go mad after a while?" she wondered miserably. "Am I already going mad? Oh, God, have mercy on me----"

From the instant when, Saturday night, she had been gripped suddenly in a man's strong arms, when another man had smothered her outcry, she had known in her heart that Bayne Trevors was taking his desperate chance in the game. But in the darkness she had had only the two vague blurs of their bodies to guess at.

They had been masked; her own eyes were covered, a bandage brought tightly over them, her mouth gagged, her hands tied behind her, her body lifted into the saddle--all in a moment. Neither man had spoken. Then, tied in the saddle, she only knew that she was riding, that one man rode in front of her, leading her horse, the other following close behind. The sense of direction which she had lost in those first five minutes she had never been given opportunity to regain. She might, even now, be a gunshot from her own ranch; she might be twenty miles from it.

For the greater part of that Saturday night they had ridden; and when trails died under them and rocks rose steeply, they walked, she and one man. The other stayed with the horses. Not once did she hear a man's voice; she did not know whether it was Trevors himself, or Quinnion, or some utter stranger who forced her into this hiding.

They had climbed cliffs, now going down into chasms, now following roaring creeks or making their way along the spine of some rocky ridge. The one man with her was masked, his eyes rather guessed at than seen through the slits of his bandanna handkerchief. He had jerked the bandage from her eyes, since blindfolded she would make such poor progress. But still he guarded his tongue.

"He would speak," she thought, "but that I would recognize his voice. Trevors or Quinnion? Which?"

Feeling the first quick spurt of hope when she saw that there was but one man to deal with, she was aquiver to seize the first opportunity for flight. But that hope died swiftly as she recognized that no such opportunity was to be granted her. Once she paused, looking to a possible leap over a low ledge and escape in a thick bit of timber. But the two eyes through the slits in the improvised mask had been keen and quick, a heavy hand was laid on her arm, she felt the fingers bite into her flesh as he sought to drive into her a full comprehension of his grim determination that she should not escape.

It was when they had clambered high upon a mass of tumbled boulders, topping a ridge, that Judith had seen the man's face. Docilely she had obeyed his gestures for an hour; now, suddenly maddened at the silence and the mask over his face, she sprang unexpectedly upon him, shoving him from the rock on which he had stepped, snatching off his mask as she did so. For the first time she heard his voice, cursing her coolly as he gripped and held her.

It was Bayne Trevors, at last come out the open, his eyes hard on hers.

"It's just as well that you know whom you are up against," he said as he held her with his hand heavy on her shrinking shoulder.

Summoning all of the reckless fearlessness which was her birthright, she laughed at him coolly, laughed as the two stood against the sky-line, upon the barren breast of a lonesome land.

"So you are a fool, after all, Bayne Trevors!" she jeered at him. "Fool enough to mix first-hand in a dangerous undertaking."

Trevors shrugged.

"Yes?" He slipped the handkerchief into his pocket and stared at her with a glint of anger in the blue-gray of his eyes. He lifted his broad shoulders. "Or wise man enough to do my own work when needs be, and when I'd have no bungling? I'm going to square with you, girl. Square with you for meddling, for a bullet-hole in each shoulder. If there's a fool in our little junketing party, it's a girl who thought she could handle a man's-size job."

They went on, over the ridge and down. Judith made no second attempt to surprise him, for always his eyes watched her. Nor did she seek to hold back or in any way to hamper him now. For, swiftly adjusting herself to the new conditions, she made her first decision: Trevors did think her a "fool of a girl," Trevors did sneer at her helplessness in that man's way of his. Let him think her a little fool; let him hold her in his contempt; let him grow to think her cowed and afraid and helpless. Then, when the time came----

Again she had been blindfolded; seeing the look in Trevors's eyes, she had offered no objection. Again she had followed him in a darkness made at sunrise by a bandage across her eyes. Again, the bandage removed, she winked at the sunlight. Again they climbed ridges, dropped down into tiny valleys, fought their way along thunderous ravines where the water was lashed into white foam. Again blindfolded, again trudging on, her whole body beginning to tremble with fatigue, the weakness of hunger upon her. And at length, out of a canon, making a perilous way up the steep walls of rock, they came to the mouth of the black cavern in which she lay now, waiting for the sound of a stirring foot.

Only an instant had Judith stood upon the ledge outside the cave before she was thrust into the black interior. But in that instant her eager eyes had made out, upon a tiny bit of table-land across the chasm of the gorge, a cabin, sending aloft a plume of smoke.

Then, after an hour, the terrible woman had come to whom Trevors had intrusted her, bringing food and water in her hard, blackened hands, carrying the flickering fires of madness in her unfathomable eyes. A lantern set on the floor made rude shadows, and out of them crept this woman, leering at Trevors, peering at Judith, licking her thin lips, and chuckling to herself.

"I have brought her back to you, Ruth," he said, speaking softly, more softly than Judith had thought the man could speak. "You will know what to do with her. And you will not let her escape you again."

The mad woman, for only too plainly was her reason strangely misshapen, stood in silence, her great muscular body looming high above Judith's, a giant of a woman, bigger than Trevors even, broad and heavy, her forearms thick and corded, her bare throat like the bull neck of a prize-fighter.

"I will know, I will know," she said, her eyes filled with cunning, her voice a strange singsong oddly at variance with the coarse bigness of her body. "Oh, no, she will never escape from me again."

"I will have a man on the ledge outside night and day," went on Trevors. "But we cannot be so sure of others as we are of ourselves, Ruth. You know that, don't you?"

"Oh, yes, I know," she answered quickly. As she spoke she suddenly shot out her long arm so that her great, bony hand fastened like a big claw on the girl's shoulder. "I have got her again! She is mine, all mine. Oh, I will keep her well."

In a little while Trevors left. He had not returned. Mad Ruth, still gripping Judith's shoulder, half led her, half thrust her farther back in the cavern. Judith made no resistance. Always, even when terror was uppermost she held one thought in mind: "If I can make them think me a little fool and a weakling, my chance may come after a while."

As the two women passed around a bend in the sinuous tunnel-like cave, the faint rays of the lantern they had left behind them died out, and heavy darkness shut them in. Judith could barely make out the huge form towering over her. But Ruth, whether her eyes were like a cat's and accustomed to this sombre place, or whether a hand on a rock wall or a foot on the uneven floor under her told her which way to go, moved on without hesitation. Judith estimated roughly that they had come fifty yards from the outside ledge in front of the cave when she was pushed down and felt the rude bed of fir-boughs under her.

"So," grunted the woman, for the first time removing her hard hand from the girl's shoulder, "I've got you again, my pretty. And this time you don't play any more little tricks on your old mother."

She was gone swiftly, all but silently, through the gloom, her form vaguely outlined against the lantern's glimmer, to bring the food and water which she had set down when she came in. Judith drank and ate.

It was only little by little, in fragments which she obtained during the slow days which followed, that she came to understand Trevors's scheme. And the scheme was in keeping with the man; so far as it was possible, Bayne Trevors was still playing safe.

Mad Ruth was an odd mixture of crazed suspicion, shrewd cunning, cruelty, and madness. Perhaps very long ago--Judith came to believe that it had occurred at the time when she had gone mad, for God knows what reason--Mad Ruth had had a little daughter. The girl had been lost to her, whether through death when an infant, or some tragic accident when a young girl, Judith never knew. But Ruth's heart had been bound up in that baby of hers; when madness came, it centred and turned upon the return of her child, "Who had run away from her, but who would come back some time." Trevors, having learned of her mad passion, had shaped it to his purpose.

But that was not all. Judith had been brought to the cave early Sunday morning. Sunday afternoon there came to the cave a well-dressed man carrying a little black bag in his hand. He talked with Ruth; he took up the lantern and came to look at Judith.

"So I'll know you again," he laughed. Then he went away. In fragments which through long, empty hours her busy mind pieced together, bridging the gaps, she grasped the rest of Trevors's plan. This man was a physician, sent here from some one of the many mining towns in the mountains, probably from a camp twenty or thirty miles away. He, too, was a Trevors hireling. Should Judith ever accuse Trevors of having brought her here, there was another story to be told. And this man would tell it: How he had been summoned here to attend a girl who had had a fall, who had wandered delirious through the mountains until Ruth had found her; whom he had treated here, not daring at first to move her for fear of permanent shock to her reason; who could give them no help to establish her identity; who had a thousand absurd fears and fancies and accusations to make; who in her babbling had at one time accused Bayne Trevors of having forcibly abducted her; who at another had cried that it was a man named Carson, a man named Lee, who had brought her here.

Judith spent many a long hour exploring her prison, hoping to find a way out. So far as she knew she had but one person to reckon with, Mad Ruth. True, Trevors had said that he'd have a man on the ledge outside day and night; Judith had never seen such a person, had never heard his voice, and began to believe that it was a bit of bluff on Trevors's part. But she had never again been where she could look out of the cave's mouth, since Mad Ruth had her own pallet on the floor at the narrowest part of the cave where it was like the neck of a monster bottle, and always at the first sound of the girl's approach, was on her feet to thrust her back. Clearly there was no way out of this place of shadows except that through which she had come.

Judith sought an explanation of her imprisonment, and after long groping she came very near the truth: Trevors would work his will with Hampton through Hampton's faith in him and admiration for him. And, in her absence, Hampton was the head of Blue Lake ranch.

Sunday night, hearing Mad Ruth moving cautiously, Judith raised herself on her elbow, listening. She was confident that the woman was moving toward the cave's mouth; she hoped wildly that Mad Ruth was tricked into believing her asleep and was going out. Her shoes in her hands, her stockinged feet falling lightly, Judith moved toward the mad woman's couch.

Ruth was going out; was in fact even now slipping out of the narrow throat of the cave and to the ledge. But Judith could not see her. For a new, unexpected obstacle was in her way. Her outthrust hands touched not rock walls but heavy wooden panels; she knew then that the narrow neck of the cave was fitted with a heavy door and that it had been drawn shut, fastened from without. In a sudden access of fury and despair she beat at it with her two hands, crying out bitterly.

It was so dark, so inky black, and as still, save for her own outcry, as a tomb sealed and forgotten. Such darkness, smothering hope, suddenly was filled with vague terrors; for one worn-out and nervous as Judith was, the darkness seemed to harbor a thousand ugly things which watched her and mocked at her despair and reached out vile hands toward her. She called loudly, and for answer had the crazed laugh of Mad Ruth which floated in to her from without, but which seemed to drop down from the void above.

"Judith, Judith," the girl whispered after the first outburst, when she found that she was shaking pitifully. "You've got to do better than this; I'm ashamed of you."

She went back to her couch, where she sat down seeking to hold her jangling nerves in check. But, despite her intention, she sat shaking, listening, listening-- praying for even the footfall of her jailer.

When Ruth was with her she attempted in a hundred ways to gauge the woman's warped brain, to seek some way to get the better of her, to gain her trust and so to slip away. But she found that here was the usual cunning born of madness, and that Ruth's one idea was to keep the girl who had escaped her once but who must never escape again. There were times when suspicion awakened in Ruth's mind, and she broke into violent rage, so that her big body shook and her eyes in the lantern-light were cruel and murderous, when Judith shrank back, and tried to change the woman's thoughts. For more than once had Mad Ruth cried out:

"I'll kill you! Kill you with my own hands to keep you here. To keep you mine, mine, mine!"

The woman carried no weapon, but after her two hands had once gripped the girl's shoulders, shaking her, Judith knew that Ruth needed no weapon. Hers was a strength greater than Trevors's, greater than two men's. If Mad Ruth saw fit to kill Judith with her two hands, she could do it.

Sunday passed and Sunday night; Monday and Monday night. Judith knew that she had accomplished nothing, except perhaps to make Ruth believe that she was very much of a coward. In Ruth's mad brain that was little enough, since this did not allay her cunning watchfulness. Then Judith began to do something else, something actively. Just to be occupied, was something. Her fingers selected the largest, thickest branch from her bed of fir-boughs. It was perhaps a couple of inches in diameter and heavy, because it was green. Silently, cautious of a twig snapped, she began with her fingers to strip the branch, tough and pliable. Then the limb must be cut into a length which would make it a club to be used in a cramped space.

She found a bit of stone, hard granite, which had scaled from the walls and which had a rough edge. With this, working many a quiet hour, she at last cut in two the fir-bough. She lifted it in her hands, to feel the weight of it, before she thrust it under her bed to lie hidden there against possible need. Poor thing as it was, she felt no longer utterly defenseless.

Once Mad Ruth, lighting the lantern, had dropped a good match. When she had gone, Judith secured it hastily, hiding it as if it were gold. She knew that now and then Mad Ruth went down the cliffs and to the cabin across the chasm. Always at night and at the darkest hour. When she heard her go, Judith rose swiftly and went to the heavy door. Always she found it locked; her shaking at it hardly budged the heavy timbers. But though she could not see it, she studied it with her fingers until she had a picture of it in her mind. A picture that only increased her hopelessness. Barehanded she could never hope to break it down or push it aside. And above it and below, and on each side, were the solid walls of stone.

She no longer knew what day it was. She scarcely knew if it were day or night. But, setting herself something to do so that she would not go mad, mad as Mad Ruth, she secured for herself another weapon. Another bit of stone which her groping fingers had found and hidden with her club; a jagged, ugly rock half the size of a man's head. Some little scraps of bread and meat, hoarded from her scanty meals, she hid in her blouse.

"If I could stun her, just stun her," she got into the way of whispering to herself. "Not kill her outright--just stun her----"

At last, seeing that she must work her own salvation with the crude weapons given her, Judith told herself that she could wait no longer. Another day and another and she would be weak from the confinement and poor food and nervous, wakeful hours. She must act while the strength was in her. And, if Trevors had spoken the truth, if there were a man to deal with outside--well, she must shut her mind to that until she came to it.

Mad Ruth was gone again, and Judith stood by the thick door, her heart beating furiously while she waited. It seemed to her eager impatience that Ruth would never come back. Then after a long, long time she heard a little scraping sound upon the rock ledge outside, the sound of a quick step. And then, before she heard the snarling, ugly voice which she had heard once and had never forgotten, she knew that this time she had waited too long, that it was not Ruth coming.

One man--and there might be others. She stepped back to her bed, hid the two weapons and waited. She must make no mistakes now.

The door was flung open. Outside it was dark, pitch-dark. But evidently the man entering had no fear of being seen. He threw down a bundle of dry fagots, and set fire to them. The blaze, leaping up, casting wavering gleams to where Judith stood, showed her plainly the twisted, ugly face of Quinnion, his red-rimmed eyes peering at her, filled with evil light.

XXVI
JUDITH'S PERIL

The better to see you by, my dear!" was Quinnion's word of greeting. Judith made no answer. She drew a little farther back into the shadows, a little closer to the things she had hidden among the fir-branches.

"Ho," sneered Quinnion, his mood from the first plain enough to read in the glimpses of his face and in the added harshness of his voice. "Timid little fawn, huh? By God, a man would say from the bluff you put up that it was all a dream about findin' you an' the han'some Lee in the cabin together! Stan' off all you damn please; I've come to tame you, you little beauty of the big innocent eyes!"

Not drunk; no, Quinnion was never drunk. But, as he came a step closer, the heavy air of the cave grew heavier with the whiskey he carried, whiskey enough to stimulate the evil within him, not to quench it.

"Stand back!" cried Judith, with a sharp intake of breath. "I want to talk with you, Chris Quinnion."

"So you know who I am, do you? Well, much good it'll do you."

"I know who you are and what you are," she told him defiantly, suddenly sick of her long hours of playing baby, knowing at the moment less fear than hatred and loathing. "Listen to me: Bayne Trevors has come out in the open at last; he has made his big play and is going to lose out on it. Your one chance now is to let me go and to go yourself. Go fast and far, Chris Quinnion. For when the law knows the sort Bayne Trevors is and how you have worked hand and glove with him, it will know just how much his word was worth when he swore you were with him when father was killed! Coward and cur and murderer!"

Quinnion laughed at her.

"Little pussy-cat," he jeered. "You've got claws, have you? And you spit and growl, do you? Want me to let you go back to that swaggering lover of yours, do you? Back to Lee----"

"That's enough, Quinnion," she said sharply.

"Is it?" He laughed at her again, and again came on toward her, the red-rimmed evil of his eyes driving quick fear at last into her. "Enough? Why, curse you and curse him, I haven't begun yet! When I'm through with you I'll go fast enough. And he can have you then an' damn welcome to him!"

"Stop!" cried Judith.

His laughter did not reach her ears now, but as he kicked the fire at his foot and the flames leaped up and showed his face, she read the laughter in his soul; read it through the gleaming eyes, the twisted mouth which showed the teeth at one side in a horrible leer. His long arms thrust out before him, he came on.

"Oh, my God!" cried Judith. "My God!"

Then suddenly she was silent. She thought that she had known the uttermost of fear and now for the first time did she fully know what terror was. His strength was many times her strength, his brutality was unbounded, she was alone with him. There was no one to call to, not even Ruth, the mad woman.

She was shaking now, shaking so that she could barely stand. Quinnion came on, his long arms out. . . .

She felt the strength die out of her body, grew for a moment blind and dizzy and sick. She tried again to call out to him, to plead with him. But her voice stuck in her throat.

He was gloating over her, a look strangely like Mad Ruth's in his eyes. Good God! He was like Mad Ruth; the same eyes, the same long, powerful arms, the same look of cunning! In a flash there came to her a suspicion which was near certainty: this man was blood of Mad Ruth's blood, bone of her bone; her son, and, like her, tainted with madness.

He shot out a long arm, his hand barely brushing her shoulder. She shrank back. He stood, content to pause a moment, to gloat further over her.

"You little beauty," he said, panting. "You little white and pink and brown beauty!"

Judith had shuddered when he touched her. But a strange thing had happened to her. His touch had angered her so that she almost forgot to be afraid, angered her so that the loathing was gone in white hot hatred, giving her back her old strength.

Now, though he had the brutal force of a strong man, Quinnion did not have the swiftness of movement of an alert, desperate girl. Before he could grasp her motive she leaped toward him and toward the bed of boughs, found the ragged stone, and lifting it high above her head flung it full into his face. The man staggered back, crying out in throaty harshness, a cry of blind rage. But he did not fall, did not pause more than a brief instant.

A little dazed, with blood in his eyes, he lunged toward her. She had found the club now and struck with all her might, again beating into his face and again and again. He sought to grapple with her and she beat him back. She saw his hand go to his hip and heard him curse her, and she leaped in on him and, panting with the blow, struck again. He flung up his arm. She struck once more. Taking the blow full across the face, Quinnion reeled back, stumbled at an uneven spot in the rock floor, balanced, almost falling. . . .

Only a moment he held thus. But there was a chance to pass him in the narrow way, and she took her chance, her heart beating wildly. And as she shot by she struck again.

She heard him after her, shouting curses, stumbling a little, coming on. The door was open, thank God, the door was open! She shot through. If she could but take time to close it! But there was no time for that; he was almost at her heels. And outside was the ledge and the dizzy climb down.

If she slipped, if she fell, well, it would just be a clean death and nothing more. Quinnion was but a few steps behind her. He had not fired. Had he perhaps dropped his gun back there in the darkness? Or was he so sure of taking her, alive and struggling, into his arms in another moment?

She was on the ledge. It was dark, pitch-dark.

But she found a handhold, threw herself flat down and thrust her feet out over the edge, less afraid of what lay below than what came on behind her. She was gripping the ledge now with her hands, already torn and bleeding, her feet swinging, touching sheer rock wall, slipping, seeking a foothold. Quinnion was just there, above her. She must move her hands so that he could not reach her. It seemed an eternity that she hung there, seeking a place somewhere to set her feet.

She found it, another, lesser ledge which she had almost missed, and knew that this way she had clambered upward with Bayne Trevors. If she could only find another step and another before Quinnion came upon her! She held her club in her teeth; she must not let that go.

Quinnion was over the ledge, following her. She heard his heavy breathing, heard him cursing her again. She was going so slowly, so slowly, and Quinnion would know the way better than she. Quinnion would make better time in the dark.

She moved along this lower ledge. At each instant she wondered if it were to be her last, if she were going to fall, if a swift drop through the darkness would be the end of life.

Suddenly there was scarce room in the girl's breast for hatred of Chris Quinnion, so filled was it with the love of life. She wanted to see the sun come up again, she wanted the sweet breath of the dawn in her nostrils, the beauty of a sun-lit world in her eyes. She thought of Bud Lee.

Clinging to the rocks, hanging on desperately, taking a score of desperate chances momentarily, she made her way on and down. She found scant handhold and, almost falling, dropped her club, heard it strike, strike again. Black as the night was, its gloom was less than that of the cavern to which Judith had grown accustomed; little by little she began to make out the broken surface of the cliffs. The chasm below was a pool of ink; above were the little stars; in the eastern sky, low down, was a promise of the rising moon.

The surge of quickening hope came into her heart. Had she hurt Quinnion more than she had guessed? For, slowly as she made her hazardous way down, it seemed to her that Quinnion came even more slowly. Could she but once get down into the gorge below, could she slip along the course of the racing stream, she might run and the sound of her steps would be lost even to her own ears in the sound of the water; the sight of her flying body would be lost to Quinnion's eyes.

Then she heard him laughing above her. Laughing, with a snarl and a curse in his laugh, and something of malicious triumph. Was he so certain of her then?

"Ruth!" called Quinnion. "Oh, Ruth! The girl's gettin' away. Goin' down the rocks. Head her off at the bottom."

Judith had found, because her fate was good to her, the long slanting crack in the wall of rock up which she had come that day with Bayne Trevors. There was still danger of a fall, but the danger was less now than it had been ten seconds ago. She could move more swiftly now and confidence had begun to com to her that she could elude Quinnion. But now, suddenly, she heard Mad Ruth's voice screaming a shrill answer to Quinnion's shout; knew that Ruth had been in her cabin across the gorge and was running to intercept her at the foot of the cliffs.

Well, still there was a race to be run and the odds not entirely uneven. Ruth must descend the other side of the canon, get down into the gorge, make the crossing, which, so far as Judith knew, might be farther up or farther down stream, come to the cliffs below Judith before Judith herself made her way down.

Again Judith took what risks the night and the rocks offered her and thanked God in her soul that it was given her to take a chance in the open, to use her own muscles in her own fight, not to lie longer, playing the part of a do-nothing. Now and then, across the void, there floated to her a little moaning cry from the mad woman's lips. Now and then she heard a curse from Quinnion above; often from above her, from below her own feet, from across the chasm, dropping stones, falling almost sheer, told of haste and death which might come from an unlucky step.

Fast as Judith went now, having a fair sort of cliff trail under her, Mad Ruth went faster. The gorge measured a scant fifty feet between them and the girl's alert senses told her that already Ruth was on a level with her. Ruth was winning in the desperate race. She knew her way down so perfectly, her heart was so filled with madness, that danger was nothing to her.

Down and down climbed Judith, caution wedded to haste, as she told herself that she had a chance yet, that that chance must not be tossed away in a fall, though it were but a few feet. She must have no sprained ankle if she meant to see the sun rise to-morrow.

The flush had brightened in the sky where the moon was so near the ridge. The moon, too, had joined in the race; with one quick glance toward it, Judith again discarded caution for haste. She must get down into the floor of the canon before the moonlight did; she must be running before its radiance showed her out to Quinnion and Ruth.

Her hands were cut and bleeding, her heart was beating wildly, already her body was sore and bruised. But these things she did not know. She only knew that

Quinnion was still coming on above her, and coming more swiftly now, quite as swiftly as she herself moved, since his feet, too, were in the better trail; that Mad Ruth had completed the descent across the chasm and by now must be crossing the stream upon some fallen log or rude bridge; that one minute more, or perhaps two, would decide her fate.

She could see the stream, glinting palely in the starlight. It seemed very near; its thunder filled her ears. Down she went and down, down until at last she was not ten feet above its surface, with a strip of gently sloping bank just under her. She stooped, took firm hold upon a knob of boulder, prepared to swing down and drop to the bottom. And, as she stooped, she heard a little whining moan just under her and straightened up, tense and terrified. Mad Ruth was there before her. Mad Ruth was waiting.

XXVII
ALONE IN THE WILDERNESS

And Quinnion was coming on. She was trapped, caught between the two of them. She heard Quinnion laugh again; he, too, had heard Ruth. "Oh, God help me!" whispered Judith. "God help me now!"

There was no time to hesitate. If she stood here, Quinnion would in a moment wrap his arms about her; if she dropped down, she would be in the frenzied clutch of Mad Ruth.

A second she crouched, peering down into the gloom below her, seeking to make out the form of the mad woman. Then she did not merely drop, but jumped, landing fair upon the waiting figure, striking with her boots on Mad Ruth's ample shoulders. A scream of rage from Ruth, a little, strangling cry from Judith, and the two fell together. Ruth clutched as she went down and a hand closed over the girl's ankle. Judith rolled, struck again with the free boot, twisted sharply and felt the grip torn loose from her ankle. She was free.

She jumped up and ran and knew that Ruth was running just behind her, screaming terribly. Judith fell, and her heart grew sick within her. But again she was up just as Ruth's hand clutched at her skirt, clutched and was torn away as Judith ran on. Quinnion cursed from above as she had not yet heard him curse. Ruth reviled both her and Quinnion for having let her go.

Judith was running swiftly and felt that she could get the better of the heavier, older woman in a race of this sort. She stumbled and fell, and fear again gripped her; it seemed so long before she could rise and clamber over a fallen log and race on. But the darkness which tricked her protected her at the same time, playing no favorites now. Ruth, too, had fallen; Ruth, too, was frenzied at the brief delay.

Stumbling, falling, rising, staggering back from a tree into which she had run full tilt, bruised and torn, the girl ran on. At every free step hope shot upward in her heart; at every fall she grew sick with dread.

The cañon broadened rapidly, the ground underfoot grew less broken and littered with boulders and logs. Through tangles of brush she went blindly, throwing herself forward, falling, rising, falling, rising again. It was a nightmare of a race, with Ruth always just there, almost at her heels. She turned as far away from the stream as she could, keeping under the cliffs where there was less brush; where the way was more open; where the shadows were thickest.

She was outdistancing Mad Ruth. Ruth's weird voice came from a greater distance; the woman was ten, maybe twenty, feet behind her.

The moon at last rose pale gold above the eastern ridge. And now Judith could thank God for it. For the cañon had widened more and more, the banks of the river were studded with big trees, there were wide open spaces between them through which she shot like a frightened deer, turning this way and that, darting about a clump of little firs, plunging into the shadows under great sky-seeking cedars, running as she had never run before and as she knew Mad Ruth could not run.

Free! She was free. The triumph of it danced in her blood. On she ran and now Quinnion's voice and Ruth's were confused with the roar of the river. On she ran and on and on, and but faintly there came to her the sound of breaking brush somewhere behind her. Never had her blood sung within her as it sang now; never had the dim, moonlit solitudes of the mountains opened their sheltering arms to one more grateful to slip into them, like a wounded child into the soothing embrace of its mother.

Now again she turned so that her flying steps brought her close to the water's edge. Louder and louder grew its shouting voice in her ears, little by little drowning out the sounds of Ruth and Quinnion behind her. Now, in all the glorious night, there was no sound to reach her but the sound of running water and her own beating feet. She was free.

But still she ran, summoning all of the reserve of strength and will-power which was hers to command. The sky was brightening to the climbing moon. She must round many a sweeping curve of the river, pass under many a sheltering, shadowing tree before she dared slow her steps.

When she felt that she was overtaxing herself, she dropped from the wild pace she had set herself into a little jogging trot. When her whole body cried out at the effort demanded of it, she slowed down to a brisk walk. She was shot through with pain, her throat ached, she was growing dizzy. But on she went stubbornly. It was a full hour after the last sound of pursuit had died out after her that she flung herself down at the water's edge to drink and bathe her arms and face in the cold stream. And, even then, she chose a spot where the shadow of a great pine lay like ink over the bank.

The moon was high in the sky, the world bright with it, when Judith left the valley into which the canon had widened and made her way slowly upward along a timbered ridge to the west. Of Quinnion and Mad Ruth she now had no fear. Their chance of coming upon her was less than negligible. She could creep into a clump of thick-standing young trees and, even if they should come, could watch them go past. But as they had dropped out of her world, another matter had entered it. The mountains had befriended her; they had opened their arms to her and that was all that she had asked of them. They had mothered her, drawing her into hiding against their bosom. But it was a barren, barren breast. And already she was hungry, daring to eat but sparingly of her handful of bread and meat.

From this ridge, finding an open crest, she stood looking out over the world. Mile after mile of mountain and canon and cliff fell away on every side. She sought eagerly for a landmark: to see yonder in the distance Old Baldy or Copper Mountain or Three Fools' Peak, any one of the mountains or ridges known to her. And in the end she could only shake her head and sigh wearily and slip down where she was to fall asleep, thanking God that she was free, asking God to lead her aright in the morning.

The stars watched over her, a pale, worn-out girl sleeping alone in the heart of the wilderness; the night breezes sang through the century-old tree-tops; and Judith, having striven to the utter-most, slept in heavy dreamlessness.

With the cool dawn she awoke shivering and hungry. Her hair had tumbled about her face, and sitting up she braided it with numb, sore fingers. She looked at her hands; they well stained with blood from many cuts. Her skirt was torn and soiled; her stockings were in strips; her knees were bruised. But as she rose to her feet and once more searched the riddle of a crag-broken world, her heart was light with thankfulness.

Last night the one friend she had with her was the north star. To-day she would seek to push on toward the west. In that direction she believed the Blue Lake ranch lay, though at best it was a guess. But going westward she could follow the course of the bigger streams, and soon or late, if her strength held, she would come to some open valley where men ran stock. Now, she would go down into the little meadow lying a mile away yonder and seek to find something to eat. If she could but dig a few wild onions, wild potatoes, they would keep her alive. West she would go, if for no other reason than because thus she would be setting her back squarely upon the cavern where Quinnion and Ruth were.

The sun rolled into a clear blue sky and warmed her. She made her way down the long flank of the mountain and into the tiny meadow. For upward of two hours she remained there, nibbling at roots which she dug up with a broken stick, seeking edible growths which she knew, finding little, but enough to keep the life in her, the heart warm in her breast. Then she went on, over a ridge again, down into a canon and along the stream which rose here and flowed westward.

By noon she was faint and sick and had to stop often to rest, her legs shaking under her. Again she made a scant meal. She had stumbled on a tiny field of wild potatoes and ate what she could of them, thinking longingly of a match for a fire. The match which Ruth had dropped she still had, but she carefully reserved it now, thinking how perhaps a trout, caught in a pool, might save her life.

In her already half-starved condition and with the demands constantly put on her strength, she would grow weaker and weaker if help did not soon come. But she was still filled with the glory of freedom. It was a heart-weary, trembling Judith who late that afternoon made her way upward along another ridge, seeking anxiously to find from this lookout some landmark which she had sought in vain last night. In her blouse were the few roots she had brought with her from the field discovered at noon. Lying in a little patch of dry grass, resting, she watched the day go down and the night drift into the mountains, filling the ravines, creeping up the slopes, rising slowly to the peak to which she had climbed, seeping into her soul. Never had the passing of the day seemed to her so majestic a thing, truly filled with awe. Never until now had the solitudes seemed so vast, so utterly, stupendously big. Never until now, as she lay staring up into the limitless sky, having given up the world about her as unknown, had she drunk to the lees of the cup of loneliness.

So great was the weariness of her tired body that as she lay still, watching the stars come out one by one, she was half-resigned to lie so and let death come to find her. It seemed to her that there in the rude arms of Mother Earth a human life was a matter of no greater consequence than the down upon a moth's wing. But she rested a little and this mood, foreign to her intrepid heart, passed, and she sat up, again resolute, again ready to make her fight as long as life beat through her blood. At last she took the one match from her pocket. She scarcely dared breathe when, with dry grass and twigs piled against a rock, her dress shielding them from the wind, she rubbed the match softly against her boot. A sputtering flame, making the blue light of burning sulphur, died down, creating panic in her breast, then flared, crackled, licked at the grass. She had a fire and she knew how to use it!

When a log was blazing, assuring her that her fire was safe, she rose swiftly and went in search of the tree she meant to burn. She found a giant pine, pitch-oozing, standing in a rocky open space where there was little danger of the fire spreading. Fagged out and eager as she was, she had not come to the point of forgetting what a great forest-fire meant. She went back to her burning log, for a blazing dry branch which she carried swiftly to the tree. Then she piled dry grass and dead twigs, logs as heavy as she could carry, bits of brush. The flames licked at the tree, ran up it, seemed to fall away, sprang at it again, hungering. Now and then a long tongue of fire went crackling high up along the side of the tree. Judith went back to a spot where, in a ring of boulders, there was another grassy plot, threw herself down an lay staring at the tongues of fire which were climbing higher and higher.

Some one would see her beacon. A forest ranger, perhaps, whose duty it was to ride fast and far to battle with the first spark threatening the wooded solitudes; perhaps some crew in a logging-camp, than whom none knew better the danger of spreading fires; perhaps some cow-boy, even one of her own men--perhaps Quinnion and Ruth? She then would hide among the rocks until they had come and gone. Even now, against the sleep falling upon her, she drew farther back through the tumbled boulders. Perhaps, Bud Lee. . . .

She went to sleep beyond the circle of bright light, tired and hungry and striving against a returning hopelessness, her young body curled up in the nest she had found, a cheek cuddled against her arm, wondering vaguely if some one would see her fire and come--if that some one might be Bud Lee.

XXVIII
BACON, KISSES, AND A CONFESSION

Throughout the night the tree blazed unseen. Judith's eyes were closed in the heavy sleep of exhaustion. The flames roared and leaped high skyward, burning branches felt crashingly, to lie smouldering on the rocky soil, the upstanding trunk glowed, vivid against the sky-line.

In the early morning at least two pairs of eyes found the plume of smoke above the still burning giant pine. A man named Greene, one of the government forest rangers, blazing a new trail over Devil's Ridge, came out upon a height, saw it and watched it frowningly across the miles. It called him to a hard ride, perhaps to a difficult journey on foot after he must leave his horse. He turned promptly from the work in hand, ran to his horse, swung up and sped back to his cabin, to telephone to the nearest station, passing the word. Then with axe and shovel, he began his slow way toward the beacon.

Bud Lee, from the mountain-top where he and Burkitt had taken Hampton, saw it. Lee judged roughly that it was separated from him by four or five miles of broken country, impassable to a man on horseback, to be covered laboriously foot in a matter of weary hours.

Lee and Greene approached the signal smoke from different quarters. Lee from the west, Greene from the northeast. They fought their way on toward it with far different emotions in their breasts. Greene with the desire to do a day's work and kill a forest-fire in its beginning. Lee with the passionate hope of finding Judith. Lee reached his journey's end first.

As he came pantingly up the last climb he discharged his rifle again and again, to tell her that he was coming, to put hope into her. And, because he was a lover and a lover must be filled with dread when she is out of his sight, he felt a growing anxiety. She had lighted the fire last night; what might have happened to her since then? Had she been wandering, lost all these days? If nothing else, then had she waited here half the night and in the end had she gone on plunging deep into some canon hidden to him? Would he find her well? Would he find her at all?

Suddenly he called out, shouting mightily, and began running, though the way was steep. He had seen Judith, he had found her. She was standing among the scattered boulders, her back to a great rock. She was waving to him. Her lips were moving, though he could not see that yet, could not hear her tremulous:

"Oh, thank God, thank God!"

"Judith," he called, "Judith!"

Now, near enough to see her distinctly, he saw that her face was white, that the hand she held out was shaking, that her clothes were torn, that she looked pitifully in need of him. But at last, when he stood at her side, one of the old rare smiles came into Judith's tired eyes, her lips curved, and she said quietly:

"Good morning, Bud Lee. You were very good--to come to me."

"Oh, Judith," he cried sharply. But no other word came to his lips then. The brave little smile had gone, the whiteness of her face smote him to the heart. And now she was shaking from head to foot, and he knew why she had not stepped out to meet him, why she had kept her back to the rock. He thought that she was going to fall, he saw two big tears start from the suddenly closed eyelids, and with a little inarticulate cry he took her into his arms.

"If you had not come, Bud Lee," she whispered faintly, "I should have died, I think."

Very tenderly he gathered her up so that her little boots were swung clear of the flinty ground and she lay quiet in his arms. He stood a moment holding her thus, looking with eyes alternately hard and tender into her face. He wanted to hold her thus always, to watch the glad color come back into her cheeks, to carry her, like a baby, back across the weary miles and home. And, oddly, perhaps, the thought came back to him and hurt him as it had never hurt him before, that he had once been brutal with her, that he had crushed her in his arms and forced upon her lips his kiss. He had been brutal with Judith, when now he could kill a man for laying a little finger on her.

"I have been a brute with you, a brute," he muttered to himself. But Judith heard him, her eyes fluttered open and into them came again her glorious smile.

"Because you kissed me that night, Bud Lee?" she asked him.

"Don't!" he cried sharply. "Don't even remember it, Judith."

"Do you know so little of a girl, Bud Lee," she went on slowly, "to think that a man can so easily--find her lips with his unless--unless she wants to be kissed?"

He almost doubted his ears; he could hardly believe that he had seen what he had seen in Judith's eyes. They were closed now, she lay quiet in his arms, it seemed that she had fainted, or, was asleep, so very white and still was she. He had forgotten that he must carry her to where he could lay her down and bring water to her, give her something to eat. He just stood motionless, holding her to him, staring hungrily down at her.

"Are you going to play--I'm your baby--all day, Bud Lee?" she asked softly.

He carried her swiftly away from the ring of boulders and to a little grassy, level spot where he put her down with lingering tenderness. Judith had not been angry with him all these months! Judith had let him kiss her because she wanted to be kissed--by him!

He raked some coals out of the ashes, hastily set some slices of bacon to fry, cursed himself for not having brought coffee and milk and sugar and a steak and a flask of whiskey and enough other articles to load a mule. He ran down into the canon and brought water in his hat, swearing at himself all the way up that he had not brought a cup. He put his arm about her while she drank; kept his arm about her, kneeling at her side, while he gave her a little, crisp slice of bacon, held his arm there when she had finished, watching her solicitously.

"The two nicest things in the world, Mr. Man," she said, with a second attempt at the old Judith brightness, "are half-burnt bacon and Bud Lee!"

Then, because, though he had been slow to believe, he was not a fool, and now did believe, he kissed her. And Judith's lips met his lingeringly. Judith's two arms rose, slipped about his neck, holding him tight to her.

The faintest of flushes had come at last into a her cheeks. He saw it and grew glad as he held her so that he could look into her face. But now she laid a hand against his breast, holding him back from her.

"That's all now," she told him, her eyes soft upon him. "Just one kiss for each slice of bacon, Mr. Lee. But--I'm so hungry!"

For a little there was nothing to do but for Judith to rest and get some of her strength back. Lee made of his coat and vest a seat for her against a rock, sat at her side, his arm about her, made her lean against him and just be happy. Not yet would he let her tell him of the horrors through which she had gone. And he saw no need of telling her anything immediately of conditions as he had left them at the ranch. Time enough for that when she was stronger, when they were near Blue Lake.

Greene, the forester, came at last up the mountain. He noted the isolated tree, nodded at it approvingly, made a brief tour around the charred circle, extinguishing a burning brand here and there.

"What sort of a fool would want to climb way up here to start a fire, anyway?" he grumbled.

Then, unexpectedly, he came upon the happiest-looking man he had ever seen, with his arms about an amazingly pretty girl. Not just the sort of thing a lone forest ranger counts upon stumbling upon on the top of a mountain. Greene stared in bewilderment. Bud Lee turning a flaming red. Judith smiled.

"Good morning, stranger," said Lee. "Fine day, isn't it?"

Judith laughed. Greene continued to stare. Lee went a trifle redder.

"If you two folks just started that fire for fun," grunted Greene finally, "why, then, all I've got to say is you've got a blamed queer idea of fun. Here I've been busting myself wide open to get to it."

"Haven't got a flask of brandy on you, have you?" asked Lee.

"Yes, I have. And what's more I'm going to take a shot at it right now. If nobody asks you, I need it!"

Now, Lee heard for the first time something of Judith's adventure. For, recognizing the ranger in Greene, she told him swiftly why she had started the fire, of her trouble with Quinnion, of the cave where Quinnion had attacked her and of Mad Ruth. Greene's eyes lighted with interest. He swept off his hat and came forward, suddenly apologetic and very human, proffering his brandy, insisting with Lee upon her taking a sip of it.

Yes, he knew Mad Ruth, he knew where her cabin was. He could find the cave from Judith's description. Also, he knew of Quinnion and would be delighted to break a record getting back to his station and to White Rock. White Rock was in the next county, but so, for that matter, was the cave. He'd get the sheriff and would lose no time cornering Quinnion if the man had not already slipped away.

"I don't know you two real well," said Greene, with a quick smile at the end, "but if you don't mind, pardner," and he put out his hand to Lee, "I'd like to congratulate you! I don't know a man that's quite as lucky this morning as you are!"

"Thank you," laughed Judith. She rose and shook hands too. "We're at Blue Lake ranch for the present. Come and see us."

"Then you're Miss Sanford?" said Greene. He laughed. "I've heard of you more than once. Greene's my name."

"Lee's mine," offered Lee.

"Bud Lee, eh? Oh, you two will do! So long, friends. I'm off to look up Quinnion."

And, swinging his axe blithely, Greene took his departure.

"There are other things in the world besides just cliffs to stare at," said Judith. "And I would like a bath and a change of clothes and a chance to brush my hair. And the bacon doesn't taste so good as it did and I want an apple and a glass of milk."

So at last they left the mountain-top and made their slow way down.

As they went Lee told her something of what had happened at the ranch, how Carson would hold off the buyers, how Tommy Burkitt was assuming charge of Pollock Hampton. And when they came near enough to Burkitt's and Hampton's hiding-place, Lee fired a rifle several times to get Burkitt's attention. Finally they saw the boy, standing against the sky upon a big rock, waving to them. From Lee's shouts, from his gestures, chiefly from the fact that Judith was there, Burkitt understood and freed Hampton, the two of them coming swiftly down a to Judith and Lee.

Hampton's face was hot with the anger which had grown overnight. He came on stiffly, chafing his wrists.

"These two fools," he snapped to Judith, "have made an awful mess of things. They've queered the deal with Doan, Rockwell & Haight, they've made themselves liable to prosecution for holding me against my will, they've----"

"Wait a minute, Pollock," said Judith quietly. "It's you who have made a mistake."

Briefly, she told him what had happened. As word after word of her account fell upon Hampton's ears, his eyes widened, the stiffness of his bearing fell away, the glint of anger went out of his eyes, a look of wonder came into them. And when she had finished, Hampton did not hesitate. He turned quickly and put out two hands, one to Lee, one to Burkitt.

"I was a chump, same as usual," he grunted. "Forget it if you can. I can't."

They went on more swiftly now, the four of them together, Judith insisting that that last sip of brandy had put new life into her. In a little, seeing that Judith did in fact have herself in hand, Bud Lee, with a hidden pressure of her hand, left them, hurrying on ahead, trying to reach Carson or some of the men in Pocket Valley and to get horses.

As he drew nearer the ranch Lee saw smoke rising from the north ridge. Again he could turn his thoughts a little to what lay in front of him, wondering what luck Carson had had in his double task of fighting fire and holding off the buyers.

At any rate, the Blue Lake stock had not been driven off. The bawling of the big herds told him that before he saw the countless tossing horns. Then, dropping down into Pocket Valley from above, he found his own string of horses feeding quietly. Beyond, the cattle. At first he thought that the animals had been left to their own devices. He saw no rider anywhere. Hurrying on, he shouted loudly. After he had called repeatedly, there floated to him from somewhere down on the lower flat an answering yell. And presently Carson himself came riding to meet him.

Carson's face was smeared with blood; one bruised, battered, discolored eye was swelling shut, but in his uninjured eye there was triumphant gladness.

"We got the sons-o'-guns on the run, Bud," he announced from afar. "Killed their pesky fires out before they got a good start, crippled a couple of 'em, counting Benny, the cook, in on the deal, chased their deputy sheriff off with a flea in his ear, an' set tight, holding our own."

"Where'd you get the eye, Carson?" demanded Lee.

Carson grinned broadly, an evil grin of a distorted, battered face.

"You want to take a good look at ol' Poker Face," he chuckled. "He won't cheat no more games of crib for a coon's age. I jus' nacherally beat him all to hell, Bud."

"Where are the rest of the men?" Lee asked.

"Watching the fires an' seeing no more don't get started."

Then Lee told him of Judith. Carson's good eye opened wide with interest.

Carson's bruised lips sought to form for a whistle which managed to give them the air of a maidenly pout.

"He had the nerve!" he muttered. "Trevors had the nerve! Bud, we ought to make a little call on that gent."

Then, seeing Lee's face, Carson realized that anything he might have to remark on this score was superfluous. Lee had already thought of that.

They roped a couple of the wandering horses, improvised hackamores from the rope cut in two, and went to meet Judith. Carson snatched eagerly at her hand and squeezed it and looked inexpressible things from his one useful eye. He gave his saddled horse to her, watched her and Lee ride on to the ranch, and sent Tommy to the old cabin for another rope, while he rounded up some more horses in a narrow canon for Burkitt and Hampton.

"You damn' fool," he said growlingly to Hampton, "look what you've done."

"Of course I'm a damn fool," replied Hampton, by now his old cheerful self. "I've apologized to Judith and Lee and Burkitt. I apologize to you. I'll tell you confidentially that I'm a sucker and a Come-on-Charlie. I haven't got the brains of a jack-rabbit."

Carson went away grumbling. But for the first time he felt a vague respect for Pollock Hampton.

"He'll be a real man some day," thought Carson, "if the fool-killer don't pick him off first."

"You may come and see me this evening," Judith told Bud Lee as he left her to Marcia's arms. "I'll be eating and sleeping and taking baths until then. Thank you for the bacon--and the water--and----"

She smiled at him from Marcia's excited embrace. Bud Lee, the blood tingling through him, left her.

"Before I come to you, Judith girl," he whispered to himself as he went, "I'll have to have little talk with Bayne Trevors."

XXIX
LEE AND OLD MAN CARSON RIDE TOGETHER

B ud Lee, riding alone toward the Western Lumber Camp, turned in his saddle to glance back as he heard hoof-beats behind him. It was Carson, and the old cattleman was riding hard. Lee frowned. Then for an instant a smile softened his stern eyes.

"Good little old Carson," he muttered.

Carson came to his side, saying merely in his dry voice:

"Mind if I come along, Bud? You an' me have rid into one thing an' another more'n just once."

"This is my fight," said Lee coolly.

"Who said it wasn't?" demanded the other querulously. "Only you ain't got any call to be a hawg, Bud. Besides, I got a right to see if there's a fair break, ain't I? Say, look at them cow brutes back yonder! Don't it beat all how silage, when you use it right, shapes 'em up?"

Few enough words were said as the miles were flung behind them; few were needed. A swift glance showed Carson that Lee carried a revolver in his shirt; his own gun rode plainly in evidence in front of his hip. What little conversation rose between them was of ranch matters. They spoke of success now with confidence. These two foremen alone could see the money in late winter and early spring from their cattle and horses to carry the Blue Lake venture over the rapids Then there were the other resources of the diversified undertaking, the hogs, the prize stock, the olives, poultry, dairy products. And soon or late Western Lumber would pay the price for the timber tract, soon, if they saw that they had to pay it or lose the forests which they had so long counted upon. Lumber values were mounting every day.

Neither man, when it chanced that Bayne Trevors's name was casually mentioned, suggested: "Why not go to the law?" For to them it was very clear that, once in the courts, the man who had played safe would laugh at them. Against Judith's oath that he had kidnapped her would stand Trevors's word that he had done nothing of the kind, coupled with his carefully established perjured alibi and the lying testimony of the physician who had visited Judith in the cave. This man and that might be rounded up, Shorty and Benny and Poker Face, and if any of them talked--which perhaps none of them would--at most they would say that they had no orders from anybody but Quinnion. And where was Quinnion, who stood as a buckler between Trevors and prosecution? And what buckler in all the world can ever stand between one man and another?

Now and then Carson sent a quick questioning glance toward Lee's inscrutable face; now and then he sighed, his thoughts his own. Bud Lee, knowing his companion as he did, shrewdly guessed that Carson was hoping that events might so befall that there would be an open, free-for-all fight and that he might not be forced to play the restless part of a mere onlooker. Bud Lee hoped otherwise.

"There's two ways to get a man," said Carson meditatively, out of a long silence. "An' both is good ways: with a gun or with your hands."

"Yes," agreed Bud quietly.

"If it works out gun way," continued Carson, still with that thoughtful, half-abstracted look in his eyes, "it don't hurt to remember, Bud, that he shoots left-handed an' from the hip."

Lee merely nodded. Carson did not look up from the bobbing ears of his horse as he continued:

"If it works out the other way an' it's just fists, it don't hurt to remember how Trevors put out Scotty Webb last year in Rocky Bend. Four-footed style, striking with his boot square in Scotty's belly."

Trevors's name was not again referred to even in the vaguest terms. The road in front of them, at last dropping down into the valley in which the lumber-camp was, straightened out into a lane that ran between stumps to the clutter of frame buildings.

"Something doing at the office," offered Carson, as they drew near. "Directors' meeting, likely."

Two automobiles stood in the road ten steps from the closed door of the unpretentious shack which bore the printed legend, "Office, Western Lumber Company." The big red touring-car certainly belonged to Melvin, the company's president. Carson looked curiously at Lee.

Bud dismounted, dropped his horse's reins, shifted the revolver from his shirt to his belt where it was at once unhidden and loosely held, ready for a quick draw. Then he went up the three steps, Carson at his heels, his gun also unhidden and ready. From within came voices, one in protest, Bayne Trevors's ringing out, filled with mastery followed by a laugh. Lee set his hand to the door. Then, only because it was locked from within, did he knock sharply.

"Who is it?" came the sharp inquiry. But the man who made it and who was standing by the door, threw it open.

"What do you want?" he demanded again. "We're busy."

"I want to see Trevors," said Lee coolly.

"You can't. He----"

Lee shoved the man aside and strode on. Carson, close at Lee's heels, his eyes glittering, stepped a little aside when once he was within the room and took his place with his back against the wall close to the door.

It was a big, bare, barn-like room, furnished simply with one long table and half a dozen chairs. Here were five men besides Bayne Trevors. All except Trevors and the man who had opened the door were seated; Trevors, at the far end of the room, was standing, an oratorical arm slowly dropping to his side.

His eyes met Lee's, ran quickly to Carson's, came back to Lee's and rested there steadily. Beyond the slow falling of his extended arm, he did not move. The muscles of his face hardened, the look of triumph which just now had stood in his eyes changed slowly and in its place came an expression that was twin to that in Bud Lee's eyes, just a look of inscrutability with a hint of watchfulness under it, and the hardness of agate. While a man might have drawn a deep breath into his lungs and expelled it, neither Lee nor Trevor stirred.

"What the devil is this?" demanded Melvin from across the table. "Hold-up or what?" He rapped the table resoundingly.

"Shut up!" snapped Carson. "It's just a two-man play, Melvin: Lee an' Trevors."

"Oh," said Melvin, and sank back, making no further protest. He was no stranger to Carson or to Bud Lee, and he sensed what might be between Lee and a man like Trevors. Then shrugging his shoulders, he said carelessly: "I'm not the man to get in other men's way, and you know it, Carson. But you might tell your friend Bud Lee that Bayne Trevors is rather a big man influentially to mix things with. I've just resigned this morning and Trevors is our new president."

"Thanks," returned Carson dryly. "I don't think that'll make much difference though, Melvin. Most likely you'll have two presidents resigning the same day."

At last Lee spoke.

"Trevors," he said quietly, "maybe the law can't get you. But I can. For reasons which both you and I understand you are going to clear out of this part of the country."

"Am I?" asked Trevors. The look of his eyes did not alter, the poise of his big body did not shift, his hands, both at his sides again, might have been carved in bronze.

Then suddenly he laughed and threw out his arms in a wide gesture and again dropped them, saying shortly:

"You're playing the game the way I thought you would. You've got a gun. I am unarmed--begin your shooting and be damned to you!"

He even stepped forward, his eyes fearlessly upon Lee's, and settled his big frame comfortably in a chair by the table.

"Go ahead," he concluded. "I'm ready."

"That's as it should be!" Lee's voice was vibrant. His hard eyes brightened. With a quick jerk he drew the revolver from his belt and dropped it to the floor at Carson's feet.

Carson, though he stooped for it quickly, did not shift his watchful eyes from Trevors. For Carson had known more fights in his life than he had years; he knew men, and looked to Trevor for just the sort of thing Trevors did.

As Lee stepped forward, Trevors snatched open the drawer of the table at his side, quick as light, and whipped out the weapon which lay there.

"Go slow, Trevors!" came old Carson's dry voice. "I've got you covered already, two-gun style."

Trevors, even with his finger crooking to the trigger, paused and saw the two guns in Carson's brown hands trained unwaveringly upon him. There was much deadly determination in Carson's eyes. Again Trevors laughed, drawing back his empty hand.

"You yellow dog!" grunted Bud Lee, his tone one of supreme disgust. "You damned yellow dog!"

Trevors shrugged.

"You see, gentlemen--two to one, with the odds all theirs."

"You lie!" spat out Carson. "It's one to one an' I see the game goes square." He stepped forward, removed the weapon from the table under Trevors's now suddenly changeful eyes, and went back to his place with his back to the wall.

"For God's sake!" cried the one nervous man in the room, he who had opened the door. "This is murder!"

Melvin smiled, a smile as cheerless as the gleam of wintry starlight on a bit of glass.

"Will you fight him, Trevors?" he asked. "With your hands?"

"Yes," answered Trevors. "Yes."

"Move back the table," commanded Melvin, on his feet in an instant. "And the chairs. Get them back."

The table was dragged to the far end of the room; the chairs were piled upon it.

"Now," and Melvin's watch was in his hand, his voice coming with metallic coldness, "it's to a finish, is it? Three-minute rounds, fair fighting, no----"

But now at last Bayne Trevors's blood was up, his slow anger had kindled, he was moving his feet restlessly.

"Damn it," he shouted, "whose fight is this but mine and Lee's? If he wants a fight, let him come and get it; a man's fight and rules and rounds and time be damned! Am I to dance around here and sidestep and fence just for you to look on? . . . Carson!"

"Well?" said Carson.

"Lee challenges me, doesn't he? Then I'm the man to name the sort of fight, am I not? Is that fair?"

"Meaning just what?" asked Carson.

"Meaning that I am going to get him, get him any way I can! You let us fight this out our way, any way, and no interference!"

"Talk to Bud there," rejoined the old cattleman calmly. "It ain't my scrap."

"Then, Lee," snapped Trevors, "come on if you want such a fight as you'd get if you and I were alone in the mountains, with no man to watch, a fight where a man can use what weapons God gave him, any weapon he can lay his mind to, his eye to, his hand to! Or," and at last the sneer came, "do you want a pair of padded gloves and somebody to fan you?"

Carson shifted his glance to Bud Lee's face. Lee merely nodded.

"Then," cried Carson sternly, "go to it! No man steps in, an' you two can fight it out like coyotes or mountain-lions for all of me."

"Your word there will be no interference?" asked Trevors. "For you're just a fool and not a liar, Carson."

"My word," was the answer.

XXX
THE FIGHT

Bayne Trevors slipped out of his coat and vest, tossing them to the pile of chairs on the table. He loosened his soft shirt-collar and was ready. All of Bud Lee's simple preparations had been made when he threw his broad hat aside.

Then came the little pause which is forerunner to the first blow, when two men measure each other, seeking each to read the other's purpose.

"It ought to be a pretty even break," muttered Melvin, his interest obviously that of a sporting man who would travel a thousand miles to see a fight for a champion's belt. "Trevors has the weight by forty pounds; Lee has the reach by a hair; both quick-footed; both hard; Lee, maybe a little harder. Don't know. Even break. The sand will do it--sand or luck."

The two men drew slowly together. Their hands came up, their fists showed glistening knuckles, their jaws were set, their feet moved cautiously Then suddenly Bud Lee sprang in and struck.

Struck tentatively with his left hand that grazed Trevors's cheek and did no harm; struck terribly with his right hand that drove through the other man's guard and landed with the little sound of flesh on flesh on Trevors's chest. Trevors's grunt and his return blow came together; both men reeled back a half-pace from the impact, both hung an instant upon an unsteady balance, both sprang forward. And as they met the second time, they battled furiously, clinging together, striking mercilessly, giving and taking with only the sound of scuffing boot-heels and soft thuds and little coughing grunts breaking the silence. Bayne Trevors gave back a stubborn step, striking right and left as he did so; caught himself, hurled himself forward so that now it was Bud Lee who was borne backward by the sheer weight of his opponent. There was a gash on Lee's temple from which a thin stream of blood trickled; Trevors's mouth was bleeding.

"Under his guard, Trevors!" shouted Melvin, on the table now, his face red, his eyes shining. "Under, under!"

"Remember, Bud! Remember!" cried Carson.

"That's it, that's it!" Melvin clapped his two big hands and came perilously near falling from his point of vantage as Trevors's fists drove into Lee's body and Lee went reeling back. "Give him hell! A hundred dollars on Trevors!"

"Take you!" called Carson without withdrawing his eyes from the two forms reeling up and down, back and forth across the room.

"Done!" cried Melvin. "Trevors, a hundred dollars----"

He broke off, forgetful of his own words. The two men met again, clung to each other in a ludicrous embrace, broke asunder, and Lee struck so that his fist, landing fair upon Trevors's chin, hurled the bigger man back, stumbling, falling----

But not fallen. For his back found the wall and saved him. As Lee came on, rushing at him like a man gone mad, Trevors slipped aside and struck back, for the critical moment gaining time to breathe. He spat, wiped his bloody mouth with the back of his hand and again eluded a rushing attack by ducking and stepping to one side. And ever, when he sought to save his own body, he struck back, grunting audibly with the effort.

They fought everywhere, up and down, back and forth, until every foot of the floor felt their heavy boots, until each of them was fighting with all of the force that lay in him, fighting with that swelling anger which grows at leaps and bounds when two men strive body to body, when the hot breath of one mingles with the hot breath of the other, when red rage looking out of one pair of eyes sees its reflection in the other. Again and again Melvin muttered: "An even break! By God, an even break!" And over and over did Carson's heart rise in his breast as he saw Bud Lee drive Trevors, and over and over did his heart sink when he saw Lee sway and reel under the sledge-hammer blows beating at face and body.

In the beginning there had been in Bud Lee's mind but the one thought: This man had laid his hands upon Judith; this man must be punished and punished by none other in God's wide world than Bud Lee. Now all cool thought had fled, leaving just the hot desire to beat at that which beat at him, to strike down that which strove to strike him down, to master his enemy, to see the great, powerful body prone at his feet. Now he was fighting for that simplest, most potent reason in the world, just because he was fighting. And, though he knew that he had found a man as quick and hard and strong as himself, still he told himself, that he must fight a winning fight--there was some good reason why he must fight a winning fight.

His whole body was bruised and battered and sore. A glancing blow now shot him through with pain. Trevors knew how to put his weight behind his blows, and his weight was well over two hundred pounds. It was like being hammered with a two-hundred-pound sledge.

Give and take it was from the first blow, with none of the finesse of a boxers' match, with less thought of escaping punishment than of inflicting it. More than once had Bud Lee felt that he was falling only to catch his balance and come back at Trevors; more than once had Trevors gone reeling backward, smashing into the wall. Many a time did Melvin count his money won and lost. And Carson, crouching now, tense, eager, a little fearful, muttered constantly to himself.

"They've both got the sand!" grunted Melvin. "Which one draws the luck?"

But luck stood by and did not enter into the battle that grew ever hotter as Bud Lee's and Trevors's gorge rose higher at every blow. It was to be simply the best man wins, and none of the six men who watched knew from the beginning until the end who the best man was. What tricks Trevors knew, he used, and they were met by what cunning lay in Bud Lee; what strength, what resistance, what power to endure was each panting body was called upon to the reserve.

Already the spring had gone out of their steps. They came at each other for the most part more slowly, more cautiously, but more determined not to give over. Faces glistening with sweat, grimy with the dust their pounding feet beat up from the floor, the roots of Lee's hair red where with a bloody hand he had pushed it back, Trevors's lips swollen and ugly, they fought on until the men who looked at them wondered just where lay the limits upon which each depended.

"Lee's tough," Carson whispered to himself. "Riding every day an' working . . . Trevors has been setting in a chair. . . . Bud'll wear him out. . . . My God! Bud, look out! Foot work. . . ."

Yes, foot work, but not as Carson expected it, not the thing Bud Lee looked for when he sensed rather than read in Trevors's eyes that a fresh trick was coming. He was ready for a lifted boot, and, instead, Trevors, rushing down upon him, threw grappling arms about him, heedless of the fist smashing again into his cut lips. Trevors doubled and twisted and got a grip about Lee's middle, at him, seeking to throw him.

Down they went together with no particular advantage to either man. But as they rolled apart and Lee threw out an arm to lift himself Trevors saw the chance he sought and mightily, brutally, cursing as he jumped up for it, he drove the heel of his boot down upon Lee's hand on the floor.

From Lee's white lips burst an involuntary groan as it seemed to him that every bone in his hand had been crushed, from Carson a choking cry of rage, from Trevors a short laugh as he called out sharply:

"Hands off, Carson! Our fight--any way----"

Again on their feet, Trevors a second first and with the advantage clearly his now rushed Lee, seeking to finish what he had begun. And Bud Lee, his face white and drawn, looking ghastly with the blood smears across it, moving swiftly but not swiftly enough, went down, Trevors's weight against him, Trevors's fist beating into his side just below the arm-pit.

"Five hundred on Trevors!" shouted Melvin. Carson did not hear him.

"At him, Bud, go at him!" he was crying over and over. "That's the last dirty trick he's got. Get him, Buddie. Oh, for Gawd's sake, Buddie, go get him!"

Trevors was upon him again, but Lee slipped aside, even rolled over, managed to get to his feet. Again Trevors bore down upon him, a new leaping fire in his eyes. Again, though barely in time, Bud Lee slipped away from him. He drew Trevors's harsh laugh after him and Trevors's questing, eager fists. Lee put up his arm, his right arm, guarding his face, and drew away, back and back. Carson was almost whimpering, calling whiningly:

"Stand up to him, Bud! Oh, go get him, Buddie!"

Still up and down the room they went, Trevors rushing at Lee, Lee taking what blows he must, striking out but little, seeking now only to pull himself together, to get his head clear of daze and dizziness. Stepping backward, he again got the wall at his shoulders, slipped to one side, strove only to get the empty room behind him, succeeded and let Trevors drive him, drive until again his back was to a wall.

"Run away, will you?" panted Trevors. "I've got you, damn you. Got you right."

Lee didn't answer. He was thinking dully that Bayne Trevors was near telling the truth, that Bud Lee was almost beaten--almost. That was as far as a gentleman ever went--just to that desperate "almost beaten." Not quite. No! not quite. Never that.

Both men were nearly spent; Carson saw that while he cursed softly in his corner; Melvin saw it and watched for the end, wondering just how it would come. Trevors should swing for the point of the jaw, put all that was in him into a final, smashing blow, beat through an insufficient guard, do it now, quickly. For both Carson and Melvin saw another thing, a thing which both had sensed at the outset: Bud Lee was harder than Bayne Trevors. Lee, slipping away at every step was getting something back which had nearly gone from him; Trevors was breathing in noisy jerks; save for the vital fact that he now had two hands to Bud Lee's one, Trevors was showing more signs of weariness than Lee.

"Bud'll get him--somehow," whispered Carson. "Good old Bud. Somehow."

What Carson and Melvin sensed Trevors knew. He saw that Lee was having less trouble in eluding him now, that Lee's feet were quicker, lighter than his, that Lee was beginning to strike back viciously at him, and when the blow landed, Trevors's big body rocked, shot through with pain. There came to him the thought which was Melvin's, but it came in Trevors's way: Now, quickly, before Lee was ready for it, must come the end. So, for the third time that day Bayne Trevors, with much at stake, resorted to "what weapons God gave him, what weapons he could lay his mind to, his eyes to, his hands to"--his feet to. Resorting to the old trick which came up from South American ports in disreputable windjammers, which is known to the San Francisco waterfront, he raised a heavy boot, striking for Lee's stomach, seeking with one low, horrible blow to double up his already handicapped antagonist in writhing pain on the floor.

"An' I gave my word!" bellowed Carson, the sweat on his own tortured brow. "Oh, my Gawd."

But just that one brief instant too late did Bayne Trevors lift his foot. For Bud Lee had expected this, never had forgotten it, had prayed within his soul that the man he fought would use it. Just by that fraction of time which has no name was he quicker than Trevors, and he knew it. Now, as he read the sinister purpose in

Trevors's glaring eyes, as he glimpsed the raised boot as it left the floor, he lowered his own head, averted it ever so little, stooped--and his hand closed like locked iron about the calf of Trevors's leg. A stifled cry from the bulkier man, a little grunt of effort from Lee, Lee straining, heaving mightily, and Trevors went back, toppled, fought for his slipping balance, and fell. As he went down Lee was upon him, Lee's arm about his neck, Lee's weight flung upon him, Lee holding his body between a powerful pair of knees which rode him as they rode daily some struggling Blue Lake colt.

Now Bud's left arm, defying the agony of a broken hand, was around him, Lee's legs were about the frantically fighting body, and at last Lee's right hand went its sure way to the thick, bared, pulsing throat. Trevors's right arm was caught at his side, held there by the body upon his. His left hand beat at Lee's face, struck and battered again only to come back like a steam-driven piston to hammer again. But Bud Lee's pain-racked body clung on, his thumb and fingers sank and sank deeper into the corded muscles of the heaving throat, crooked like talons, white and hard and relentless.

Trevors's eyes were terrible, filled with hatred, red-flecked with rage. He sought, with a great sudden heave, to roll over. But he could not shake off the legs which were like stubborn tentacles about him, could not free his throat of the tensing clutch. He tore at the wrist, smote again at Lee's head, set his own hand to Lee's throat. In an instant his hand was back at the hand worrying him, but he was unable to drag it away.

His face went white, flamed red, grew purplish. His eyes bulged up at Lee's, his deep chest contracted spasmodically. Lee, summoning the force within him, drove thumb and fingers deeper.

"Got enough?" he panted.

For the last time Trevors strained with him and they rolled like death-locked mountain-lions. But still Lee's left arm was about Trevors's neck, his legs about the tossing body, his hand at Trevors's throat. Trevors's breath caught, failed him. . . .

Then and then only did a new look come into the bulging eyes. A look of more than fear, of utter, desperate terror. Trevors threw up his hand weakly, then let it fall so that it struck the floor heavily, a dead weight.

Lee's grip at the strangling throat relaxed. But he did not move his hand.

"Got enough?" he panted again.

The answer came brokenly, weakly, almost inarticulate. But it did come and the men drawn close heard it:

"Yes."

"You'll get out of the country?"

"Yes."

Bud Lee drew back and rose, going to the door swiftly. He stooped for his hat and passed out. And as Bayne Trevors got unsteadily to his feet and sank slumping into the chair offered him, two big tears formed in his eyes and rolled down his cheeks. The first tears in many a year, the tears of a strong man broken for the first time in his life.

"Sand did it!" grunted Melvin. "Just sand, Carson."

"I'll stick aroun' an' see he moves on, Bud," Carson followed Lee to say. "Oh, he'll go. But I'll just tell him how the boys is headed this way by now an' it's tar an' feathers for him if he don't mosey right along. That's something he couldn't stand right now. An', Bud----"

He put out his hand and locked Lee's in a grip that made the sore fingers wince. Then, swinging upon the heel of his boot, he went back to collect a hundred dollars from Melvin and help Bayne Trevors shape his plans.

But Bud Lee did not wait. He was on his horse, swaying a little, an arm caught in a rude sling, glad to be out in the late sunlight.

"Fog along, little horse," he was saying dully. "Fog right along. She's waiting, little horse. Judith is waiting! Think of that. That's right--fog right along."

XXXI
YES, JUDITH WAS WAITING . . .

At the old cabin above the lake Bud Lee dismounted. His hand in its rude sling was paining him terribly, demanding some sort of first-aid treatment. To-morrow he could take it to a doctor; perhaps in an hour or so he could get Tripp to look to it; just now he must do what he could for it himself with hot water and strips torn from an old shirt.

The hand treated first, it was slow, tedious business seeking to remove the traces of his recent encounter with Trevors; and, though he could wash his face and manage a change of clothes, there was nothing dapper about the result. But at length, shaking his head at the bruised face looking at him from his bit of mirror, he went out to his horse and rode down the trail that led to the ranch headquarters. Judith was waiting for him--that was vastly more important than the fact that he had a crippled hand and a cut or so upon his face.

Night had descended, serene with stars. He wondered if the boys were back yet from the lumber-camp. He had met them, as Carson had predicted he would, riding in a close-packed, silent, ominous body. He felt assured that they would find no work for them to do at the company's office, that Carson was right and Trevors would "be on his way." But he stopped at the bunk-house.

No, the boys hadn't come in yet. But there was a message for Lee, just received by the cook. It was from Greene, the forester, brief and to the point:

Greene had lost no time in finding the sheriff of the adjoining county at White Rock and in going with him to the cave. They had found Quinnion. He was dead, the manner of his death clearly indicated. For he lay at the foot of the cliffs straight below the cave's mouth, his face terribly torn and scratched by a mad woman's nails, the mad woman herself lying huddled and still close beside him. He had allowed the escape of her captive; she had accused him after the two of them had gone back to the cavern, had thrown herself upon him, tearing at his face, and the two had fallen. Mother and son? Lee shuddered, hoping within his heart that Judith had been mistaken. It was too horrible.

But, such is youth, such is love. Bud Lee promptly forgot both Chris Quinnion and Mad Ruth as he went through the lilacs to the house. He remembered how Marcia had flown once to Pollock Hampton when he had made a hero of himself, how again just to-day she had gone swiftly to him because he had made a fool of himself and because it seemed she loved him. In due time there was going to be a wedding at Blue Lake ranch. A wedding! Just one? Lee hurried on.

Yes, Judith was waiting for him. She was there in the living-room, curled up on a great couch, lifting her eyes expectantly as his step sounded on the veranda. A wonderfully gowned, transcendently lovely Judith; a Judith of bare white arms, round and warm and rich in their tender curves; a Judith softly, alluringly feminine even in the eyes of Bud Lee, no longer theorist; a Judith whose filmy gown clung lingeringly to her like a sun-shot mist, a Judith whose tender mouth was a red flower, whose eyes were Aphrodite's own, glorious, dawn-gray, soft with the light shining in them, the unhidden light of love for the man who came toward her swiftly; the Judith he had first held in his arms and kissed.

He came in quickly, his heart singing. The color suddenly ran up hot and vivid in the girl's cheeks. Standing over her he put out his hand. But she slipped her own hands behind her.

"Good evening, Mr. Lee," said Judith brightly. "Really, you have taken your time in making your first call. Won't you sit down?"

"No," said Bud Lee gravely. "I'll take mine standing, please!"

"Like a man to be shot at dawn?" cried Judith. "Dear me, Mr. Lee, that sounds so tragic. What, pray, are you taking?"

"A new job," said Lee. "I've come to tell you that just being horse foreman doesn't suit me any longer. What you need and need right away is a general manager. That's what I want to be, your general manager, Judith. For life!"

Judith laughed softly, happily. Her hands flew out to him like two little homing birds, and she followed them--home.

"You'll find your work cut out for you, Mr. Lee," she told him.

"It's the kind of work I want," answered Bud Lee.

Then suddenly her arms went about his neck and tears sprang into her eyes and she set her lips to the cut he had sought to cover with his hair, and took his sore, swathed hand tenderly into her own two hands, laying it against her cheek.

"Carson telephoned me," she whispered, her lips trembling all of a sudden. "He told me how Trevors fought . . . and how you fought! And he was half crying over the telephone, he was so proud of you. And I am proud of you! And--oh, Bud Lee, Bud Lee, I love you so!"

From without came the sound of the Blue Lake boys returning, Carson at their head. Riding close together they were singing, their voices floating through the night in an old cowboy song. Mrs. Simpson heard and ran out into the courtyard to listen. Marcia and Pollock Hampton, lost to all save each other in the shadows far down the veranda, listened, and Marcia clapped her hands. The voices were to be heard from afar, the strong voices of a score of men. The strange thing is that neither Judith nor Bud Lee heard; that neither had the vaguest consciousness just then that there were in all the world any other, mortals than--Judith and Bud Lee.

www.bookjungle.com *email: sales@bookjungle.com fax: 630-214-0564 mail: Book Jungle PO Box 2226 Champaign, IL 61825*

The Codes Of Hammurabi And Moses
W. W. Davies

QTY

The discovery of the Hammurabi Code is one of the greatest achievements of archaeology, and is of paramount interest, not only to the student of the Bible, but also to all those interested in ancient history...

Religion   **ISBN:** *1-59462-338-4*   **Pages:**132
MSRP $12.95

The Theory of Moral Sentiments
Adam Smith

QTY

This work from 1749. contains original theories of conscience amd moral judgment and it is the foundation for systemof morals.

Philosophy   **ISBN:** *1-59462-777-0*   **Pages:**536
MSRP $19.95

Jessica's First Prayer
Hesba Stretton

QTY

In a screened and secluded corner of one of the many railway-bridges which span the streets of London there could be seen a few years ago, from five o'clock every morning until half past eight, a tidily set-out coffee-stall, consisting of a trestle and board, upon which stood two large tin cans with a small fire of charcoal burning under each so as to keep the coffee boiling during the early hours of the morning when the work-people were thronging into the city on their way to their daily toil...

Childrens   **ISBN:** *1-59462-373-2*   **Pages:**84
MSRP $9.95

My Life and Work
Henry Ford

QTY

Henry Ford revolutionized the world with his implementation of mass production for the Model T automobile. Gain valuable business insight into his life and work with his own auto-biography... "We have only started on our development of our country we have not as yet, with all our talk of wonderful progress done more than scratch the surface. The progress has been wonderful enough but..."

Biographies/   **ISBN:** *1-59462-198-5*   **Pages:**300
MSRP $21.95

The Art of Cross-Examination
Francis Wellman

QTY

I presume it is the experience of every author, after his first book is published upon an important subject, to be almost overwhelmed with a wealth of ideas and illustrations which could readily have been included in his book, and which to his own mind, at least, seem to make a second edition inevitable. Such certainly was the case with me; and when the first edition had reached its sixth impression in five months, I rejoiced to learn that it seemed to my publishers that the book had met with a sufficiently favorable reception to justify a second and considerably enlarged edition. ..

Reference   **ISBN: *1-59462-647-2***

Pages:412

MSRP $19.95

On the Duty of Civil Disobedience
Henry David Thoreau

QTY

Thoreau wrote his famous essay, On the Duty of Civil Disobedience, as a protest against an unjust but popular war and the immoral but popular institution of slave-owning. He did more than write—he declined to pay his taxes, and was hauled off to gaol in consequence. Who can say how much this refusal of his hastened the end of the war and of slavery ?

Law   **ISBN: *1-59462-747-9***

Pages:48

MSRP $7.45

Dream Psychology Psychoanalysis for Beginners
Sigmund Freud

QTY

Sigmund Freud, born Sigismund Schlomo Freud (May 6, 1856 - September 23, 1939), was a Jewish-Austrian neurologist and psychiatrist who co-founded the psychoanalytic school of psychology. Freud is best known for his theories of the unconscious mind, especially involving the mechanism of repression; his redefinition of sexual desire as mobile and directed towards a wide variety of objects; and his therapeutic techniques, especially his understanding of transference in the therapeutic relationship and the presumed value of dreams as sources of insight into unconscious desires.

Psychology   **ISBN: *1-59462-905-6***

Pages:196

MSRP $15.45

The Miracle of Right Thought
Orison Swett Marden

QTY

Believe with all of your heart that you will do what you were made to do. When the mind has once formed the habit of holding cheerful, happy, prosperous pictures, it will not be easy to form the opposite habit. It does not matter how improbable or how far away this realization may see, or how dark the prospects may be, if we visualize them as best we can, as vividly as possible, hold tenaciously to them and vigorously struggle to attain them, they will gradually become actualized, realized in the life. But a desire, a longing without endeavor, a yearning abandoned or held indifferently will vanish without realization.

Pages:360

Self Help   **ISBN: *1-59462-644-8***

MSRP $25.45

The Rosicrucian Cosmo-Conception Mystic Christianity *by Max Heindel*   ISBN: 1-59462-188-8   **$38.95**
The Rosicrucian Cosmo-conception is not dogmatic, neither does it appeal to any other authority than the reason of the student. It is: no. controversial, but is: sent forth in the, hope that it may help to clear...   New Age/Religion Pages 646

Abandonment To Divine Providence *by Jean-Pierre de Caussade*   ISBN: 1-59462-228-0   **$25.95**
"The Rev. Jean Pierre de Caussade was one of the most remarkable spiritual writers of the Society of Jesus in France in the 18th Century. His death took place at Toulouse in 1751. His works have gone through many editions and have been republished...   Inspirational/Religion Pages 400

Mental Chemistry *by Charles Haanel*   ISBN: 1-59462-192-6   **$23.95**
Mental Chemistry allows the change of material conditions by combining and appropriately utilizing the power of the mind. Much like applied chemistry creates something new and unique out of careful combinations of chemicals the mastery of mental chemistry...   New Age Pages 354

The Letters of Robert Browning and Elizabeth Barret Barrett 1845-1846 vol II   ISBN: 1-59462-193-4   **$35.95**
by Robert Browning and Elizabeth Barrett   Biographies Pages 596

Gleanings In Genesis (volume I) *by Arthur W. Pink*   ISBN: 1-59462-130-6   **$27.45**
Appropriately has Genesis been termed "the seed plot of the Bible" for in it we have, in germ form, almost all of the great doctrines which are afterwards fully developed in the books of Scripture which follow...   Religion/Inspirational Pages 420

The Master Key *by L. W. de Laurence*   ISBN: 1-59462-001-6   **$30.95**
In no branch of human knowledge has there been a more lively increase of the spirit of research during the past few years than in the study of Psychology, Concentration and Mental Discipline. The requests for authentic lessons in Thought Control, Mental Discipline and...   New Age/Business Pages 422

The Lesser Key Of Solomon Goetia *by L. W. de Laurence*   ISBN: 1-59462-092-X   **$9.95**
This translation of the first book of the "Lemegton" which is now for the first time made accessible to students of Talismanic Magic was done, after careful collation and edition, from numerous Ancient Manuscripts in Hebrew, Latin, and French...   New Age/Occult Pages 92

Rubaiyat Of Omar Khayyam *by Edward Fitzgerald*   ISBN:1-59462-332-5   **$13.95**
Edward Fitzgerald, whom the world has already learned, in spite of his own efforts to remain within the shadow of anonymity, to look upon as one of the rarest poets of the century, was born at Bredfield, in Suffolk, on the 31st of March, 1809. He was the third son of John Purcell...   Music Pages 172

Ancient Law *by Henry Maine*   ISBN: 1-59462-128-4   **$29.95**
The chief object of the following pages is to indicate some of the earliest ideas of mankind, as they are reflected in Ancient Law, and to point out the relation of those ideas to modern thought.   Religion/History Pages 452

Far-Away Stories *by William J. Locke*   ISBN: 1-59462-129-2   **$19.45**
"Good wine needs no bush, but a collection of mixed vintages does. And this book is just such a collection. Some of the stories I do not want to remain buried for ever in the museum files of dead magazine-numbers an author's not unpardonable vanity..."   Fiction Pages 272

Life of David Crockett *by David Crockett*   ISBN: 1-59462-250-7   **$27.45**
"Colonel David Crockett was one of the most remarkable men of the times in which he lived. Born in humble life, but gifted with a strong will, an indomitable courage, and unremitting perseverance...   Biographies/New Age Pages 424

Lip-Reading *by Edward Nitchie*   ISBN: 1-59462-206-X   **$25.95**
Edward B. Nitchie, founder of the New York School for the Hard of Hearing, now the Nitchie School of Lip-Reading, Inc, wrote "LIP-READING Principles and Practice". The development and perfecting of this meritorious work on lip-reading was an undertaking...   How-to Pages 400

A Handbook of Suggestive Therapeutics, Applied Hypnotism, Psychic Science   ISBN: 1-59462-214-0   **$24.95**
by Henry Munro   Health/New Age/Health/Self-help Pages 376

A Doll's House: and Two Other Plays *by Henrik Ibsen*   ISBN: 1-59462-112-8   **$19.95**
Henrik Ibsen created this classic when in revolutionary 1848 Rome. Introducing some striking concepts in playwriting for the realist genre, this play has been studied the world over.   Fiction/Classics/Plays 308

The Light of Asia *by sir Edwin Arnold*   ISBN: 1-59462-204-3   **$13.95**
In this poetic masterpiece, Edwin Arnold describes the life and teachings of Buddha. The man who was to become known as Buddha to the world was born as Prince Gautama of India but he rejected the worldly riches and abandoned the reigns of power when...   Religion/History/Biographies Pages 170

The Complete Works of Guy de Maupassant *by Guy de Maupassant*   ISBN: 1-59462-157-8   **$16.95**
"For days and days, nights and nights, I had dreamed of that first kiss which was to consecrate our engagement, and I knew not on what spot I should put my lips..."   Fiction/Classics Pages 240

The Art of Cross-Examination *by Francis L. Wellman*   ISBN: 1-59462-309-0   **$26.95**
Written by a renowned trial lawyer, Wellman imparts his experience and uses case studies to explain how to use psychology to extract desired information through questioning.   How-to/Science/Reference Pages 408

Answered or Unanswered? *by Louisa Vaughan*   ISBN: 1-59462-248-5   **$10.95**
Miracles of Faith in China   Religion Pages 112

The Edinburgh Lectures on Mental Science (1909) *by Thomas*   ISBN: 1-59462-008-3   **$11.95**
This book contains the substance of a course of lectures recently given by the writer in the Queen Street Hall, Edinburgh. Its purpose is to indicate the Natural Principles governing the relation between Mental Action and Material Conditions...   New Age Psychology Pages 148

Ayesha *by H. Rider Haggard*   ISBN: 1-59462-301-5   **$24.95**
Verily and indeed it is the unexpected that happens! Probably if there was one person upon the earth from whom the Editor of this, and of a certain previous history, did not expect to hear again...   Classics Pages 380

Ayala's Angel *by Anthony Trollope*   ISBN: 1-59462-352-X   **$29.95**
The two girls were both pretty, but Lucy who was twenty-one who supposed to be simple and comparatively unattractive, whereas Ayala was credited, as her Bombwhat romantic name might show, with poetic charm and a taste for romance. Ayala when her father died was nineteen....   Fiction Pages 484

The American Commonwealth *by James Bryce*   ISBN: 1-59462-286-8   **$34.45**
An interpretation of American democratic political theory. It examines political mechanics and society from the perspective of Scotsman James Bryce   Politics Pages 572

Stories of the Pilgrims *by Margaret P. Pumphrey*   ISBN: 1-59462-110-0   **$17.95**
This book explores pilgrims religious oppression in England as well as their escape to Holland and eventual crossing to America on the Mayflower, and their early days in New England...   History Pages 268

QTY

The Fasting Cure *by Sinclair Upton*
ISBN: *1-59462-222-1* **$13.95**

In the Cosmopolitan Magazine for May, 1910, and in the Contemporary Review (London) for April, 1910, I published an article dealing with my experiences in fasting. I have written a great many magazine articles, but never one which attracted so much attention... New Age/Self Help/Health Pages 164

Hebrew Astrology *by Sepharial*
ISBN: *1-59462-308-2* **$13.45**

In these days of advanced thinking it is a matter of common observation that we have left many of the old landmarks behind and that we are now pressing forward to greater heights and to a wider horizon than that which represented the mind-content of our progenitors... Astrology Pages 144

Thought Vibration or The Law of Attraction in the Thought World
by William Walker Atkinson
ISBN: *1-59462-127-6* **$12.95**

Psychology/Religion Pages 144

Optimism *by Helen Keller*
ISBN: *1-59462-108-X* **$15.95**

Helen Keller was blind, deaf, and mute since 19 months old, yet famously learned how to overcome these handicaps, communicate with the world, and spread her lectures promoting optimism. An inspiring read for everyone... Biographies/Inspirational Pages 84

Sara Crewe *by Frances Burnett*
ISBN: *1-59462-360-0* **$9.45**

In the first place, Miss Minchin lived in London. Her home was a large, dull, tall one, in a large, dull square, where all the houses were alike, and all the sparrows were alike, and where all the door-knockers made the same heavy sound... Childrens/Classic Pages 88

The Autobiography of Benjamin Franklin *by Benjamin Franklin*
ISBN: *1-59462-135-7* **$24.95**

The Autobiography of Benjamin Franklin has probably been more extensively read than any other American historical work, and no other book of its kind has had such ups and downs of fortune. Franklin lived for many years in England, where he was agent... Biographies/History Pages 332

Name	
Email	
Telephone	
Address	
City, State ZIP	

☐ **Credit Card**   ☐ **Check / Money Order**

Credit Card Number	
Expiration Date	
Signature	

Please Mail to: Book Jungle
PO Box 2226
Champaign, IL 61825
or Fax to: 630-214-0564

ORDERING INFORMATION

web: *www.bookjungle.com*
email: *sales@bookjungle.com*
fax: *630-214-0564*
mail: *Book Jungle PO Box 2226 Champaign, IL 61825*
or PayPal *to sales@bookjungle.com*

Please contact us for bulk discounts

DIRECT-ORDER TERMS

**20% Discount if You Order
Two or More Books**
Free Domestic Shipping!
Accepted: Master Card, Visa,
Discover, American Express